QUEEN OF
THE LIGHTNING

QUEEN OF
THE LIGHTNING

Kathleen Herbert

ST. MARTIN'S PRESS / NEW YORK

Fic.

ACKNOWLEDGEMENT

The poem on p.129 is from 'The
Exeter Riddle Book' translated
by Kevin Crossley-Holland.
Copyright the author.

QUEEN OF THE LIGHTNING. Copyright © 1983 by Kathleen Herbert.
All rights reserved. Printed in the United States of America. No part of
this book may be used or reproduced in any manner whatsoever without
written permission except in the case of brief quotations embodied in
critical articles or reviews. For information, address St. Martin's Press,
175 Fifth Avenue, New York, N.Y. 10010.

Library of Congress Cataloging in Publication Data

Herbert, Kathleen.
  Queen of the lightning.

  I. Title.
PR6058.E623Q4   1984   823'.914   83-21104
ISBN 0-312-65996-2

First published in Great Britain in 1983 by The Bodley Head Ltd.

10 9 8 7 6 5 4 3 2

R00342 11285

List of Characters

CUMBRIA

Rhun ap Urien, former king of Cumbria, now Prince-Bishop
  of Caer Luel
Penarwan, former wife of King Owain ap Urien, now
  Abbess of a convent near Caer Luel
Riemmelth, Rhun's granddaughter, last heir of the
  Cumbrian Royal House
Arianrhod, her cousin, daughter of one of King Owain's
  love-children
Elidir, a Manx chieftain, grandson of Llywarch
Guriat, his foster-brother
Arthgal ⎫
Congair ⎭ warriors of Elidir's war-band
Enid ⎫
Nesta ⎭ Riemmelth's maids
Idwal, captain of the palace guard   Nesta's brothers
Rhodri, warrior of the palace guard
Gereint, a warrior of the palace guard
Merchiaun, chamberlain of the palace
Afaon, the royal bard
Bleddri, a story-teller
Drutwas, gate-warden of Glannaventa
Meirion, usher of Glannaventa

NORTHUMBRIA

Oswald of Bernicia, King of Northumbria, saint and martyr,
  killed 642 by Penda

Oswy, his younger brother, later Bretwalda (High King) died 670

Ebbe, their sister, foundress of Coludesburh, died 679, revered as a saint

Hild of Deira, their cousin, foundress of Whitby, died 680, revered as a saint

Elfwyn of Deira, her cousin, descendant of the Deiran royal family

Cyneburg of Wessex, Oswald's wife

Aidan, Oswald's bishop, an Irish monk from Iona, founder of Lindisfarne, died 651, revered as a saint

Liadan, Oswy's lover, an Irish bard

Mildred, a Deiran farmer's daughter

Cadman ap Cadwal, or Cadwalsson, Oswy's Horse-Thane (Master of Horse)

Godric, Oswy's shield-bearer

Dunnere, Oswy's oldest retainer

Beorn, a pagan hill-farmer in Gefrin

Godwin, Oswald's Horse-Thane

Westerfalc, thane of Deawesbyrig

Edyth of Hrypum, one of Oswy's mistresses

Teleri, a Welsh farm-woman of Elmet

Cynric
Hewald } palace servants in Eoforwic, loyal to Elfwyn

Helmstan, a Deiran thane, loyal to Elfwyn

Wulfstan
Guthlac } warriors of Oswy's war-band
Brand

Liodwald, Dish-Thane (Steward) of Eoforwic

Weybrand, Dish-Thane of Bebbanburh

Hunwald, Gate-Warden of Bebbanburh

Edgar
Ashferth
Wermund } folk of Gefrin
Sigerun

also Talorgan of Pictland, Oswy's nephew, later king of the Picts

6

MERCIA

Penda, the heathen warrior-king, defeated and killed 655 by
Oswy
Eobba, his brother, killed 642

THE DEAD

The memory of the following people is still active and potent
in the lives of their kin. In fact, to a society dominated by
the blood-feud, they can hardly be considered 'dead'.

Pascen, Riemmelth's brother
Urien, the greatest king of the Cumbrian Royal House,
murdered c.585 by his own allies in the moment of
victory. He appears in the Arthurian legends as the
husband of Morgan le Fay
Owain ap Urien, his eldest son, a great warrior, hero of later
Arthurian romances
Llywarch, Urien's cousin, central character in a cycle of
Powys poems lamenting the death of Urien and the fate of
the Cumbrian House
Dunawd ap Pabo, a cousin of the Cumbrian House, at bitter
feud with them. His family caused the death of several
Cumbrian princes
Cadwallon, warrior-king of Gwynedd. He occupied and
devastated Northumbria for a year in alliance with Penda.
Killed 633
Ethelfrith of Bernicia, last great pagan ruler of
Northumbria, killed 617
Edwin of Deira, first Christian king of Northumbria, killed
633
Acha, his sister, forced into marriage with Ethelfrith
Eanfrid, eldest son of Ethelfrith and Acha, apostasised and
murdered 633

7

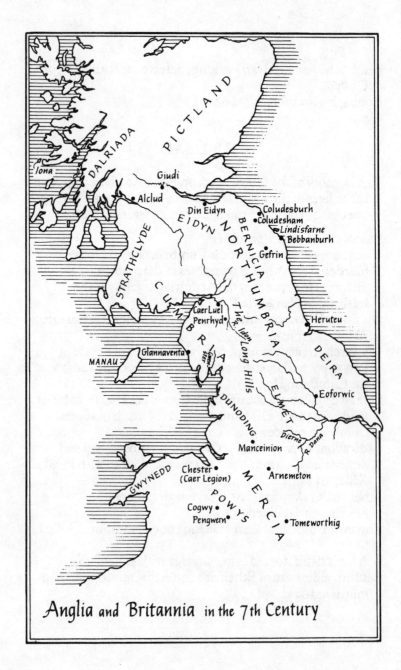

Anglia and Britannia in the 7th Century

The Royal Houses of Cumbria and Northumbria 6th–7th Century

CUMBRIA

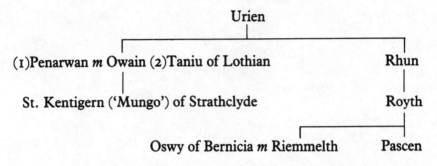

Urien
- (1)Penarwan *m* Owain (2)Taniu of Lothian
  - St. Kentigern ('Mungo') of Strathclyde
- Rhun
  - Royth
    - Oswy of Bernicia *m* Riemmelth
    - Pascen

NORTHUMBRIA

1.Bernicia

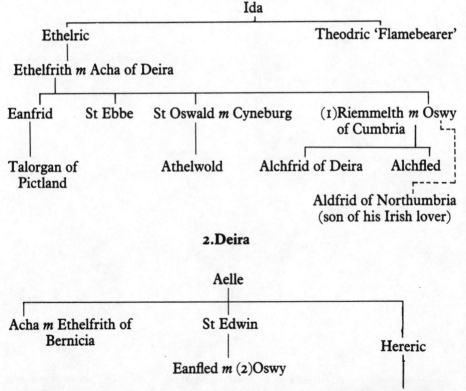

Ida
- Ethelric
  - Ethelfrith *m* Acha of Deira
    - Eanfrid
      - Talorgan of Pictland
    - St Ebbe
    - St Oswald *m* Cyneburg
      - Athelwold
    - (1)Riemmelth *m* Oswy of Cumbria
      - Alchfrid of Deira
      - Alchfled
      - Aldfrid of Northumbria (son of his Irish lover)
- Theodric 'Flamebearer'

2.Deira

Aelle
- Acha *m* Ethelfrith of Bernicia
- St Edwin
  - Eanfled *m* (2)Oswy
- Hereric
  - St Hild of Whitby

1

The hounds had the scent; the pursuit was coming up as fast and furious as the wild hunt hungry for the souls of the dead. They were not far behind now; the thudding hoofs could be felt as well as heard on the turf, the hounds in full cry, the crash of bodies breaking through the undergrowth. Still, the rider on the grey horse took time to pause and listen, head lifted, keen eyes piercing the thickets. The grey had stretched his neck to snatch a mouthful of grass when a heel in his side kicked him into action again. The rider took him to the edge of the track, where a little stream ran across the pebbles, then turned the horse into the flow of water, keeping him to a leisurely walk as his hoofs slipped on the loose stones. They made no haste though the woods were crying out with many voices that the pursuers were almost on them.

As the trees thinned into the water meadow the quarry paused again for the space of a heartbeat; glanced behind, then raced like the wind for the Esk, splashed across and vanished into the woods on the other side.

The trees crowded closer to the water's edge here, barring the way with outstretched arms rank on rank till they halted at the foot of a sheer wall of crags. There seemed to be no road and no way out, but the rider was throwing the horse forward with the recklessness of total despair—or total confidence.

The pair halted again, the rider scanning the earth. Sharp eyes might have seen that there was a parting of the ways. The path, hardly more than a thread among the brushwood, wound away to the right. Another track—and surely only a fox or a wolf could have seen or used it—went steeply uphill to the left, making for the cliff wall. The rider, who had a spear, swung it and drove the point savagely into a pool of sunlight lying across a gap between the trees. The shaft, bathed in gold, stood like a pointer—or a challenge—by the right-hand path. The rider put the grey to the wolf-track on the left.

The ground was rising so steeply now that care was needed to ward the face against scourging from overhanging boughs. A thorn tree clawed the fugitive's head, waved a cap aloft in triumph, then dropped it behind the horse's heels. A mass of black hair cascaded on to the rider's shoulders and streamed below her waist. She checked and turned in the saddle, shielding her face with her arm. The cap was soft leather, dyed green and trimmed with a raven's feather pinned in a blue brooch. The colours, emerald, sapphire and glossy blue-black, shone up from the softer green turf like an illumination in a Gospel-book.

The rider looked at her cap for a moment. She laughed, a strange little sound, soft, wild and breathless; then fled on leaving the cap lying there.

The ground was far too steep for speed now, and jagged with rocks. If she went on at the same crazy rate she would be in as much danger from her own recklessness as from capture. The grey slowed to a walk, heaving himself up at every pace. When the track turned a shoulder of rock, it became a flight of natural steps, precipitous, uneven and slippery with damp. The horse stopped determinedly.

His rider made no attempt to argue with him. She reached up, careless of scratches, and pulled a spray of flowering hawthorn. She balanced it, took aim and threw it up on the rock-face. It caught and hung on one of the steps as if it had been broken off when someone scrambled past. Smiling wickedly, she rode back a few paces, dismounted and led her hard-tried mount off the track into the darkness under the trees. The noise of their passing was soon drowned by a loud rushing ahead.

Beyond the river, the hunters were sweeping through the

skirts of the forest, glints of sunlight catching on their spearpoints and gilded armrings. Their hounds sprang over the streamlet where the rider on the grey had paused a few minutes ago, and raced on unheeding, the hunters yelling after them. From his watch-tower on the rocks, a raven swore at them. These human rivals would carry their kill away, and scare all other prey for miles. He took wing and made for the far side of the river, croaking another curse as he went.

The shadow of his wings darkened a patch of sunlight on the track. One hunter checked his horse instinctively and looked up, following the bird's flight. He watched it soar over the trees beyond the Esk and make for the bare crag wall above. He glanced uncertainly in the wake of the hunt getting lost down the valley; then back again to the raven's path, as if he heard someone calling. Then he turned his horse's head and rode slowly beside the stream, carefully scanning the ground.

At the edge of the trees he found what he was looking for—a horse's track making straight across the meadow. She must have gone at full gallop, but she had not had so much start; besides, she could not have kept up her speed among the trees yonder. Also, the cliff wall would turn her back.

He went fast over the open ground and the ford. It was not hard for a skilled hunter to pick up the trail in the woods; she had been hurrying too frantically to hide her tracks.

When he came to the parting of ways and saw her spear like a sign in the path, he laughed. The bravado of it was like her; she was warning her hunters that it was hopeless to follow her. *She* had no need of weapons, she could elude them by woodcraft and jeer at them from some safe lair.

He took her spear and set off briskly to the right; then slowed to a halt. This was too easy. Neither the path nor the undergrowth showed any signs of her passing. He got down and cast about like a hound; remounted, retraced his steps and took the faint track up the rocks.

His pursuit had lost much of its speed and most of its

confidence. His horse, a powerfully-built bay, was disliking the track more and more at every step, twitching his ears and rolling his eyes back in disbelief, expecting every second that his master would correct his foolish mistake. The rider was almost of the same mind. Nobody in their senses would ride such a path. But was she in her senses? Or rather, could you measure her acts by what was possible to an ordinary woman—or even an ordinary warrior, for that matter?

Even so it was more likely that she had outwitted him after all, in spite of his hunter's skill, and had doubled back. In that case, she could have crossed the river again and would now be trailing the hunters down the valley, insolently confident that that was the last place anyone would seek her.

He swore at the thought, but was going to turn back when he saw something brighter than the turf under the thorn trees. Her cap, with the sapphire brooch and the sign of the Raven, the badge of the Cumbrian Royal House.

He was sure of her now, and decided to follow on foot. He dismounted, drove the spears into the ground, looped his bridle-rein round a branch low and supple enough to let the bay browse, gave him a reassuring pat and set off. He went up the steep, hardly visible track almost at a run, for he was as swift and light-footed as a wolf, turned a shoulder of crag and saw the rocks rising in front of him like a flight of broken, uneven steps. There, just at the top, where the steps turned abruptly out of sight, hung a spray of white hawthorn.

He laughed again, triumphantly; she was almost in hands' reach now. There was no other way down the rock and the path must end soon as he was almost at the foot of the crags. There was a waterfall near; he could hear the water rushing and the stones were wet with spray. Maybe she was lying there, crouched like a vixen a few feet above, watching him. He scrambled up the rocks and stretched to pick up the flowers that had betrayed her.

Perhaps he was too excited by the thought of catching her; perhaps he wanted to show her by his reckless ease and swiftness how little he cared for any efforts she could make to delay or escape him. As he reached for the hawthorn spray his foot slipped, he stumbled, and kicked out. The rock broke away under him. He caught the last edge and pulled up his knee to swing himself round the turn in the path. He stopped in time, and hung frozen with shock and horror.

The beck flowed out of the high fells and came tumbling down the cliff to run through the woods and out to join the Esk in the valley. Just in front of his face the rock was split by a deep crack; the water poured down fifty feet or so into a whirlpool swirling over jagged stones. The fall had polished the sides of the crack till they were as slippery as ice, not a chink or a knob where a falling body could catch or hold itself. Another pulse-beat and he would have thrown himself over.

His sight blurred, his head seemed to be spinning round. He tightened his fingers on the ledge, shut his eyes and made himself breathe steadily till his heart quietened. Then he inched himself down the rock till his foot found the next step. Moving only one hand or foot at a time he crawled slowly backwards until he reached the shoulder of rock and leaned his back hard against it, staring down at his hands and feet as if he could hardly believe they had got him back to safety. He saw that he was still clutching the flowers of the White Goddess that had beckoned him to his death.

He looked up the rocky stair. She had won. How she must have enjoyed watching his fearful and undignified crawl back to safety! He listened for the sound of her laughter, more than half expecting to see her appear on top of the rocks to taunt him with being both near and out of reach.

There was neither sight nor sound of her, yet she seemed to be all round him—in the rush of the waterfall, in the dappled green and gold of the sunlit woods, above all in the faint, perilous scent of the crushed may blossom. He moved vaguely in search of her, turning towards the sound of the water.

His persistence was rewarded. The ground was not so steep here and he found a path going downhill. A horse could pass here, indeed, a horse had passed that way not so long ago. Here and there a print showed clearly on a patch of moist earth. The flies were thick and noisy over a pile of warm droppings. He hurried back for his own mount and led him down warily, watching every step.

They came to a broad glade and the hunter paused at the edge of the trees. Ahead of him, a great rock barred the course of the stream. The water swirled and beat against it, then split into two arms that held a little island shaped like a spear-head. Beyond the spear's point, the waters joined again and swept on towards the Esk.

He couldn't see on to the island. Hawthorns were growing there, and a wild apple tree up by the rock. On the lawn by the waterside, a grey horse was grazing peacefully. The whole place—the island with its may blossom and apple tree, the pale horse—was so full of the presence of the Goddess that he felt the skin crawl at the nape of his neck. He dropped his bridle-rein but the bay, reassured by the company of the other horse, just lowered his head and began cropping the fresh turf. Then, with her cap and hawthorn spray for talismans, he took a flying run and jumped the stream on to the island.

It was only a few yards across, a ring of green turf girdled with may trees. She was lying with her head pillowed on the black masses of her hair; she had unlaced her leather hunting jerkin and opened the neck of her shirt. Her limbs were as loose as if she were asleep but he could tell by the slight quiver of her lashes that she was awake and aware of him. He knelt over her.

'Why?'

'You said you wanted to hunt,' she said tranquilly, without opening her eyes. 'A careful hostess tries to give her guest whatever he wants,'

'Careful!'

'Didn't I show good enough sport?' Her eyes opened and

she laughed. 'Ah, I made a mistake! Your heart was set on baying some mighty boar—you're disappointed, you didn't want me in the least!'

'Not want you?' he whispered. 'Why did you run away?'

'To see if you could catch me. Your fame as a hunter arrived before you. My brother says there's no game so swift or wily that you can't track it down and take it, if you've a mind. I wanted to see if it was true.'

'If what was true? That I'm a skilful hunter—or that I've a mind to take you?'

'That you're a skilful hunter, of course. So only the swiftest or wiliest game would serve if I wasn't to insult your skill. It should have been a milk-white hind with red ears, of course, sent from Avallon to lure you away. As that's beyond my powers, I had only myself to offer, as a makeshift.'

She was no makeshift for the magic of Avallon, thought the young hunter, she was enchantment itself. His eyes and mind were so bewitched by her that he had never even asked himself if she were beautiful. Any lusty huntsman or warrior, used to giving full-bodied satisfaction to a hearty appetite, would have said 'No' to the question, objecting that she was too thin, her bones too long and fine, her nostrils and lips too sharply cut.

But no one watching Riemmelth could ever take her apart like that, without her charm of grace and warmth, and lovely subtle colour. She was light and swift as a bird, even her stillness was a gull's or hawk's, poised weightless on spreading feathers before sweeping down on its prey. Just so, her fine dark brows slanted across her forehead like a raven's wings, so that her thoughts and feelings seemed to be flying out of her eyes. And no one who had been caught by those eyes and drawn to look into their depths could ever doubt her beauty. They were as soft as blue woodsmoke and as luminous as the heart of a candle-flame, their brilliance set off by their fringe of long black lashes.

Riemmelth wore no roses in her face and hardly ever

17

flushed, even in excitement or anger, but her pallor had no trace of sickliness. Her skin was like fresh cream; without much colour, it had the sheen and warmth of life. This vivid life of hers came flowing out of her even to the tips of her hair—what fools could say black was no colour? Hers had the bluish gloss of her ravens' feathers; it was warm to the touch and when he sank his hands in it on either side of her face, as he was doing now, it seemed to curl up and twine between his fingers, binding him to her in an unbreakable net.

With a little spurt of resentment that she was not his prisoner, as he was hers, in spite of the fact that he was holding her down, he said with some bitterness, 'You tried to kill me.'

She shook her head, smiling up at him.

'Don't you have bards and story-tellers in Manau—or are you too busy hunting to stop and listen to them? Only the clumsy and the stupid fail on a quest.'

She drew him down, offering her lips. He caught her to him and took possession of her mouth, tasting and probing with eager delight. But when his face flushed and he began to fumble at her belt, she drew away gently and sat up, beginning to comb and braid her hair with her long fingers. He lay with his face turned away, pressing his cheek into the turf.

'You use men for your game, Riemmelth, when you ride out hunting. "Didn't I show good enough sport?"' mocking her tone viciously, 'or do you want to torture me some more before you strike and make an end?'

'Torture you? How do I torture you?'

'What else do you think it is? You're well named, Riemmelth, Queen of the Lightning! You dazzled my eyes when I dared to lift them up to you. Then, when I touch you, you strike!'

'There's nothing in the world that I'd deny you, Elidir,' she said with serious tenderness, 'and nothing of mine that isn't yours already.'

18

She dropped the stream of hair that she was braiding and drew the end across his face. 'But a princess of Cumbria doesn't mate in the greenwood like a peasant girl.'

'Could you find a better place for mating?'

He rolled round towards her and caught her braid, playing with the end of it as he went on, half-coaxing, half-laughing at himself.

'Is your church in Caer Luel more splendid than this?'

He pointed to the aisle of tree-columns, with their roof of leaves and dappled sunshine, hesitated a little, then added in a whisper, '—and we've brought the body and the blood ourselves, for the offertory.'

She twitched the plait out of his fingers.

'Fine talk—as good as a bard and just as heathen! If my grandfather knew, they'd hear him crying heresy all the way to Rome! But for all your talk, we'll be married in his church in Caer Luel with all the nobles of Cumbria to witness.'

He sighed and sat up, hugging his knees.

'I'm not a king or a prince. Your rich Cumbrian nobles will say it's a poor match you're making—not worthy of you.'

'You're my kinsman!'

She flamed out at once to hear him belittle himself. 'Your grandfather Llywarch was cousin and sword-friend to Owain ap Urien himself. All the treasures of Britain couldn't buy a share in our blood. You're the only match in the whole island who is worthy of me!'

'And I've got a good estate in Manau!' he said eagerly. 'Or there's my uncle in Powys. His son was badly crippled in a hunting accident. They say he means to turn monk—he'll never be able to lead a war-band or even father a son. My uncle wants one of my family as his heir. I could take you to Powys.'

'Why go looking for lands in Powys when I own the whole of Eskdale? And if that isn't enough, Pascen's taken to you like a brother—he'll be overjoyed to have you as his brother, in law as well as in friendship.' She laughed. 'His sister's husband won't be landless in Cumbria—he'll give you as much as you ask.'

She saw him frown and could have bitten her heedless tongue. Three days had been enough to teach her that Elidir would rise happily to any challenge of his daring or huntsman's skill, but resented anything he saw as a slight to his dignity or comparative poverty—and he had a hawk's eye for slights.

She added quickly, 'Do you know, when Pascen first came back from Manau, I was jealous, he talked about you so much! Elidir's skill in hunting, how Elidir bayed the boar! I couldn't believe there was anyone whose company he'd set above mine!'

'He talked about you, too—how he had a sister who could sit the wildest horse, and handle a spear and sword as well as any warrior. I couldn't believe it either; or, I thought, if it was in any way true, you'd be some hulking ogress.'

'And am I?'

'Not when I look closely.'

Riemmelth lay back in his arms with a sigh of pleasure. Even her teasing of Elidir was part of her joy in him, like the toss and slap of waves on a summer sea over her deep happiness. Though the sea was not a fit image for Elidir—he belonged to the woodlands, in looks as well as spirit. He was very dark, as if he had grown up out in the sun and wind. His hair and eyes were such a deep brown that they seemed to be black until the sunlight brought out their hidden warmth. He was a little over middle height, broad-shouldered and strong-limbed, though there was nothing clumsy or coarsely-made about him. He moved with the pride of a stag and the light-footed speed of a hunting wolf. His features had something of Riemmelth's fineness; anyone could see they were of the same blood.

Perhaps that was why her own blood leaped to greet him as she felt his body-heat and the hardness of his strong young muscles against her flesh. She thrust her fingers into his curly hair, picturing with a shiver of delight how it grew thick and springy across his body and between his thighs. Why not give herself now, under the leaves as he wished, since she meant to give herself anyway?

Everything around her seemed to merge with the strength of his body, urging her to give—the rush of water embracing the island where they lay, the hard earth against which she was pressed, the heavy female scent of the hawthorn blossom. And still her will said 'No' to the giving—for the moment.

It was partly her own pride, but mainly for his sake, though it would be hard to make him believe that. As he said, he was not a great lord; while she was the king's only sister. She wanted her proud people to see that her brother gave her to Elidir proudly, out of choice, and not in shameful haste before too many of the nine months had gone by.

But it'll be too late soon for choice because I'll be beyond choosing. I'll be having a greenwood marriage whether I will or no—and it'll be more 'will' than 'no', I don't doubt!

He felt her shake with laughter in his arms and looked at her with quick suspicion. He was too far from feeling sure of her to be able to bear mockery.

'I'm not laughing at you.' She kissed him. 'Oh, Elidir, don't you ever laugh just for the joy of it, because you've got everything you could possibly want?'

'But I haven't got everything I want!'

'Yes, you have, if it's me you're wanting. When you're offered a cup of good wine, you don't swill it down like a horse at the trough. You hold the cup in your hands for a minute or two, let the light shine in it, savour the scent. And then, when you put it to your lips at last, you sip it slowly.'

'You don't if you're dying of thirst!'

'Thirst makes the wine taste better.' She took his face between her hands. 'We've got all our lives to love each other. But this moment, before we love, it'll never come again. Let's enjoy its full sweetness.'

'But if I should lose you—?' His voice sharpened with foreboding.

21

'How can you lose me now? Haven't I given you my word?'

He couldn't argue against that, though his body protested at the needless delay. She pulled her cap on; they got up, jumped across the stream and mounted their horses in silence. He let her lead down the narrow path until they came to the open meadow, then drew alongside as they followed the Roman road beside the river. The water meadows gave rich grazing, the grass was like gold under the westering sun. Riemmelth saw Elidir's appraising look and laughed triumphantly.

'Why go looking for lands in Powys?' she asked again. 'There isn't a fairer lordship than this in all Britain. And I couldn't live anywhere but Cumbria.'

The road crossed a ford and began to climb the fell-side for the last few miles to Riemmelth's stronghold, guarding the river-mouth at Glannaventa. On the bare slope ahead they could see the moving dots that were the huntsmen and their hounds. They must have been keeping a lookout behind for they halted to allow the two strays to catch up. The girl made no attempt to quicken her pace, and finally rode among them with a tranquil greeting and a query about their day's sport, as if she had met them by chance on their homeward road. The Glannaventa retainers received them with profound respect. Elidir's Manxmen were grinning. He threw them a murderous look as he passed but it would take more than that to quell them.

When the road dipped down to the shore, Riemmelth turned aside, signing to the others to go on, and put her horse to the brow of the fell. Elidir followed her without question. When she halted at the crest, he had no need to ask why she had brought him there. He caught his breath, marvelling.

Glannaventa was below them on the cliff-edge, girdled, almost moated, by the last bend of the Esk, which made a wide curve to the south and then looped northwards round the fortress. But the wonder of the place was this: that where it flowed past the walls it was met by two other estuaries, one from the west, the other coming from the north in a matching curve. The three became one, making the sacred sign of the Goddess's own trefoil, and flowed out into the path of the setting sun. Straight ahead, the peaks of Manau rose on the horizon; there was a belt of cloud at sea level, so that the island seemed to be floating. The tide was on the ebb; the wet sands, the trinity of rivers and the sea were bathed in rose and gold, dissolving into light.

'Avallon's not so far away,' said Riemmelth softly, gazing at the sea.

'Just a step,' said Elidir, looking at her. 'It'll be a lovely night, and it's as warm as if summer had come already. It's a shame to spend it under a roof.'

She laughed, following his thought, but turned her horse's head.

'Nights are cold under the stars.'

'I'd keep you warm.'

'You're my guest—it's for me to see to your night's lodging. There's firelight and feasting and music for you under my roof, and good wine for that thirst you were complaining about.'

'Not for *that* thirst.'

'That too. Don't be so impatient.'

She set off down the slope at a canter, without looking back. She knew he would come after her.

2

Riemmelth prided herself on keeping the ancient British customs. Her hospitality was famous. A visitor was sure of meat for his hounds and corn for his horse without stint. Anyone who came too late for the day's feast knew that in the guest halls there would be hot peppered chops, mead and ale

23

brimming over, and a woman to sleep with from among the light-hearted, welcoming girls of her court.

In the Manxmen's quarters the drink had already started to flow when Elidir came in at last, to be greeted by cheers and stamping.

'Welcome to the great hunter!' shouted Guriat, his foster-brother, waving a drinking horn till the mead splashed like a fountain. 'We were looking for you in vain at the kill today!'

Elidir ducked out of range, flung himself on a bench and stretched his legs for a page to pull off his boots.

'And it's I'll be looking for you in vain at the feast tonight. You'll be under the table in a stupor.'

Guriat shook his head solemnly. 'You don't know what you're talking about, man. When a hunter's followed the chase all the way to the death, he needs his drink. You should try doing that, one time.'

'Ah, be fair, Guriat!' called Congair. 'It wasn't Elidir's fault his cousin's horse ran away with her like that, and she so little used to riding. He only did his duty as a kinsman, going after her to the rescue.'

Guriat nodded. 'And then they lost their way, since she doesn't know the country. Nasty places, woods, to get lost in—I hope you weren't too scared!'

Elidir aimed a boot at Guriat's mead-horn, so that he soused himself. When Guriat charged, he tripped him neatly and sent him crashing on to Congair and Arthgal. While they were disentangling themselves, he set about shifting from his soiled hunting gear, helped by the sniggering page.

He got into a clean shirt of saffron linen from Ireland, breeches of dark green plaid and a crimson tunic embroidered with gold. He was not used to spending much time and thought on clothes; but now he was eager to appear with credit before Riemmelth's people, as he would soon be their lord. While the page knelt to buckle the golden clasps of his doe-skin shoes, he thought of the steps that had brought his feet to that place. Even now, he could hardly believe his luck.

24

It was not strange that King Pascen, who had a Manx grandmother, should come to the island to visit his kin. The rumour went that he was following his grandfather's footsteps, and probably the old man's orders, in search of a bride. Once on the island, it was a matter of course that he should visit Elidir's father, who was descended from the Cumbrian Royal House through Llywarch, cousin of the great king Owain ap Urien. Naturally, Elidir, the youngest unmarried son, was picked out to be the special escort and companion to the young king, who was as reckless and hunting-mad as himself.

Perhaps there was some foreshadowing of what was coming, in the warm friendship, brotherly-close, that sprang up at once between them, so that when the king left, he had been urgent for Elidir to visit him in Cumbria as soon as possible. Fate had already directed the young Manxman's path to Britain. His uncle was a prince of Iâl, in Powys, stricken now at the maiming of his only son and bitter against the cousins he blamed, quite unjustly, for the accident that had left the boy crippled beyond all hope of rule or child-getting. He had sent to his sister's family for an heir, and Elidir had been picked out for inspection.

'Best call at Caer Luel on your way,' advised his father. 'That's a friendship worth keeping.'

Glannaventa was the nearest port from Manau. Elidir had landed three days ago, to learn that Pascen was away on progress in the south. The king's sister was at her palace in the caer. Courtesy demanded that he should visit this grim warrior-woman; from Pascen ap Royth's account of her feats with horses and spears, he imagined a muscular giantess with a leathery skin and a voice gruff or strident with hallooing to hounds. He hadn't realised that his face had betrayed this idea, and that Pascen had deliberately fostered the mistake. The young king was looking forward with evil amusement to the moment when Elidir would meet Riemmelth and show her all too clearly what he had expected.

25

, So he had climbed up from the harbour and passed between the menacing gate-towers of Glannaventa, all unknowing of his fate, and the world's wonder had come smiling to greet him, as she was coming now to lead them to the feast.

Riemmelth was not a wild huntress any longer. In her sky-blue tunic and gown of green silk from Constantinople, brocaded with gold and silver flowers, she looked like the goddess of the summer woodlands. She took Elidir's hand; they went together to the great feasting-hall and took their places on the dais. The horn sounded for the last time, and the outer gates were shut.

Most of the company around them was young. Riemmelth had chosen her household—her bower-maidens and bodyguard, even her scullions and grooms—from those who were as carefree and lively as herself. They gave a hearty welcome to the great platters of roast meat, the pasties and oat-bread, the generous flow of wine, mead and ale.

When the meats were cleared away, it was time for music and story-telling, while the feasters lingered over their drink, or nibbled honey-cakes and sweet withered apples from the winter stores. The din and laughter hushed, and a shiver of expectancy went along the tables as Bleddri stepped out to the hearth. He was the most famous story-teller in the North; he could change his voice and face, he could make you believe while you listened that he changed his shape as well, so that the people of his story came before your eyes.

'First choice to the guest,' said Riemmelth. 'What story would you like?'

'I'll have the tale of Blodeuedd,' cried Elidir, 'the girl the wizards made out of flowers!'

He looked meaningly at Riemmelth in her flower-sprinkled gown. 'Give me the girl made of flowers!'

Though the hall was aglow with fires and torches, she suddenly felt cold.

'Blodeuedd betrayed her husband,' she said, low-voiced.

26

'She took another lover and gave her first man to his death.'

'That's because the wizards didn't use the right flowers!' Elidir laughed. He was slightly drunk, with happiness as much as wine. And so was she—or why did it seem that she was back on the rocks by the waterfall and sliding, sliding over the edge? She gripped the table to steady herself.

'If I were making a girl out of flowers,' Elidir went on loudly to the hall in general, 'I'd take wild apple blossom and may—with blue speedwell for her eyes, that's the stuff to make a girl. Begin!' he shouted to Bleddri. 'Let's have the Flower-Face!'

He picked up his goblet and hammered on the table. In answer, there was a knocking at the hall door. The feasters became silent.

Into the stillness came Drutwas, one of the gate-wardens. Meirion, the usher, hurried to meet him and they exchanged a few low-voiced words. Then Meirion came up to the dais.

'By your leave, lady. There's a rider come from Caer Luel. He knows you're at table but he says he must speak with you.'

'Let him enter.' Riemmelth's mouth was dry.

The gate-warden left, making way for the visitor. She knew him; it was Idwal, captain of the palace guard. He bowed before the dais.

'Forgive me for disturbing the feast, lady. I've been sent to bring you to Prince Rhun as soon as may be.'

'My grandfather! Has he been taken ill?'

'He's sorely stricken, lady.'

In spite of her pang of shock and pity, Riemmelth felt a sense of relief, though she did not know what she had feared. She loved and respected her grandfather, but he was old. Such tidings must have come soon.

'I'll set out at once. I'll be ready by the time you've taken refreshment; you can get a fresh horse from the stables. There's no moon tonight, but the sky is clear enough to ride.'

'We couldn't ride fast in the dark of the moon. Wait till

27

dawn, lady—that was Prince Rhun's wish.'

'He can still speak?' she asked eagerly. 'He's not just at the point of death?'

'Not when I left Caer Luel, lady.' He looked at her compassionately.

'My brother must be brought back at once.'

'They've already gone to fetch him.'

'That's well. Thank you for your pains. Now go with my chamberlain and take your rest.'

She stood up. 'I don't want any one of my guests to lose a moment's mirth because of me. Welcome to all that my hall holds and my servants can bring you. But I beg you to forgive me—I can't feast while my grandfather may be dying.'

Elidir stood up by her side.

'Is there anyone here with the heart to be merry-making while the princess is in grief? Break up the feast.'

'Riemmelth! Where are you? *Riemmelth!*'

She crouched lower. She was struggling not to laugh but her heart was thumping so that the laughter nearly escaped in noisy gasps. It was a wonder Elidir didn't hear her.

'I know you're there!'

But there was a note of doubt in his voice and he sounded further away. She didn't want to lose him. She decided to show herself, temptingly near but just out of reach at the top of the rocks. As she jumped up into the sunlight, her shadow jumped too.

'Where are you, Riemmelth? Where are you?' called Elidir, but his voice was faint in the distance. She was just about to call, 'I'm here, Elidir! Come back!' when the shadow rose out of the ground and loomed across her path. Startled, she stepped back and lost her balance. She caught the rock ledge as she fell and hung across it over the depths, clutching desperately and trying to scream, 'Elidir, Elidir, *help me!*'

But the shadow was all around her, blinding and choking

28

her; something was prising her hands from the rock.

'Lady! Dearest heart! Oh, Mother of God!'

She was gripping the edge of her bed, with her head hanging over the side, half smothered in her hair. Enid lifted her up, resting her mistress's head against her breast and smoothing her hair away from her face. Nesta was kneeling at the bedside, holding her hands and looking up at her. The maid's round, merry little face seemed pinched with worry.

'You've been riding the Night Mare, lady,' murmured Enid.

Riemmelth laughed shakily.

'Bless you for your charity, my dear! I drank too much last night, and then got shocked back too fast into sober sadness—that's what ails me! Now, go back to bed and finish your sleep.'

Enid went on stroking her face. 'I'll come into your bed, lady. The Night Mare won't carry you off again if you're not alone.'

'Don't trouble yourself, child.'

Riemmelth was ashamed that she, with her name for daring, should need comforting against the dark by her own bower-women. How Pascen would laugh at her! She did nothing, though, to stop Enid sliding into bed with her. The worst of the terror, strangely, had not been of death, but cold loneliness and the loss of Elidir. It was good to feel warm arms round her. Nesta snuggled down at her other side; the two maids, in spite of their heroic efforts, were soon asleep again. Riemmelth stayed awake, watching the window for the dawn greyness, but warm and peaceful. The Night Mare had gone away on the wind, back to the high fells and the standing stones that guarded the desolate places.

It was a weeping morning when they set out for Caer Luel; rain as light as mist sweeping in from the sea in brief showers, with a pale sun blinking through at ghosts of rainbows, and the peaks of Manau glimpsed at moments above the cloud veils.

Riemmelth's mood was like the morning, smiles and tears mixed, all along the coast road, then inland by Derwennydd and Guasmoric. It was hard to be sad on horseback in the fresh morning, with Elidir by her side. She was looking forward to showing him Caer Luel, meeting Pascen, making plans for their future. Then she would see her grandfather's thin form, propped helpless in his bed, watching for her coming with the sad patience of the old, drifting further and further from the shores of this life. Yet surely it would be a comfort to Rhun to know that she was bringing Pascen a trusty friend and sword-brother.

'I think we should get married as soon as possible after the funeral,' she said suddenly.

Idwal and his spearmen were riding ahead, while her own and Elidir's people kept discreetly to the rear; they were, in effect, alone.

'It'll strengthen Pascen's hand to have a brother by his side when Grandfather's gone.'

'Prince Rhun must be very old?' Elidir was not quite sure what to say. It was hardly decent to talk about the death of her kinsman while beaming with pleasure but to have her so close, the loveliest and richest prize in all Britain, and think how soon he would possess her, stirred his blood like the sound of a hunting-horn.

'Very old, he's well over seventy.'

They were both silent for a moment, awe-stricken at the thought of anyone living so long.

'I can't think of Cumbria without him. He's always been there, like the mountains. Imagine waking up one morning and finding Helvellyn had just vanished! He took the kingship when Owain ap Urien died, but he went into the Church when my father came to manhood. I think that was what he'd always wanted, though he was a very great warrior, too. Then, when my father was killed, he held the kingdom again till Pascen grew up.'

'It's strange to think he knew Owain and Urien—like

meeting someone who'd seen Arthur.'

Riemmelth sighed. 'Yes, when he dies, there'll be no one alive who remembers them—except the Abbess. She must be even older than Grandfather, but I never think of her as old.'

'The Abbess?'

'Lady Penarwan. She was Owain ap Urien's first wife, but she took the veil when Urien was murdered. She must have loved him very much, turning away from the world like that to pray for his soul. Yet there's nothing gloomy or deathlike about her. I spent a couple of years in her convent to get my letters—I like her, she's the best company in the world.'

Once again, Elidir was at a loss for words. This talk of the great dead heroes of her House seemed to set her more than ever out of his reach. Elidir was strong-willed and hot-blooded; he was used to taking the game he tracked. If Riemmelth had been anyone else, he would have had his greenwood marriage the first moment he got her alone under the trees. But as well as being her own lovely self, she was the living incarnation of Cumbria—of Urien and Owain, who had passed out of life into legend and bards' songs. That blood was not to be taken lightly, even the little drop that would come when he broke her maidenhead.

Riemmelth had also been thinking about her family.

'When Grandfather dies, Pascen and I will be the only ones left,' she murmured, then her voice brightened. 'And that's another good reason why we should marry as soon as we decently can. Pascen's in no hurry to celebrate *his* wedding—except in the greenwood! He's had more than one of those!'

She laughed, and so did Elidir, though he didn't meet her eyes, recalling some wild moments on Manau during Pascen's recent visit.

'I see you as Pascen's chief war-leader, holding the southern marches. Glannaventa commands the coast of course, but we'll have another court to the east—Alauna in Kent Dale, I think. That's where the main danger lies.'

'To the south-east?' Elidir made a hurried effort to gather up the scraps of fact about Britain that he had collected when he knew he might be an heir in Powys. 'I didn't think there were any great kingdoms on your border there.'

'No. It would be simpler if there were—at least we'd know where to find our enemies. It's Dunoding—Dunawd's land.'

She saw this meant nothing to him. 'They're faraway cousin-kin, but *that's* no bond of love. There's been bad blood ever since Urien's murder—'

Her voice broke; no Cumbrian could ever talk calmly about that crime. Her knuckles were white on the reins. Gwylan twitched his ears, feeling the lightning current of anger running from his mistress.

'We were so near to victory! We could have destroyed the English, or driven them back oversea! We could have retaken Llundain, restored the High Kingdom of Arthur—had Britain to ourselves again, as it was before the Romans came! And so they murdered Urien, those high-born British princes—our countrymen, our kinsfolk!—struck down our king for jealousy, because he was so much greater than they could ever be! He was as high above them—' her glance flashed across the land around her—'as our mountains are above the Solway mud!'

She smiled. 'Well, we didn't leave them long to gloat over their noble exploit. Look for them now in their kingdoms—in Eidyn or Bernicia or Elmet—you won't find them, or their heirs. The English hold their lands and their halls. They made their own fates when they threw away our friendship.'

'But Dunawd's folk keep up the feud?'

Her eyes were gleaming with scorn and anger. 'They daren't do much—mice scratching a mountain! They're not great lords or mighty warriors. But the land down there is wild—forest and swamp. They run away when we hunt them; they've got ties with Gwynedd as well, so they can always bolt there and lie low. We have to keep watch all the time or they come sneaking in.'

'That's where my kinship with Powys will help,' put in Elidir, eagerly. 'Powys can hold Gwynedd—stop the bolt-hole.'

Elidir was feeling confident now. This hard-headed talk lacked the magic of their island in Eskdale but it made him feel more her equal. After all, his help was worth something, Cumbria could be grateful for it.

He was not like Pascen; he had known that very soon after their meeting. For all his liking of the Cumbrian and enjoyment of their shared amusements, he had felt a stirring of envy and impatience that the other should have so much power and so little sense of it. Pascen had hunted, as he feasted and made love, for the joy of the moment and sheer delight in his own young body. Elidir followed the chase to pit his strength, his wiliness and his courage against wolves and boars and king stags, because he had no other outlet.

Now, with Riemmelth at his side talking of war and statecraft, he felt like some cattle-raiding chieftain looking down from a narrow, barren mountain pass to where the land widened out into the rich lowlands, the booty that was his for the taking.

I'll take Iâl and make it the strongest lordship in Powys— perhaps I'll make myself king down there, but not if it gets in the way of higher game. Anyway, I'll make myself champion; the warriors will follow me whatever I call myself. Then I can come north while Pascen marches to meet me—we'll clear out these Dunoding vermin once and for all, and join their lands to mine. Pascen will do whatever I tell him. Maybe he'll never marry— he doesn't stay long enough with one woman to ask the question! Riemmelth will give me fine sons, direct heirs of Urien. The High Kingdom of Arthur isn't lost. It's just waiting for a man with the strength and vision to rebuild it.

Elidir's ambition had soared higher than the Cumbrian mountains; it hovered like a peregrine falcon watching the wide lands below. He already felt like the High King, deciding the fate of his subject kingdoms.

'That's our southern border taken care of. What about the wolves to the east—the English?'

'The English?' The rage had gone out of Riemmelth's voice, it was coolly dismissive. 'They're no wolves to us. They're our tamed dogs. Owain thrashed them into obedience, they haven't shown *us* their teeth since. The King of Northumbria was our pensioner for years. Grandfather took him and his family in when their father was killed and they all had to run for their lives.'

'Whatever for? He should have cut their throats when he had the chance and got rid of the whole brood at once.'

'He couldn't, he's a churchman.' Riemmelth's heart was tender to Prince Rhun. He was old and helpless, soon she would lose him, she had to defend his judgement, even against Elidir. 'He's very wise, he knew what he was doing. He made Christians of them; then, when they were grown up, he turned them on our enemies—on Gwynedd and Eidyn.' She laughed. 'A wolfcub can be trained if you catch it young enough—you should know that! We whistle them on to our enemies, and give them scraps, and straw to lie on when someone else thrashes them out of their kennels!'

Elidir laughed with her. His spirits sank again though, when they came out of the forest at last and saw Caer Luel looming ahead of them across the Caldew bridge. The rain had cleared and the westering sun turned the red sandstone to dried blood.

Elidir the hunter had never seen a city. When he entered it, seventy acres of stone and brick bounded by massive walls, he felt as much horror as wonder. Even some of the people and horses had been turned to stone; he could see them standing stiff and cold in the great square stone field on his right. Or perhaps they were all stone, these folk who were bustling about their stony halls and trackways, and only took the form of life by Druid magic. His flesh crawled, and his dark eyes were wary.

Riemmelth's eyes were also anxious and busy. She was feeling the mood of her city like a hunter sniffing the air, but she could not sense anything amiss in the streets or among the many shops and taverns. The folk were chaffering over their bargains as if their very lives depended on them; one group broke apart in a burst of guffawing and back-slapping; through the window of an upper room a woman's voice was raised in a screech of giggles; the open front of an ale-booth was raucous with song as they rode past:

> 'I took her by the toe—
> She said, "You've far to go";
> I took her by the shin—
> She said, "You can't come in";
> I took her by the thigh—
> She said . . .'

the noise mounting with the lover's upward progress.

Caer Luel was strongly placed on a low hill rising from the water meadows to a steep bluff above the Idon. At the summit, dominating the hill and the river, stood the royal stronghold, one-time governor's palace of the province of Valentia. It was cut off from the city by a mighty wall overlooking the forum. If the rest of Caer Luel was taken, a garrison could still hold this citadel, or trap the enemy in its maze of courtyards.

Riemmelth looked keenly at the warriors by the gate and guardhouse as they rode in. Again, there was no sign of mourning. They dismounted in the great outer court; glancing after the horses as they were led under the stable arch, she saw one of the grooms walking a long-legged roan.

'Look! There's Breichir! Pascen's got here before us!'

Merchiaun the chamberlain came panting up with his attendants.

'You've come on wings, my lady! I'm afraid you've tired yourself—and such a damp, dreary morning to ride in! There's fire in the king's rooms—and spiced wine, all ready to warm you—or would you prefer to go to your own apartments first? I had them stoke the bath—'

He was clucking like a hen over a strayed chick. She cut abruptly through the fuss.

'My grandfather?'

Merchiaun jerked silent and swallowed.

'He is in the chapel, my lady.'

'I'm too late!' she cried, with a pang of grief.

'There's wine for you in the king's rooms,' repeated Merchiaun, anxiously. 'Allow me—'

'My brother! Is he there? Is he waiting for me?'

She was about to dart away when she saw Merchiaun shake his head.

'He is in the chapel. My lady, let me get you some wine first, while you take breath after your journey—'

But Riemmelth was already running towards the inner court. She was whipped on by grief and regret that her grandfather had died without her; asking for her perhaps, and thinking she took no heed of him. She raced along the colonnade that flanked the king's apartments. Forgetting all ceremony, Elidir ran after her.

She threw open the door of the royal chapel and stopped for a moment, blinking. A stream of light had come in with her; beyond it, all was darkness, except for pin-points of candlelight up by the altar around a more solid blackness that was the bier.

'Pascen?'

She strained her eyes across the bowed, black-cloaked heads and backs, trying to make out her brother. There was no answer but the whispering of Latin all around her, like dead leaves rustling.

'*Libera, Domine, animam servi tui ex omnibus periculis inferni . . .*'

She took a step inside and called loudly, 'Pascen! It's Riemmelth!'

One of the kneeling figures turned, rose and came towards her.

'Riemmelth! For shame, this is unseemly!'

She stared at the tall figure looming over her in the

36

darkness. Grief and watching had worn the face to a skull; the dark eyes were deeply sunken but alive and angry.

'How dare you break the rites of the dead?' demanded her grandfather. 'I told them to take you to the king's rooms. Go now, and wait till I come to you.'

Riemmelth was still for a heartbeat, then darted past Rhun to the bier and snatched back the heavy black pall. Pascen faced her, stern and remote. She had never before seen him when he wasn't alight with love and laughing; she didn't know this Pascen. As she stared at the cold face, it sank down, down under the black pool, the waterfall was rushing in her ears, the dark figure of her nightmare towered over her; she staggered and fell over the cliff-edge.

3

Rhun saw his granddaughter carried out and then knelt again in his place. His heart was hammering at his thin frame but he forced himself to recite his *Dirige* to the end. Rising painfully, he left the chapel and returned to the king's apartments across the garden court.

His face was calm and he was holding himself as erect as the pillars of the colonnade. Nevertheless, when he came into the king's chamber, the stout woman sitting comfortably by the brazier took one look, signed to her attendant nuns to bring another chair up to the warmth, and herself poured him a goblet of warm spiced wine.

'Thank you,' whispered Rhun, falling into the chair. 'You were always a kind sister to me.'

Abbess Penarwan gave him another of her bright looks. A slight movement of her hand sent her nuns out into the antechamber. She sat down and sipped her wine to give Rhun a few moments of silence.

'I came as soon as I got your message. Merchiaun told me to wait here.'

'I wanted you to help break the news to Riemmelth. I'd left strict orders for her to stay here but, as usual, she took no heed. She came rushing into the chapel and made a disgraceful commotion.'

'Yes, I saw the end of it as I arrived.'

The Abbess sounded interested, almost amused. 'Who was that very handsome young man that carried her out? The captain of her bodyguard?'

'No, he's a visitor from Manau—Elidir, Llywarch's grandson. He's going to his kin in Powys, but,' his voice shook, 'Pascen asked him to visit here—he'd taken a liking to him.'

'Can you bear to tell me—?'

'He'd gone south to make a progress. There was a cattle-raid, only a small affair; he needn't have concerned himself, the local chief could have handled it. But he rode out after them and was killed by a chance arrow in his throat.'

His mouth twisted with bitterness.

'No great battle. No single combat with an enemy champion. Nothing for the bards to sing about. The man who killed him didn't even know what he'd done.'

'Dunawd's folk?'

'Who else? My father, my brother, my son—and now my grandson. When has harm ever come to us, that they haven't had some finger in it?'

'What will you do now? You can't keep the death a secret very long.'

'I shall resume the kingship, of course.' Rhun looked weary to death. 'I don't know what I've done that God should reject me. I wanted to turn from the world and give Him my life and service. But again and again, He's driven me back—when Owain died, and my only son. And now this. I don't know how I can bear it.'

'You can bear it.' Penarwan's voice was compassionate. 'God never tries folk beyond their strength—you're strong.'

Rhun sighed.

'Well, it'll soon be over—I can't last much longer. I must try to see Cumbria safe before I go—and Riemmelth. She's the last of our House.'

'You must get her safely married off.'

'Of course. While she's unwed, she's a danger to everyone. A female heir's worse than a child. The country might rally to a young prince of Urien's line, if the war-band keeps faith—and I trust Idwal. But that girl will be bait for every ambitious chief in Cumbria, as well as an invitation to our enemies to take advantage of her weakness.'

'Where will you look for a husband then? A Cumbrian will mean civil war—the ones you don't choose will be mortally insulted.'

Rhun pressed his bony fingers into his forehead as if he was trying to prod his tired mind. 'I haven't had much time to think. Strathclyde's our trusted friend, and their blood is as good as ours—'

'Eugein ap Beli's sons are children. She needs a husband in fact as well as name—someone who'll get her with child as soon as possible.'

Penarwan's brilliant hazel eyes were sparkling with interest. She had a head for statecraft; an intrigue was better play than a board game to her.

'Gwynedd then? Make peace at once with our most dangerous enemies?'

'Set the wolf to guard the sheep-fold?' She shook her head. 'No, Rhun, there are too many bitter blood-feuds to settle with one marriage. All you'd do would be to throw the gate open for them to walk in and take revenge at their leisure.'

'You know there's only one power strong enough to take Cumbria and hold it against all comers.'

Rhun drew a long breath.

'Northumbria?'

'Northumbria.' She saw the look on his face and almost laughed. 'You don't like it—there's the old war-leader still

39

alive in you, Rhun ap Urien.'

'What would Urien have said, or Owain, if they'd ever thought of English blood in our veins?'

'I think they'd both ask what would serve Cumbria best. And at least, these English are Christians, because of you. Our enemies aren't so squeamish. When Cadwallon of Gwynedd came north with an English ally, it was Penda of Mercia he brought.'

In spite of his courage and rock-like control, Rhun could not help wincing at that name. Penarwan smiled persuasively.

'Grant that you hate it as a Cumbrian prince—but as a Christian bishop, what better ally could you ask than Oswald? He's the holiest king in the North, and the Church's dearest friend.'

'Yes, Oswald is Christ's own warrior, one of the saints. But he's married already, to some Saxon king's daughter from the South.'

'He's got a younger brother, unwed. And he would be even better, from our point of view. Cumbria won't be lost inside Northumbria. He'll rule apart, as Riemmelth's husband.'

When Rhun remained silent, she leaned towards him and spoke more urgently. 'You know, Rhun, if we don't give, they'll take. Saintly though Oswald is, he won't let Cumbria be snatched by his enemies or have war on his borders.'

'So we must yield to the foreigners at last?'

'It won't be yielding. They're your debtors over and over again. Who got them away to safety when their father was killed? Who lent Oswald the horsemen to flank him when he marched to win his kingdom back? And he destroyed Cadwallon at Heavenfield, he's kept Penda at bay for seven years—our people remember that. They'll accept this marriage—they won't rejoice at it but they'll take it quietly if we put it to them properly. We make the offer from strength—one more favour to our loyal henchmen. But however it happens, happen it will, believe me.'

'I think you're right.'

'I am right. And we must be quick about it, before Cumbria's enemies smell blood.'

'Very well. Tell them to bring my granddaughter to me as soon as she's recovered.'

Riemmelth came to herself lying on her bed. Some grief was pressing on her heart, fit to break it; she groped bewildered for a few moments before she remembered she would never laugh with Pascen again. Pain came flooding back over her, but she fought against it, pushing herself up, and shaking her hair from her face.

Her watchful maids came to her at once. They dressed her in the mourning robes that Rhun had ordered to be laid ready, and bound up her hair under a heavy black veil. Enid's gentle face was wrung with pity and Nesta's eyes were red and swollen. She had slept with Pascen, one of many who had enjoyed his light-hearted love-making; she was sobbing quietly for him and for herself as much as for her mistress. Riemmelth stayed calm.

I'm the heir of Urien, she kept telling herself. *I'm the last. I'm the Queen of Cumbria. I've got to be strong for everybody.*

So she was ready when Rhun's summons came. She hugged her girls and went to the meeting with gathered courage—the first Council of her reign.

Rhun and Penarwan were seated at a table; she made a reverence to the Abbess, kissed the Bishop's ring and took the chair that was placed between them.

'I'm sorry to call you so soon, my dear,' said her grandfather, relieved to see her calm, 'but our state is urgent. We must put our grief aside and act at once.'

'Of course. I'm ready.'

He smiled at her kindly. 'I shall take back the kingship, as long as God spares me but, naturally, my time is short. We must choose my successor; we must choose now and make it known. There must be no doubt that could start a civil war.'

Riemmelth's eyes were wide with shock and anger.

41

'Doubt? I'm Pascen's sister, Royth's daughter. Has there ever been any doubt of that? I'm the heir of Cumbria—who dares deny it?'

'Nobody doubts you're the heir,' said Rhun impatiently. 'You'll be Queen of Cumbria, of course, but you can't rule.'

'Why not? Boudicca did, and made the Romans run like thrashed curs. And there were all the great queens and goddesses that the bards sing about.'

'Heathen nonsense, as stupid as wicked! So long as you're unmarried and unprotected, neighbouring kings will attack you. Who'll lead your army for you? Your nobles will be competing for the crown themselves.'

'*I'll* lead my army.'

Rhun choked so hard that for a few moments he was unable to speak. Riemmelth swept on confidently. 'I can handle a spear and a sword as well as most men—better, Pascen said, better. And Father used to praise me.'

She glanced at the Abbess for support; Penarwan was smiling tolerantly.

'My son and grandson indulged you too much.' Rhun had recovered his breath and his voice was bitter. 'It's time you learnt that you're a woman.'

'I don't need to learn that, I've already noticed. If a woman has got strength, skill and spirit equal to a man's, why shouldn't she do a man's work? Why shouldn't she rule?'

Rhun compressed his lips; the Abbess was more forthright.

'Because whatever else happens to a king who's taken in war, including gelding or rape, he can't be got with a bastard heir by the victor.'

Riemmelth gasped as if she had been hit in the face. The Bishop looked his distaste, but after a glance at his granddaughter he went on more gently, 'It's woman's work we're asking from you, my dear. You carry our life-blood in your veins. You must bear an heir to Urien, by some worthy father who'll hold your lands and see your sons to manhood.'

Riemmelth swallowed her sense of insult. What did words matter, when the end was unchanged?

'Of course, I must bear a son. And what better father could he have than our kinsman Elidir?'

Rhun sighed. 'Riemmelth, if you can't help me, at least don't hinder! The youngest son of an obscure Manx chieftain, what sort of match is that?'

'The best! He's our own blood—his grandfather was Urien's cousin. So none of our nobles could challenge his right. And because he's never lived here, he hasn't got any feuds of his own in Cumbria. Don't you see?'

She looked eagerly from one to the other. Penarwan seemed amused; Rhun was as unbending as the rocks of Helvellyn.

'And he's kin to the lords of Powys.' She struggled to sound calm and prudent. 'I do want to help you, Grandfather, I've thought hard about this. It would guard us to the south—if Gwynedd threatened, we could set Powys on them.'

'Powys? Do you know how far it is from Caer Luel to Pengwern? We want an ally on our border, not two hundred miles to the south.'

'But—'

Rhun suddenly slammed his palm on the table. 'You've wasted enough time with childishness. I have considered the matter carefully and decided that our best policy is an alliance with Northumbria. So—'

She stared at him. She didn't believe she had heard aright.

'Northumbria? You're asking me to marry an *Englishman*?'

'Yes, the king has a younger brother who is suitable. I've kept Pascen's death secret, to hoodwink our enemies, but it must be known soon. So you must marry their prince as quickly as possible—'

'I'll see him damned in Hell first, and you as well, before I do!'

'You forget yourself!'

'*You* forget yourself! Or you forget the stock you come from! But don't deceive yourself that I ever will! How dare you insult me? You say Elidir's no fit match for me—and then tell me to marry into a foreign pirate's brood, a flock of carrion crows that came scavenging along our coasts—'

'Hold your tongue!'

'I will not! And if you tore my tongue out, every drop of Urien's blood in my veins would pour shame on you. Have you forgotten how he drove the English into the sea at Metcaud? Have you forgotten how Owain cut down the Flamebearer and his host at Argoed Llwyvein?'

'And have you forgotten who killed Urien and Owain?' Rhun's temper was ice to Riemmelth's fire, but he was just as furious. His anger was the more bitter because the deepest part of his own nature shared his granddaughter's sense of outrage. 'It wasn't the English. But they took Elmet and Eidyn for us, and brought the traitors down at last.'

'What of it?' She forced her quivering lips to smile. 'I've always said they made good dogs to whistle on to our enemies. But that's no good reason why I should marry one of them and breed a mongrel.'

Rhun could hardly bear to look at her. That pale, clear-cut face framed in raven hair, the mocking mouth, the luminous eyes under winged brows stared back at him out of his own lost youth. It was Owain, he saw, Cumbria's hero and his idolised brother; it was Owain who reproached him. He hardened himself, he dared not break.

'The good reason is that I order you,' he said calmly. 'I am your king and I'll make your marriage as I see fit.'

'You can't make me take the marriage oath,' she taunted him. 'Not if you had me dragged to the altar in chains.'

'If I could, don't imagine that I would so profane the holy sacrament. No, Riemmelth, I can't make you marry, but I can make you safe. I'll name the strongest chief in the country as my successor—and God help him, and Cumbria! Do you want to call Penda back into the North? To see Christian churches blazing as burnt offerings to the

44

Mercians' gods? To see Cumbrian warriors hanging naked on ash trees as sacrifices to Woden?'

Anger and pain made him bitter with his granddaughter, though he loved her.

'Children of your age only see the moment's pleasure—never look before or behind. Have you never troubled to ask yourself why all Pascen's councillors are so old and his warriors so young? Have you forgotten the day Merchiaun held you up to wave when your father rode south with his war-band?' His mouth quivered, he tightened his lips. 'There was no need to wave or cheer for their home-coming! Don't you remember when the ships were ready loaded to sail for Manau, and the watchers waked all night by the beacons on the fells to warn us when to flee?'

He sighed. 'There was no need, that time, Northumbria took the brunt. We held our borders, though your father died to do it. I won't leave you loose now to plunge our country into invasion and civil war. If you won't take the protection of a husband, you'll have the protection of Holy Church to guard you from capture and rape. I'll send you under escort to the Abbess's convent.'

He saw her answer in her face and smiled grimly. 'No, of course you wouldn't be forced to take the veil without a vocation. You'd just stay in your cell till you found one. Now go to your rooms and don't leave them till I send for you.'

Riemmelth looked desperately at Penarwan. The Abbess was still smiling, but there was no comfort in the smile. She turned on her heel and slammed out.

'Oh, God give me strength!'

Rhun hardly had voice for the prayer, he was white and shaking. Penarwan rose and put a comforting hand on his shoulder.

'The child was shocked out of her wits—she didn't know what she was saying. Remember, you didn't feel so very different yourself at the first idea. Don't worry, she'll think better.'

'I hope so.'

'I know so. There's no nun's vocation there, believe me.'
Remembering Riemmelth's praise of Elidir, she added,
'We'd better get our embassy on the road to King Oswald at
Bebbanburh without delay.'

Rhun sighed. He looked exhausted.

'You're weary to death, and no wonder. Leave it to me,
I'm an old hand at negotiations, I haven't presided at synods
for nothing.'

She gave him a reassuring pat. 'Now try to rest. I'm going
to pray beside Pascen for a while. Then I'll choose the
envoys and give them their instructions.'

Rhun nodded gratefully and Penarwan went out to the
antechamber. She sent a couple of pages to attend on Rhun
and beckoned her nuns to go with her.

'I'm going to the chapel,' she said quietly. 'I want you to
gather fresh herbs to strew the corpse—and look in the rose
garden, too, there may be some early buds.'

The nuns bowed their heads. She added, 'The princess is
very upset over her brother's death, she went to her rooms
almost distraught. If you see her wandering, send for me at
once.'

She watched them on their way, then set off towards the
chapel, moving with graceful majesty for all her bulk. Her
ample black robe was hemmed and cuffed with costly fur,
her veils were of the finest lawn; her cross and ring seemed
about to break into leaf, the gold work was so rich. A
stranger would have thought it was the Cumbrian queen-
dowager who came sailing down the colonnade like a fat
black swan.

When she was young and beautiful, Penarwan had
queened it in the palace for some years, and had once been
Queen of Cumbria in fact. Her reign had lasted five days, the
time it took for her young husband Owain to bring his troops
back from Northumbria, where his father had just been
murdered by their own allies. Returning unannounced, he
had found her in bed with the Saxon captain of her
bodyguard. Owain had buried the scandal with the lover,

46

whom he killed on the spot; Penarwan's father was too powerful for an open quarrel. She had been allowed to retire with all honour to a convent, in grief—so it was said—for her father-in-law.

It was all over, fifty years and more. She was a venerated abbess; the two who knew the truth about her were safely dead. Yet it was of those two she was thinking, as she went into the chapel and made her way towards the altar.

She drew back the pall and gazed at the young, dead face for a moment before lowering herself painfully to her knees.

'*Kyrie eleison* . . . Lord have mercy . . .'

Poor boy, you should have lived to pleasure many more women with your love-making.

So there's an end of your House and name, Owain. All gone now, except poor old Rhun, and he's going fast. I've seen you all dead, Owain, since the night I saw Wulfric die on your sword.

'*Miserere mei Deus* . . . Have mercy on me, O God . . .'

I'm asking to be damned, I suppose, bringing such thoughts to the altar. But if fifty years of chastity haven't earned me the right to gloat . . .

She tried to shift her weight, her knees were paining her.

Why do I still care? I've had more power inside the Church than I ever would have had as a queen. And if I'd been Queen of Cumbria these fifty years, what man would want me now? This old carrion is what we all come to, if we last long enough.

They were the lucky ones, she thought bitterly, *they were young—Wulfric in his forgotten grave; Owain who had passed beyond death to live for ever in his country's songs and legends.*

'*Delicta iuventutis ne memineris* . . . Remember no more the sins of his youth, O Lord . . .'

Was it such a sin, that fire in the loins, that I had to be cold for fifty years to pay for it? And I had such beauty, the ashes of Ovid or any long-dead poet would have glowed red and burst into flame if I'd only straddled his grave. All wasted. Haven't I a right to demand payment in my turn? What wrong am I doing? I told Rhun the truth. It is the best marriage for her—the only safe one.

47

And I shall see your face, Owain, your eyes, with your spirit looking out of them—but helpless, quite helpless, because they're in a woman's body. Lying down, Owain, and being ridden at will by one of Wulfric's blood, as he used to ride me.

'Requiem aeternam dona ... Eternal rest grant to him, O Lord, and let perpetual light shine upon him. May he rest in peace, Amen.'

4

Riemmelth threw herself on her bed and punched her bolster. It was anger, not despair. She was not wondering if she could possibly upset her grandfather's plans, simply thinking how best to do it.

Why are old people so blind—and stubborn with it? And they call it wisdom! Grandfather lamenting the dead and crying doom on us all if our enemies find us kingless—and all the while the one man who could save us is here, under his roof, and he won't see! A hero, a champion, our own blood! Father would have been proud to take him as a son. Pascen loved him like a brother—urged him to come here—it's as if he'd known Cumbria would need him as heir—

If only I'd given myself to Elidir yesterday, it would all be settled now, and no arguments. I'd just tell Grandfather I was already betrothed by word and deed to our kinsman, and that all he had to do was give us the Church's blessing! He wouldn't dare attack Elidir—he's got enough trouble without bringing Manau and Powys against him. And the Northumbrian prince wouldn't want me, with all his people asking who'd fathered my eldest child!

She hit the bolster again. *The fool I was to say 'No', when I had the chance!*

Well, that could soon be put right. She lay still, planning

48

the details, then sat up, gave her orders to Nesta and called Enid to comb her hair.

Elidir paced the courtyard length for the hundredth time. He stooped, picked up a pebble and hurled it into a group of pigeons who were strolling and chatting on the roof. The pebble struck the tiles, the pigeons clattered away and Elidir swore.

'Who do they think I am?' he demanded, also for the hundredth time. 'Do they take me for some travelling juggler, come in for a free meal and a bed? I'm Pascen's guest. Why haven't I been brought to his wake? Why haven't I been called to the feasting-hall? Are they trying to insult me?'

'Ah, be easy, Elidir,' said Guriat. 'There'll be no feasting here for a while. The chief's an old man—a priest. And this place—the folk here—they're different.'

This was too true for Elidir's comfort. The guest chambers were splendid, but he felt trapped inside them. He hated the way they all looked inward, into a courtyard. It was like a prison with hidden locks and bars. He had not had time to notice much about the building when he ran after Riemmelth to the chapel and then carried her fainting to her room. He felt she was hidden from him inside a maze of courts and passages, and that he'd need a witch's help to find her again.

He brightened when two young warriors of the palace guard came for him, Idwal and Rhodri, Nesta's brothers. To his surprise they took him through the stables and on past the guards' quarters. They walked one on each side of him, swinging their long red cloaks. Their heads were close to his, as if the three of them were deep in talk. He realised, indignant and bewildered, that they were hiding him from notice.

They led him through the kitchen gardens and into the orchard under the walls, where they handed him over to the waiting Nesta. His anger grew as she took him in by a narrow back door and along a dark corridor to the fountain courtyard, where he remembered carrying Riemmelth. Nesta stopped, peeped down the colonnade, then bundled him along to the princess's room. Riemmelth pulled him inside and bolted the door. He glared at her.

'Am I a spy or a beggar? Why bother to meet me at all, if you're ashamed to be seen with me?'

'Ashamed? Oh, don't say that, even to tease me.'

She was surprised to find herself crying. Her grief for Pascen, the violent quarrel with Rhun, and now Elidir turning on her—it was all too much.

'If only we were married! If Pascen were alive we could be together.'

Elidir relaxed. 'Don't cry. I'll see your grandfather now and ask for you.'

'No, don't!' She clutched him in alarm.

'Why not?' he demanded, suspicious at once.

Riemmelth hesitated. She had come to know, and rather to dread, Elidir's touchy pride. If he heard that her grandfather had already said he wasn't a good enough match, he'd be likely to go storming to confront Rhun and wreck everything.

'He's old. He doesn't understand, he wants everything to be ceremonious. He said I must stay in mourning for a year,' she lied. Elidir looked horrified. 'God knows I'll be mourning for Pascen as long as I live, but Grandfather doesn't realise our danger. All our enemies will be on us at once, when they know our war-leader's dead.'

'I'll take care of you. I'll go and tell him—'

'No! I told you, he doesn't understand. If you tell him we're pledged, he'll forbid the marriage for a year. He's the bishop, remember.'

'What do you want me to do then?'

'If I were yours already, he'd have to give the Church's blessing.'

'Why, of course!' Elidir looked eagerly at the bed. Riemmelth had a vision of the Abbess coming in and finding them. She had seen the nuns going to and fro in the courtyard and wondered if it was only flowers they were looking for.

'Not here. It wouldn't be saf—seemly, with poor Pascen unburied.' She pressed his hand. 'We'll have our greenwood wedding after all! Do you know anyone in Cumbria—is there any friend of your family that you should visit for courtesy?'

Elidir looked puzzled. 'There's Enniaun, my father's old sword-friend. He lives at Penrhyd—I was going to visit him on my way to Powys. Why—?'

'Excellent! Penrhyd's on the South Road, beyond Inglewood. Take leave of my grandfather tomorrow morning and set off to visit Enniaun—say your father told you to. It's not twenty miles away, if you made haste you'd arrive within the morning—but you won't be making haste. Once you're away from Caer Luel, go into the forest, west of the road, and camp by the Petteril—if anyone asks what you're doing, say you followed a boar or a stag. Now, listen carefully. In three days' time I shall go to St Nynia's Well at Brisco to keep a vigil. The spring that flows from the well runs down to the Petteril about a quarter of a mile north of the ford. Can you find it?'

'I can find it.'

'I'll wait for you by the stream after dark on the third night.'

'I'll be there before you.'

'Don't forget!'

Elidir opened his mouth to protest; she put her arms round him and kissed him fiercely.

'Take that to remember me by.'

When Nesta had guided him away, Riemmelth sat on her bed hugging herself and smiling triumphantly. She'd defeated the old ones. How Pascen would have laughed!

Rhun gave Godspeed to his unwanted guests, kindly politeness masking relief. It was unfair to blame the boy for

51

his granddaughter's headstrong whims; still, when he was gone they might have some peace.

Rhun's hopes were answered within two days. His granddaughter asked for an audience and came to him, meek and downcast. She knelt to kiss his ring and stayed on her knees while she begged his pardon for her folly and disobedience. It was her shock and grief for Pascen; she hadn't known what she was saying. As a penance, and for the repose of her brother's soul, she had vowed to spend the next night in vigil at St Nynia's shrine, if he would allow it.

'That is a blessed thought, my dear.' He stroked her hair. 'I wouldn't lay a penance on you—grief is no sin. But since the vow has come from your own heart, go and God be with you.'

Riemmelth would not have found the Abbess so easy. Penarwan had kept vigils too, in her youth, in ways that would have surprised the Church. But she had been called back to her convent by the news that one of her oldest nuns was dying, so Riemmelth made her plans unhindered.

The shrine was so near that she didn't need a large escort, only her maids and a couple of grooms. She went in a litter, to keep herself unseen, and to please her grandfather, who disapproved of her galloping across country in men's breeches. She hated the litter. She felt smothered in it, as if she were lying on her bier under a pall, like Pascen, being carried alive to her grave, not a bride going to her chosen husband.

Her spirits were already low when they arrived in Brisco just before sunset, where there was a small farm with a cluster of huts for pilgrims. As she was keeping a private vow, she told her attendants to stay there and gave strict orders that she was not to be disturbed in her vigil till sunrise. They were glad to obey. The grooms wanted to drink; Enid and Nesta were scared by the holiness of the place—they needed firelight and laughter.

Riemmelth went alone through the dusk, down the muddy path that skirted a damp meadow. The well had been

52

roofed over and a little oratory opened on to the inner shrine, where steps in the middle of the floor led down to the holy spring. Devout pilgrims, or those under strict penance, would strip and pray there, sunk to their necks. The water ran away through a culvert, appearing outside as a streamlet trickling down to the Petteril.

The place had been holy for more than a thousand years before Nynia put the name of Christ on it. Caer Luel was so near, with its rivers and springs, that the saint would hardly have chosen Brisco for his baptistery if some Power had not been there already which he needed to sanctify because it was too strong to be driven out. The old hawthorn trees growing all around that no one would dare to cut down showed who She was.

Riemmelth dropped to her knees, because the place made her, though there were no human eyes to see. She had left her gown and shoes with her maids, as if intending a penance, and had only her shift under her cloak. She was shivering with more than the cold, though the place was dank and cold as a tomb. Wasn't she bringing a curse on herself and Elidir by blasphemy, and disobedience to her grandfather the bishop?

But I'm fighting for love, she protested to the accusing silence. *God told us to love. And it's my life—I can't live without Elidir. How could I stay quiet and be destroyed, like a blind kitten taken out for drowning?*

She waited till well after nightfall before venturing out. There was only a thin shell of new moon, but the sky was brilliant with stars. When her eyes were used to the night, she could make out the massed hawthorn blossoms, the pale feathery hemlocks and the spectral arms of mist beckoning her along the stream towards the Petteril.

She had stepped into an eerie world; for the first time in her life she knew the terror of the hunted creature. There were mist-wraiths lurking under the great oaks that reached out to grasp her; the call of a hunting owl brought her heart quaking up to her mouth. Blodeuedd had been turned into

53

an owl for betraying her man and taking another—why should that cry come to haunt her on this night of all? One of the trees stirred and came towards her and she nearly screamed, then Elidir's mouth was on hers and his arms tight around her.

He carried her under the trees, pulled off her cloak and shift and laid her naked on the couch of ferns he had prepared, covered with the sheepskin from his saddle. After her fear and cold loneliness, it was a miracle to feel his warm strength. She pulled him down on to her, into her, with a desperate urgency that left no time for love-play. He could not be too close for her to feel safe enough, if his mouth sucked the breath from her lungs and his weight crushed her ribs. Even the second's pain when he broke her flesh was a triumph, because it was Elidir who had entered and taken possession of her. The thrust of his hard young flesh inside her was her safeguard that he would hold her and keep her against the world. She twined her legs behind his thighs and clutched him closer.

When they slackened and drew apart a little, and he had wrapped her in his cloak, she snuggled back into the safe cradle of his arms, rubbing her skin against his body hair, comforted by his warmth, rocked by his breathing. Sometimes they dozed for a while, then lay caressing each other and whispering love-names; or watched the glimmer of the stars through the branches, while the scent of crushed grass and leaves rose around them.

Elidir was too delighted to talk much. Since he had known Riemmelth, there had been times when his awe of her had almost killed his desire. While he waited for her, he had worried whether he could please her. Now, the completeness of her surrender, her open need of him, soothed his pride and swept away his self-doubt.

Nights are short in May. A faint greyness came into the eastern sky, there was a stir and flutter of wings. Elidir took her again, for the joy of knowing that he owned her. She pressed her lips against his breast.

'I belong to you now—don't ever desert me.'

He raised his head and stared at her. His lips were drawn back from his teeth.

'If anyone tried to take you from me now, I'd kill him.'

She was startled by the savagery in his voice; for a moment his handsome young face looked ugly and vicious.

Elidir dressed, then went to pick up her clothes, damp with dew. She stood passively, letting him dress her; he was amusing himself playing maid, laughing at her as he plaited her hair in two braids. Then he swung her up in his arms to keep her bare feet from the cold, and carried her until they were almost up to the shrine.

'I don't want to let you go.'

'You must. My maids will come at sunrise. Go on to your father's friend at Penrhyd and come back on the third day— say you want to attend Pascen's funeral before you leave for Powys, but don't speak of me or come near me by daylight. Come to my room after nightfall—the way Nesta brought you. In the morning we'll go to my grandfather together and I'll ask him for Pascen's ruby—the royal ring of Cumbria— to put on your hand as my betrothed husband.'

He held her to him for another heartbeat, then set her down and vanished among the trees.

Nesta and Enid found her crouching on her knees by the well, speechless with weariness. Her shift and hair were damp, she had done strict penance in the well-water. They rubbed some warmth into her limbs, gowned her and covered her with cloaks in the litter. It was no wonder that she slept through the rest of the day and the following night.

The next two days passed in dreamy contentment. She was gentle but absentminded with her maids. Penarwan had come back to the palace, but she was closeted with Rhun and Riemmelth was left in peace.

As the third day dragged on, she got restless. Towards evening she went up on to the ramparts, and walked to and fro, enjoying the freedom of sky and wind. Elidir was somewhere in the palace below; she was hungry for him, just

55

a glimpse or the sound of his voice to live on till their meeting. She had too much sense, though, to prowl round the walls above the guest courtyards where curious eyes could see her. She stayed gazing to the south-west, where the mountain wall loomed black against the rosy sky. Her thoughts lifted across and hovered over her own Eskdale, the shining river-mouths, Manau beyond the flame-gold sea—then came homing back to Caer Luel.

Light and colour drained from the landscape, the mountains melted into dusk, the last cattle were driven in from the water meadows. Only the hemlocks and may blossom still showed white, and the drifting veil of mist where Caldew flowed into Idon. She felt the same enchantment as on her first night with Elidir, they could never lose it now.

We've come to Avallon, she thought, *we've found the Grail.*

She went back to her rooms and let her maids put her to bed. Then she dismissed them, saying she wanted to spend the night alone. That was no wonder, with Pascen's funeral in the morning, and they went at once. She listened for silence, then rose and dressed herself in a soft white robe. Hooding and muffling herself in a heavy black cloak, she crept out into the colonnade to wait for him.

The fountain shimmered under the waxing moon; there was no sound but the tinkling drops and the cry of a night-owl at its hunting. The stars moved, the shadows shifted, the moon set. Riemmelth waited, leaning against a column as if she had been frozen into its stone. When the first blackbird fluttered down into the courtyard she went back to her room. Her face was as grey as the dawn sky. Elidir had not come.

When they led her into the chapel, she looked through her heavy veils for the Manxmen, but they were not there. After that, she was as still and quiet, and heard as little, as if it was her own requiem they were chanting. When it was over, they led her back to her room and left her, respecting her grief.

Next day she was like a sleepwalker, staring at those who

tended her, dark-circled eyes in a corpse's face. No one mentioned Elidir; she wanted to ask questions, but was terrified of answers.

Rhun sent for her. He was worn with grief, but upright and dignified as ever. He put a ring on her finger, a great ruby set in gold.

'Here is the royal ring. I took it from Pascen's hand, as I took it from your father's, and from my brother Owain. Only the king should wear it, but I'm giving it to you, because you have our royalty in your keeping. You will give it to your husband on your wedding day, and he will give it to your son.'

She stared at the ring, like a gout of blood on her hand.

'I'll give this ring to my husband, I promise. May I die if I don't.'

Rhun closed her fingers over her palm and pressed her hand. 'I'm proud of you—the dignity and calm you've shown—but you mustn't try yourself too hard. Go and rest, my dear.'

The word 'husband' had unfrozen her blood. She had to know the truth and decided to question Idwal. She couldn't wait till he was summoned, but went herself, walking boldly into the warriors' court. Then she stopped in amazement. Guriat was sitting on the steps in front of the main doorway. When he saw her, he tried to get up and sat down again clumsily, his left leg stiff and unmanageable. She hurried across.

'What's happened, Guriat?'

He grinned at her, rather ashamed.

'You'll think I'm a fool, princess, not fit to go out with the warriors, if I can't even stay on a horse's back once I'm up. We were having a bit of a gallop after a hare—my beast put its foot down a rabbit-hole and threw me.'

'Did—where's—was anyone else hurt?'

'No, they're all away on your errand, lady—and so will I be as soon as my leg will hold me. I'd never willingly lag behind when you begged for speed, believe me.'

'What errand?'

Her voice was sharp. Guriat looked at her anxiously.

'Don't think Elidir blabbed. He's not one for chattering his affairs to the four winds. He had to tell me what he was doing, because I'm his foster-brother, you see. I'd have stuck with him, only I'd have slowed him down.'

'What did he tell you?'

'Your messengers caught up with us just after I'd taken my toss.' Guriat was more concerned to justify himself than to answer her question. 'The others were just picking me up, when Elidir came and told me we were turning south again. I asked to borrow one of the Cumbrians' horses, as mine was lame—I said they could tie me on. Then Elidir sent the others aside and told me he had to go on as fast as possible, it was urgent, he couldn't lose time. So they brought me back here, till my leg's ready to go with me.'

'But what did he *say*?'

'That you'd had word Gwynedd was planning to attack in force. That your only hope was Powys, and you'd begged Elidir to go to his kinsmen there and win their help for Cumbria.'

Riemmelth struggled to make sense of it. She wanted to take Guriat's mind to pieces and get at the truth, but she couldn't do it there and then. Members of the guard were going in and out; they were too polite to interrupt her, but they glanced at her curiously. Besides, she didn't know the right questions to ask; she needed time to think. Guriat was feeling worried at her silence.

'You're not angry, lady? Elidir had to tell me, to stop me hobbling after him. You needn't worry about Gwynedd. Not even Heaven can help your enemies once Elidir starts on them.'

'Oh no!' She forced her pale lips to smile. 'In fact, it's lucky you came back here—you can tell Elidir the truth. Those messengers were fools, the danger isn't as urgent as that. Tell him to give our greetings to Powys and come back to me at once. I need him here.'

His face was bewildered.

'Don't worry, I'll see you again before you leave. Idwal will bring you to me—don't talk about this to anybody else.'

She had to make him realise what a serious business it was, give him a message simple enough for him to understand. She glanced round quickly, pulled off her ring and pressed it into his hand.

'Hide this. Keep it safe and give it to Elidir. Tell him I love him for ever.'

She hurried away without looking back. Guriat blinked, then set about stowing the ring carefully in a pouch he wore inside his shirt, thinking about women's moods and panics. Three days ago she'd been urgent to have Elidir go, now she was urgent to have him back.

A shadow fell across him and he glanced up to see one of the Cumbrians looking at him.

'Leg still bothering you?'

'It's on the mend,' said Guriat, shifting it cautiously, 'but it's a hellish nuisance.'

The stranger sat down beside him, pulled out a leather flask and handed it over. 'I can feel for you. I know myself what it is to be tied by the leg—steward to the Lady Abbess.' He pulled a long mouth. 'Not that I've a word to say against her, she's a great lady, everything of the best for herself and her household. Wine all right?'

'It's good.' Guriat took another swig to make sure. 'Very good.'

'That's from her cellar. She doesn't grudge what she's got. Still, there are some things you can't get in a houseful of nuns—a man needs more than wine to keep his insides warm.'

He winked at Guriat. 'That's why I'm always glad to come to Caer Luel. There's a place by the North Gate where the wine's nearly as good as this. "The Golden Lily"—calls itself an inn. It's that, of course, a traveller can always have a bed, any hour.' He winked again. 'Good service. Willing maids and a kind-hearted hostess, she doesn't mind how

59

often her girls go and lie down during the day. I always call there when I'm in the city. Care to come?'

Guriat was bored and lonely. The warriors of the guard were friendly enough but they had their duties to busy them; he felt very much an outsider. He hesitated.

'I'd like that—but is it far? I don't know if my leg'll hold up.'

'Just a step. Don't worry. They've got good beds at the "Lily"—and it isn't your leg that needs to stand up in that house! Here, hang on to my arm.'

Riemmelth's mind went back and forth over the same beaten track. Who had sent that message to Elidir—and why? After all, she had talked so much about danger from the south, and the help Elidir could bring. Rhun might have had second thoughts, she might have won him over in the end. In that case, she mustn't say anything to offend him now.

She was called to her grandfather's room next day. She entered alert and wary, to find him with the Abbess. The attack came at once.

'Where is your ring?' demanded Rhun, sternly.

'It isn't mine— I'm not the king. I've put it in a safe place till my wedding day.'

The Abbess shook her head, smiling.

'You believe you did, I'm sure. Oh, girls, girls! I often tell my novices we need more lay-sisters just to sweep up their scattered brains!'

She took a ring off her plump hand and gave it to Rhun. 'I think we'd better ask your grandfather to look after this till your wedding day,' she said pleasantly. 'And that's what I want to see you about. Time's getting short, you'll need to have your wedding clothes ready. I know you've not given it a thought, poor child—how could you, at a time like this?— so I've come to help you.'

Still smiling, she gripped Riemmelth's arm and led her firmly out, not letting go her hold until she had sat the shocked girl down on her bed. Penarwan reached out her soft little hand and slapped her lightly, playfully, on the cheek.

'Silly child, silly child!'

She sat down opposite, fixed her brilliant hazel eyes on Riemmelth's face, and laughed.

'Don't look so scared, I'm not going to scold you! I've been young myself, I know what girls are like about keepsakes at your age. Of course you want your dead brother's friend to have something to remember him by—and so he shall. We'll pick out something splendid for him, a brooch, a hound, Pascen's best hawk. But, oh dear! not the royal ring of Cumbria!'

'How did you get it?' whispered Riemmelth. Penarwan looked grave.

'You should have known better than to trust it to one of those drunken islanders. What can you expect when they're let loose in a city for the first time in their lives?'

She clicked her tongue, weary but tolerant. 'Of course, he went straight to a brothel—a house called "The Golden Lily"—and then behaved as if it was a farmhouse he'd just looted and the girls were for anyone's taking. He wouldn't keep his turn and got into a brawl. One can't blame the house—it's quite a well-conducted place by all accounts, and the other man had already paid. As soon as knives were drawn, they were all bundled outside and they carried on the fight in the street. The Manxman got stabbed and the others ran away.'

Riemmelth had shut her eyes but tears were forcing themselves under her lashes. Poor simple Guriat, with his mop of red hair and his grin. He'd have been safer if they'd left him in Inglewood with his injured leg than on his own in Caer Luel.

'Luckily, my steward happened to be passing—a very reliable man and a true Samaritan. He went to the victim at once, but he was already past help by then, God rest him. My steward found the ring on the body and brought it straight to me—thank Heaven, he's discreet. I've told him to see the poor creature has decent burial.'

Her voice hardened. 'It doesn't bear thinking about—the royal ring of Cumbria on the hand of some whore. Still, all's well that ends well. I won't tell your grandfather, he's got enough cares on his shoulders. About your wedding clothes, where are the keys of your chests, my dear? Give them here. Now, you've nothing more to worry about, you can leave it all to me.'

Riemmelth gave up her keys without a word of protest, stunned by the disaster. Elidir had been ruthlessly swept out of her reach, she was trapped. There was no way she could get word to him in time. And if there were a way, she dared not take it. They would destroy him, like Guriat, if she sent for him.

For herself, it no longer mattered what they did to her. She couldn't live without Elidir. They had already destroyed her.

5
———

The wind was from the east, like the morning sun. It had come across miles of ocean, bringing a chill touch to skin and a salty tang to lips and nostrils. The cliff was so high above the sea that the crash and drag of breakers rose to it as a distant sighing. Unshuttered windows high under the roof opened on nothing but clear blue space and the white flash of soaring, wheeling gulls.

The pair on the bed had thrown off the coverlet and were letting the sunlight wash over their long limbs as if they were playing in the summer sea. The man raised himself, reached for a wine jug on the bedside chest and filled a goblet. He was very fair, his body hair like silver spray over his tan. The woman lifted her arms above her head and stretched to the

tips of her toes; she was as tall as the man. She warmed the
sunlight with her honey-gold skin, mass of wiry copper-red
hair and eyes like autumn beech leaves.

The man drank to her, then handed her the wine.

'A parting cup to your journey. The sun on your path,
Liadan.'

She smiled at him over the rim of the goblet, without
speaking.

'Must you go today?'

'Will go. That's the same as "must" to me. I'm making a
bardic circuit in Dalriada, then going back to Ireland.'

He looked along her body with slow relish: the broad
shoulders, the full firm breasts, the smooth belly and big
round thighs.

'Why don't I hold you here, now I've got you back?'

'Nobody holds a bard or a Druid. We come and we go.'

'You're not a Druid to my war-band, they're English. To
them, you're just a woman I happen to fancy, that I haven't
finished with yet. They'd hold you, all right, if I told them.
So why don't I keep you, since I want you?'

She laughed softly, unafraid. Reaching across him, she
took a book from the chest and opened it at a great
illuminated capital of blue, red and gold, curve within curve
breaking out into interwoven blossoms and tendrils, a
miracle of beauty and patient art.

'Why don't you tear this page out and use it in the privy?'

'Why don't I?'

'Because you love your own fine pleasure too much to
destroy it for a small bodily satisfaction. Whenever you just
want to relieve yourself, you can get a slave girl up from the
kitchens.'

He drank the last wine, then suddenly rapped the goblet
down on the chest.

'Marry me.'

'We'd be unfaithful. I'd betray you to the first poem that
ordered me to compose it. You'd leave me for every council
or battle that your kingdom demanded.'

'I haven't got a kingdom.'

'You will. I see a crown on your head.'

'Don't!' he said violently. 'I won't have you prophesying Oswald's death.'

'I don't make the future, only foresee it. Besides, you want to be king, Oswy, you know you do; just as I must be a bard. If you ever found a woman who loves king-craft as I love word-craft, that's your wife.'

'There's no such woman. And so, our roads part here?'

'They'll cross; that I do know.'

'You can say that because you've got the second sight. But how can I be sure we'll meet again?'

'I'll always come back, because you'll always let me go. The surest way to make a woman strike roots in your bed is to tell her the door's open behind her for the going.'

He took her face between his big hands and stared at every line of it, so that his memory could draw it later: the broad brow and widely-set eyes, the heavy cheek-bones scattered with freckles, the generous mouth.

'You're very presumptuous for a woman, Liadan, with your "I'll go" and "I'll come". You never think that I might intend coming to you.'

She lay back, laughing, and raised her knees.

'Come now, if you're ready.'

They were both gifted players and were enjoying each other's skill, when someone tapped urgently outside the door. Oswy swore, and lay still for a moment or two. The knocking was repeated louder. Someone called, 'Oswy? My lord!'

'What is it?'

'My lord, the King wants you. There are envoys come— Welshmen from Cumbria.'

Oswy reached for his clothes and began to dress without haste. Under his breath he was sketching a further journey for the Cumbrian envoys to go. The voice called again.

'Do you need any help, my lord? Shall I call your men?'

'No!'

64

Liadan, who was making no attempt to help, chuckled. Oswy buckled his belt over his embroidered tunic, threw a cloak round him and pinned it on his shoulder with a great square-headed brooch. He stared down for a moment at Liadan lying on the bed, smiling in the sunshine; then turned and strode to the door. He opened and shut it so quickly behind him that there was no glimpse into the room. His face showed no expression.

The messenger tilted her head to his height. Large pale-blue eyes, as guileless as a kitten's, gazed out innocently from a frame of light-brown curls. It was a pretty, gentle face, though the lower lip, unusually small and thin, and the sharp but slightly receding chin gave it a pinched look.

'I'm so sorry to break your pastime, cousin. The Irish singing-woman was performing for you, wasn't she? Will she make sport for the men tonight after the feast? Does she tumble as well as play?'

She had a clear, high-toned voice; it was pitched to get into the sleeping-chamber. Oswy smiled at her.

'You're ignorant, Elfwyn. An ollave—a master-poet—doesn't stoop to act as gleeman or juggler for a pack of drunken spearmen or empty-headed kitchen wenches. It's only fellow poets, or kings, who are privileged to enjoy her skills.'

Elfwyn's mouth pinched tight on her smile.

'Forgive my ignorance! *I* didn't spend years getting my book-Latin among the Irish.'

'We can all make mistakes,' he said blandly. 'Now, anyone seeing you come running errands to my bedroom door might take you for a captive bondmaid, not a lady of the royal kin.'.

It was said lightly, with a smile, but his eyes were not smiling. She winced as if he had hit her across the mouth. Oswy took her pointed chin between his thumb and forefinger and lifted her face.

'And now you can sheathe your sword. I've had enough weapon-play for one morning.'

65

He kissed her pinched little lips and strode away. If he had cared to look back, he would have seen in her face that Elfwyn had not been playing, and that she had not sheathed her sword.

He guessed that his brother wanted to see him before the envoys were brought from the guest chambers, so he went straight to the king's private apartments, behind the towering royal hall. The wind tugged at his cloak as he crossed the courtyard; the wind was at home in Bebbanburh.

Oswald's rooms were far more simply furnished than his brother's. His most precious possessions were his psalter, his reliquary and his crucifix. Anyone coming on him unawares was likely to find him kneeling; he spent so much time at prayer that even when he was at leisure, his big hands rested palm-upwards on his knees, as if every minute of his life was an offering.

He was sitting like this, deep in thought, when Oswy came in, but looked up at once and smiled. Oswy pulled up a stool.

'I'm told there's an embassy from Cumbria?'

'Yes, and a letter from the Bishop. They're in sore trouble.'

'And want us to pull them out of it?'

'Their king's dead. He had no brothers or uncles. The Bishop's holding the kingdom at the moment, but he's very old. He writes that he expects to die soon.'

'Are there no heirs at all?'

'One girl. They've offered her to you.'

Oswy's eyes gleamed. 'So I'll be a king! Liadan said she saw a crown on my head.'

Not Northumbria then, it wasn't Oswald's death she saw.

'You'll like that.' Oswald's face was knowing and affectionate. 'Well, be ready to start for Caer Luel fairly soon—and you'd better make sure that woman is out of your bed before you bring your bride into it.'

'*That woman* is a Bandraoi. She goes and comes as she decides.'

As Oswy spoke the Irish word, Oswald's face tightened towards a frown, then softened into a pained sigh. It could not please his austere piety that his younger brother was an unrepentant fornicator, but this had to be accepted, regretfully, as one of the facts of a young prince's life. What he hated to remember, and could not bring himself to speak of, was that the woman who had first lured Oswy into the sins of the flesh, who even after twelve years still gave him most delight, was a Druid, sorceress as well as poet. It was lucky that she never stayed with him long, moving with unwomanly and immodest freedom from one court or bardic school to another.

He chose the words of his answer carefully. 'If she's your friend, she'll decide not to hinder your marriage. This is a good offer, it means we get Cumbria without fighting.'

'Without fighting *them*, perhaps—but how did their king die?'

'Not in war. He was driving off cattle-raiders and took an unlucky blow.'

'Young fool, to throw his life away in a petty brawl.'

'A king might have to throw his life away for his people's sake—or if his honour called.'

'Well, don't you make that mistake, Oswald. I won't honour you—just call you a fool and leave you to face the destruction you've brought on yourself.'

'I know you will. I've seen you do it.'

The brothers laughed, and went into the royal hall to meet the envoys. They had both spent years of exile in western courts and monasteries; as fluent in Welsh and Irish as in English and Latin, they could speak to the Cumbrians without interpreters. It was a perfectly satisfactory meeting. There were no blood-ties of love or hate to tangle the negotiations and each side knew what they had to offer and what to gain. Cumbria had an old king and an unmarried princess; Northumbria had a king's younger brother and a long western border to guard. The two Houses had made bargains before, which had been kept on both sides.

When the main details of the alliance had been settled, the Cumbrians spoke of the wedding itself. As there was a danger that their enemies might attack to prevent the union, and as their royal House was in mourning, it would be well that the marriage should be soon and as secret as possible, without great celebrations. The Northumbrians agreed; the bridegroom could be on his way within a few days.

On his way back to his own hall, Oswy reflected sardonically that the Welsh would never want to celebrate such an alliance anyway. He wondered what the princess was thinking about it at that moment.

'Riemmelth'—that meant 'Queen of the Lightning'. That was a pretty name to sweeten a love-song! One of Woden's waelcyriges couldn't do better.

The wind had shifted to the south-west and there were heavy rain-clouds coming up from Cumbria over the Cheviots. When he came back to his room the sunlight had gone, and so had Liadan.

6

When she was first stabbed by despair, Riemmelth had felt that her life was ended. Unluckily, that was not so. The dead may remember, but at least their earthly worries have flown. Riemmelth's came flocking round her like carrion crows, and the flock grew bigger every day.

She had long empty hours to count them, sitting silent in her room. Rhun was closeted with the great nobles and churchmen he had summoned quietly to Caer Luel. Penarwan sat in on their councils or busied herself with the wedding preparations; she was queen in the palace again.

Riemmelth wondered what Elidir would think when he heard of the wedding. She felt sick. In her mind, she saw him turning on her in rage and disgust; he would believe she had betrayed him, had decoyed him away while she took a prince to her bed. She tried to plan an escape, a dash to the south, but it was hopeless. If the Cumbrians didn't catch her, Dunoding would.

She considered Rhun's other offer, a nun's cell, but she couldn't face that; she had no vocation, it would be a living burial—and she might be with child. As the wedding day neared, this one dread grew so strong that it drove all the others away. She was no maiden; perhaps she was pregnant, and in two days they were going to give her as bride to an English war-lord. What would he do to her when he came to take her maidenhead?

She remembered what this man's father had done to the twelve hundred monks of Bangor-is-y-Coed, who had come out to pray for Christ's protection on their warriors against the heathen invader. When it was explained to him who they were and what they were doing, King Ethelfrith had said grimly that praying against him was fighting against him. It was only fair that they should get what he gave to other enemy warriors. They did.

If the English counted a monk's prayers as an act of war, what would they do about a bride who took a lover as soon as she knew she was betrothed? One of those savages could strangle her in the marriage-bed, or hack her to pieces with his axe (they fought with axes!) and feed her to his hounds. He might drag her out to the public shame and torture of burning. He might accuse Rhun of cheating him with damaged goods and call in the English hordes to ravage the whole country. It was no good telling herself that since Cumbria had destroyed her, what did it matter if Cumbria got destroyed too? It mattered very much; she was Urien's last heir, as well as Elidir's lover; she would die rather than bring destruction on Cumbria.

Once, when she was alone, she took out her hunting dagger and held it under her breast. It was no good, life was too strong in her; while she lived she could never stop believing that some time, somewhere, she must win her way back to Elidir.

She heard someone crossing the ante-room, sheathed her dagger and hurriedly thrust it inside her jewel box. If Penarwan thought she might take her way out along a knife blade, she'd be watched day and night and she couldn't endure that.

Nesta came in.

'There's a woman outside, begging to see you.'

'Begging?' Riemmelth spoke without interest. She pointed to a tray that Enid had brought in earlier on which food and wine were still untouched. 'Take that out to her— tell her she can keep the silver dish and goblet.'

She went back to her brooding. The poor had simple problems. The scraps from a feast, a cast-off trinket or a few coins, and their worries were over, for a while at least. She wished that her own cares could be bought off so cheaply. When Nesta returned some time later and was airing her robes, she asked casually if the stranger had taken her alms and gone.

'No, lady. She wouldn't touch anything. She's still there.'

Riemmelth could not help following Nesta's glance through the ante-room door out to the colonnade, striped with shadows and early morning sunshine. At the threshold a grey figure was crouching, its head bowed and shrouded in a black veil.

'She said she had no hope if she couldn't see you.' Nesta seemed frightened, her voice quavered and sank to a whisper. 'She said she'd fast to death.'

'Hope! Who could look at me and see hope? She'll change her mind when she gets hungry and smells the evening feast at its cooking.'

Morning wore on. The shadows of the pillars shifted, but the figure at the threshold made no move or sound. It began to haunt the rooms, it was there in every corner; it came into Riemmelth's mind and drove out everything else, even Elidir, even her own plight. The stranger did mean to die, then. She had come to the dark frontier where Riemmelth had halted but she would go across. What dreadful compulsion was driving her to do what Riemmelth could not?

At last she surrendered. 'Oh, let her come in.'

She can earn whatever boon she's seeking, she can teach me how to will my death.

The stranger looked like a nun, shrouded in her grey robe, her veiled head on a level with Riemmelth's. Only her hands were visible: thin, fine-boned, long-fingered hands. Riemmelth kept her eyes fixed on these hands, the only part of the figure that looked alive, to hush a mad whisper of fear inside her mind that the woman had no face.

'Well, I've let you see me, as you asked. Now show yourself and tell me why you're here.'

The stranger made no move. A low-toned, husky voice spoke from behind the veil.

'Forgive me, lady, I've made a vow. The day's light will never touch my living face again if you won't help me.'

'What do you want of me?'

The stranger took a step nearer. 'My family are trying to force me into a loathsome marriage—'

Riemmelth felt herself choking.

'And you come to *me*—'

The woman stretched out her hands as if she were in a sinking boat.

'You have the power—you're a woman, you're young—surely you can feel for me—?'

Riemmelth suddenly screamed with laughter. The woman recoiled. She was backing to the door but Riemmelth sprang after her and gripped her arm savagely, feeling the thin bone under her fingers.

'Do you hate me so much?—Or did some enemy bribe you, teach you how to stab me?'

'What have I done, lady? I wouldn't hurt you! I wouldn't willingly rob you of one moment's pastime—only I've been driven to despair—'

71

'You don't take much driving! Who are you to complain of a fate that levels you with queens?' She flung the stranger's arm so that it struck across her body like a blow. 'Get back to your home, girl, and be dutiful to your kin, like me. Think of your wedding gown and laugh for joy, as I do!'

The woman made no protest; she moved away obediently, head bowed and shoulders drooping. Riemmelth felt herself drowning in self-disgust and shame that she could strike in mockery at someone who was already beaten.

'No! Come back!'

The grey figure stilled for a moment, then turned its shapeless head towards her again. Riemmelth was shaking with the violence of her change of feeling and she sat down.

'You can lift your veil. I'll help you if I can.'

The stranger moved her hand vaguely, as if she were blind; her fingers caught the edge of her veil and pulled. It floated down and lay, a black shadow, between them. Riemmelth's heart nearly stopped with shock. The face looking back at her was her own.

It was her wraith, of course; that second self which comes to meet you at the turning point of your life. And the sun had passed its noon—the token was death.

I asked for this. I willed my death. I called her, and she came.

She glanced at the mirror standing on her clothes-chest, to confirm that the visitant cast no reflection, that there was no other living thing in the room. But there were two girls in the mirror. The stranger came to her shoulder and looked at their two faces side by side.

Seen close, they could never be mistaken. They had the same dark hair, winged brows and fine-boned features, but while Riemmelth's face, even after all her grief and loss, was burning with life, the stranger's seemed to lie under a film of ash. Her hair was dead black, with no raven gloss to it, her eyes were slate-grey, faint lines showed above the corners of her mouth. The stranger saw the difference and her thin lips twisted in a smile without amusement; she said an eerie thing:

72

'I was born at the dark of the moon.'

Riemmelth's skin crawled.

'Who are you? Where do you come from?'

'I come from Guasmoric. You won't know my father, but my mother's mother was wife to Madog ap Morfran, armour-bearer and close friend to King Owain.'

'And your grandmother was an even closer friend to King Owain. I know our family history. You're welcome, cousin.'

Riemmelth was smiling with relief. Cumbria's great hero was famous in song and story for his beauty as well as for his courage, and for a charm of manner that was like enchantment. More than one Cumbrian lady, wife as well as maiden, had given him a living proof of her devotion.

She ran for the tray of food that had been refused before, the savoury pasties, delicate honey-cakes and fruit that Enid had chosen to tempt her lady's fading appetite. She poured wine for them both.

'What's your name?'

'Arianrhod.'

Riemmelth raised her goblet. 'I'm truly glad to meet you, Arianrhod.'

She noted with pity and shock that her cousin's thin hands were trembling, her cheeks sunken with hunger, her robe worn as well as travel-stained.

'But how do you come to be in such a plight? Did Owain ap Urien provide so ill for your grandmother and the daughter she bore him? That wasn't usually his way.'

'My mother was beautiful but unlucky.' Arianrhod shook her head impatiently, with that bitter twitch of her mouth. 'No, "unlucky" is a word for a child snivelling over a broken toy. My mother was beautiful but a fool. She wed a flashy spendthrift—whimpered till she got her kin's consent—a handsome face and a boastful voice, nothing behind it— that's my father!'

She sneered. 'Nearly everything went. What little was left was for my brothers, to help them make a show when they

73

went wife-hunting. I had no dowry, or other love-charm, to bring any man hunting me.'

Again the bitter smile.

'But they didn't neglect me—my loving family. They found me a husband. A widower from the fells at Cumrew who could afford a dowerless wife, so he could boast he had King Owain's granddaughter under him in bed. A pinched, mean man, in a pinched, mean homestead.'

She was staring down into her wine as if reading her own fate in the goblet.

'I couldn't believe that this was all life would offer me, for years, for ever. My kin didn't see why I should complain. I'd got a husband, hadn't I? What more did a woman expect?'

She beat her fist on her knee. 'So I ran away before the wedding. I was coming to—King Pascen.' Her eyes pleaded with Riemmelth not to be angry. 'I—I share—the same blood. I'd heard he was light-hearted, laughter-loving—I was sure he'd take my side—'

Riemmelth was sure of it too. Pascen would have laughed at the idea of out-witting the widower; he would have dowered Arianrhod—bedded her, if she'd taken his fancy— and found her a handsome husband among the young nobles of his war-band, who would have honoured her for being the king's choice.

'—then, when I got here, I learnt—what had happened. Three days I've been in Caer Luel, picking up scraps from the market, drinking at the fountain. I hadn't even a ring to barter for food.'

She laughed drearily at herself. 'I'd been telling myself fine tales on the road: some great lord would make me his lover, there'd be music and laughter and bright robes.' She drew her fingers across her shabby, nun-like dress. 'By the second day, I was ready to sell myself to anyone for the price of a meal—only I didn't know how to set about it, and because of the way I look, nobody made me an offer!'

She gripped her hands till the knuckles strained white. 'But I won't go back to live with that man—I can't. Live!—

it would only be a longer dying. I daren't ask the Lord Bishop for help—if he knows I'm in the palace, he'll order me home to obey my family—'

. She broke off and snatched her veil over her face as someone knocked from the ante-room. Riemmelth opened an inner door.

'This is my oratory. Get on your knees—and keep your veil on!'

She turned as Nesta and Enid came in.

'Bishop Rhun wants you to come to the feast tonight, to greet the nobles of the Council.'

Before Riemmelth could refuse, Enid added under her breath,

'He said, "Tell her I order her."'

While the embassy had been on its way to Bebbanburh, the news of Pascen's death had been discreetly doled out to the Cumbrians. In spite of their shock and grief at the loss of the popular young king, the people had taken it calmly enough, thanks to Rhun.

Urien's son, Owain's brother; a great warrior once, a holy bishop in his old age—Rhun towered over the land like Helvellyn or Blencathra, as strong and seemingly as ageless. Prince Rhun would hold the land safe, he had been doing so since before they were born, he would never fail them. And there was the beautiful young princess, heiress of the true blood. In a decent while she would marry some great king or famous warrior-lord. Then she would bear another Pascen or Owain for them, nothing would be changed.

When he knew that the Northumbrians had accepted his offer, and the bridegroom was on his way, Rhun summoned the nobles of the Council. Fighting men in their youth, they were now prudent landowners, anxious to hold on to their estates and leave them to their sons, unwilling to provoke civil war or invasion. It was easy enough for Rhun and Penarwan to present the Northumbrian alliance as the least of a choice of evils. If an English bridegroom brought no joy, at any rate he brought a shared grumble. Nothing promotes unity like a good grievance; if Rhun had chosen a Cumbrian lord to beget his heir, he would have had one ally and nineteen embittered rebels. So Rhun had the Council behind him; he also had their retainers in Caer Luel to join the palace guard if need be in stopping a riot when the English arrived.

As Riemmelth came into the Great Hall, sombre in her mourning robes, they all rose to greet her. She was seething with distaste for these greybeards. Her rage at her own fate, the haunting presence of her brother's laughing ghost, her pity for Arianrhod as another victim of selfish old age made her like a thundercloud with the lightning beginning to flicker at the edges. Under her grandfather's stern eyes, however, she kept her feelings under decent restraint until near the end of the feast. The guests saw nothing amiss with her courtesy; no one expected merriment from her at such a time.

After the feast, Afaon the bard came forward to entertain them and asked the princess to name the first song. She would have liked to remind the whole gathering that she was in no mood for songs, but that would have slighted the bard. Then her hostile spirit prompted her:

'Thank you, Afaon. Give me the tale of *Trystan and Essyllt.*'

She had named that most famous and saddest of all love stories because it matched her mood and her fate: loving one man, forced into marriage with a foreign king, yet bound to her lover by a chain of unbreakable passion till they were united for ever in death. Her grandfather could silence her own protests with threats of imprisonment in a nun's cell but bards were sacred. So let my Lord Bishop Rhun, and all these other withered ancients, sit in respectful silence while Afaon set her grief to music, sang her faith and defiance to their faces.

Rhun saw the point as clearly as she wished; he knew his granddaughter was in a dangerous mood. Suppose she chose her moment, when the Councillors were heated with wine and moved to tears by Afaon's poetry, to appeal to them in the names of Urien and Owain, call on them to rise against the English?

He could not forbid the song, for fear of raising the storm there and then, but his eyes were grim.

Afaon had the bard's uncanny sense for moods and tensions in his audience. He thought the song was dangerously sad; like all young girls, the princess was half in love with her own tears, with no thought of how she would bring the feast to a damp and dreary end. He wanted to cheer her, to brighten the spirit of the gathering. He thought of her coming marriage—a wedding night was always a good source for jests.

So he chose the episode of Essyllt's wedding night; when the Irish queen, to hide the loss of her virginity, had asked her faithful maid Branwen to take her place. She blew the candles out and slid from the bed, while the waiting Branwen slipped into King March's arms.

Afaon was pleased to see that he had caught the princess's attention; she no longer looked like the chief mourner at her own funeral.

What a neat ruse, Riemmelth was thinking, *how simple life was for the heroines of bards' stories—always some loyal bower-woman at hand to save her mistress's honour!*

Both of her own maids would have done it for her without a qualm, but neither was like her. Nesta was short, plump and curly-haired, while Enid was slender and about her height, but fair. It would not be pitch-dark on a May night with the moon waxing, some light would come through the window. Besides, she wasn't sure about Enid's maidenhead; she knew poor Nesta's was gone.

Then she remembered, with a stirring of hope that was almost a thrill of awe, her own face appearing from behind a black veil, looking across her shoulder in a mirror.

Arianrhod, her kinswoman, poor and desperate—and a virgin.

77

'*I had no dowry, or other love-charm, to bring any man hunting me.*'

Riemmelth's eyes began to shine with excitement. *There's some Power taking my side. This was meant. I called her, and she came.*

Looking at his hearers, Afaon congratulated himself. Rhun had relaxed, the Councillors were chuckling over their wine. And, for the first time since her brother's death, the princess was smiling.

At the proper time, Riemmelth bade the guests a courteous goodnight, left them to such decorous drinking as Rhun would permit in his presence, and hurried back to her oratory. She found her cousin huddled on the floor at the foot of the crucifix and thought the girl had fainted but Arianrhod was asleep. There were tears on her dark lashes.

She woke as Riemmelth stroked the hair away from her face; she lifted her hand and touched her cousin's cheek wonderingly.

'You said—you'd save me.'

'We can save each other. Kinsfolk should come to each other's aid. I've few enough left now, and none other to help me.'

'You want my help? What help could I ever be to you?'

Riemmelth had her story ready, worked out while Afaon was singing.

'My grandfather has found me a husband too. An English prince from Northumbria. You're Owain's granddaughter, you can guess how I feel about mating with one of Flamebearer's brood. I made a vow that no Englishman would ever be able to boast of what he did to me on his wedding night. But I'm trapped, like you, because I'm a woman. I must make this marriage for my people's sake.'

She looked at Arianrhod for sympathy. 'Only—there's my vow. No one cares to be forsworn. Would you take my place, just for one night? I'll give you half my jewels and a rich estate in Gwensteri.'

Arianrhod shook her head in her sad wisdom.

'That would sound well in a bard's tale—not so easy to do in real life.'

'I've thought how it can be done. I'm in mourning, I'll insist that things are kept quiet, without the bedding, the bridegroom's entry, and all the riot. I'll have you as my only chamber-woman—I'll tell my maids it's because you're bereaved like me, that you'll suit my mood and I won't take them away from the merrymaking in the hall. Till then, you can stay in the inner room, next to my oratory—you can spend most of your time there, I'll say you're under a vow of silence and prayer. Then, when I come to bed on the night, we'll change places, and exchange again in the morning while the man's asleep.'

Arianrhod lifted her brows. 'What wonderful forethought you have—you should be planning campaigns for the war-host!'

'It's a slight matter to take so much trouble about—but I have my pride. I want that much triumph, at any rate, over an Englishman.'

Arianrhod was smiling. 'There's just one little thing. Next night—how will you explain your restored virginity? A miracle, granted to the saintly Oswald's House?'

Riemmelth was silent, unable to meet her mocking eyes.

'You've got a lover, haven't you?'

'I had a lover—they tricked him away from me. They'll kill him if he comes back—they murdered his foster-brother when I tried to send a message. I'm trapped—but I daren't go to my marriage-bed without my maidenhead.'

'So you want to buy mine?'

'Could you bear to do it for me? Even with an Englishman?'

'I was ready to do it with anyone for a plate of food. You're offering a higher price for my maidenhead than I was going to ask—and a prince to break it for me, too!'

Riemmelth jumped up. 'I'll get the inner room prepared for you. Remember to keep your veil over your face, even

79

while you eat—you're under a vow of silence and prayer, remember—a heart-broken orphan.'

'Widow, I think. If I play your part successfully, I may need a husband to my name in a month or two—even a dead one!'

The cousins looked at each other. Suddenly they burst out laughing, and for a fleeting moment they were as like as twins. Nesta and Enid, who were coming to help their mistress to bed, hurried across the outer room and stood at the oratory door, gaping. Arianrhod had snatched up her veil at the sound of footsteps, but Riemmelth met her maids' eyes boldly.

'This woman is a suppliant, and I've promised to help her. Her family are treating her most unjustly; but if they knew she was here, they'd persuade the Bishop to force her back home in the name of family duty. So I've said she can take refuge here in my oratory for a day or two—no one else is to know anything about her.'

The maids nodded and smiled. They would have followed Riemmelth's orders in blind love and obedience if she had led them over a precipice—but this task was a pleasure. It was part of the endless conspiracy of youth against age.

7

When Riemmelth woke early next morning, all her energy and much of her high spirits seemed to have flowed back during the night, and her blood was dancing through her veins. It was wonderful to be doing something, making decisions, taking her life back into her own hands.

She had Arianrhod's life in her hands now, as well; she meant to do the best for her cousin. Showering her with jewels was easy, but that would only be enriching her for her family and the widower at Cumrew. She meant to make Arianrhod safe, to settle her on an estate of her own in the south, far from Caer Luel and its gossip. She had land to bestow, but that meant a deed of gift. Rhun had his clerks and lawyers in the palace who would be at her service, but to go to one of them would publish Arianrhod's story to the whole court.

Riemmelth puzzled over this for a while, then decided to find one of the cheap scribes who hung about the market, picking up a living among the craftsmen and visiting merchants. He would wonder, of course, why a woman of wealth should conduct her affairs in such a way. She told herself confidently that there was no question that could not be answered in the alleys of Caer Luel with the gleam of gold; so she took a leather bag of bezants, enough to buy a whole farm, let alone a deed.

I'll be a rich young widow with a helpful woman friend, hurrying to endow my lover behind her skirt before my husband's family claim the property.

She played the part in her mind, chuckling a little as she dressed in one of Enid's robes and cloaks, making sure that her veil completely hid her face and hair. She took Nesta with her, leaving Enid to guard her guest from intrusion at her prayers, and set off in high spirits. No thought of the appalling difficulties of the scheme clouded her mind which was full of bards' stories with their successful ruses and magical turns of fortune. She was still young enough to believe that her own life would be like them.

She had begun to have some doubts, though, while she and Nesta were struggling across the great market-place that had once been the forum, making their way towards the network of cattle-pens, inns, tanneries, smithies, craftsmen's workshops, weaving-sheds, ale-booths and hovels, that made up the south-east quarter of the city. She had no idea where she would find a scribe; she could hardly see where she was going among all the folk and was being rudely jostled.

The crowd was thickest where the road went downhill from the market towards the southern gate. A large booth jutted out into the roadway, with a line of stolid or sullen-faced girls squatting in front of it. A gang of young men blocked the narrow crossroads, hindering passers-by, swaggering and talking at the tops of their voices.

'—and her rump was as big as Carrock Fell and nearly as—'

Feeling more and more uneasy, Riemmelth clutched her cloak tight and kept a firm hold on Nesta, trying to edge her past without notice.

Suddenly there was an outcry from the slave-booth—a scream, then angry abuse. The leather curtain bulged as if a body had hurtled against it, then it was torn aside. An odd-looking creature dashed out with a man and a garishly-dressed woman hot on her heels. She had been stripped to her shift for a customer's inspection; her bare limbs were straight and nimble, but the long hair which fell in elf-locks over her back and shoulders was as white as a hag's.

The crossroad idlers joined joyfully in the hunt, grabbing at the quarry and tripping the pursuers with a generous spirit of fair play.

'Over here, darling!'

'Give us a kiss before you go!'

The creature writhed frantically among the clutching hands and grinning men's faces, glimpsed the two soberly-dressed women standing apart and threw herself at the feet of the taller one, clasping her knees, reaching up to seize her hand.

'Help me! If you're a decent woman, please, please buy me—I'll work to death—she's a bawd and she wants to make me a whore—'

Riemmelth tried to step out of reach. She could hardly understand her own language, mangled by the girl's accent; she noted with a shiver of distaste that the strange hair was not white but silver-fair. With that voice and colouring she could only be English. Riemmelth had no pity to spare for

82

the English. At that moment, tormented and harassed as she was, there was even a thrill of malicious pleasure in seeing one of that masterful race as trapped and shamed as she felt herself. She was about to pull her hand away when the man from the booth grabbed the girl by her long silvery hair and pulled her head back; the bawd's be-ringed hand lashed across her face.

'Be quiet, you stupid bitch,' said the trader. 'You don't know your luck, working at "The Golden Lily"—you'll live like a princess.'

Riemmelth stiffened at that name, she was sure that poor Guriat had not died there by unlucky chance. Without knowing, her fingers tensed on the English girl's hand. The bawd saw it.

'None of your interference, mistress. She's bought and paid for.'

Riemmelth stared at the painted face—as sleek, hard and handsome as a well-gorged buzzard. She saw the face smiling at Guriat as he was welcomed in to his murder.

The bawd was impatient. 'Didn't you hear what I said? Take your fingers off my goods.' She put her hand on Riemmelth's breast and pushed.

Riemmelth's hand whipped across her wrist like lightning. 'Take your fingers off me, you filthy whore!'

There was a howl of laughter from the bystanders. A voice from the edge of the crowd called down the alley that two bitches were fighting in the gutter, come and see the sport. There was a rush towards them and, with some jostling, a ring was formed. The bawd pulled at Riemmelth's veil, trying to claw her hair and eyes, but Rimmelth moved with the speed of a huntress who had often faced the spring of a cornered wolf. Her fist drove into the bawd's face like a spear-head and the woman's mouth was cut against her teeth. A cheer went up. Someone started to call odds.

Little Nesta, frantic, was tugging at the bawd's skirt to pull her back, when she was snatched up by a burly drover.

'Hey, none of that! Two against one's not fair! Have a

tumble with me, if you want a bit of sport!'

He tossed her up, to swing her head over heels and bring her skirt down over her head. The bawd spat the blood out of her mouth, then drew a knife. Riemmelth threw off her veil and braced herself to catch the bawd off balance and twist or snap the wrist. Nesta, hurtling upwards, caught a glimpse of the red cloak of a palace guard, some yards away, watching a juggler and his girl in a corner of the market-place; she shrieked to him.

'Help! *Gereint!* Help, they're killing the princess!'

Gereint glanced round, saw Nesta over the heads of the mob, stared for a second, then started towards them, yelling for a couple of his comrades, who were inside an ale-booth. These came out, wiping their mouths, then shouldered their way after Gereint.

The onlookers had fallen as still and quiet as an enchanted stone circle. The bawd was on her knees, whimpering, 'How could I know—?' The trader had dashed for a cloak to put on the English girl whom he then pushed towards Riemmelth. 'Here she is, my lady, I won't keep you waiting a moment! Will you take her now—or shall I bring her—?'

Gereint scowled them into silence, then said quietly, 'Do you want to have them flogged, princess, before I throw them back in the sewer?'

Riemmelth shook her head. She was going to be the night's talk on every ale-bench in Caer Luel and at every farmer's hearth within reach of the city; she didn't want the story scored on people's memories with weals and blood. She gathered her tattered dignity as best she might, speaking coldly at the bawd.

'If you want to be good at your craft, you should learn to know your tools. This girl won't do for your work.' She threw down her bag of gold. 'Pay yourself back out of that.'

The crowd's goodwill came surging back to her like a Solway tide. Pascen had played such pranks more than once, roaming among his people like one of themselves; standing his drink and taking his knock with a good grace, then

84

ending the jest with a laugh and the chink of gold. Looking at Riemmelth, they saw Pascen in her face; the old blood still ran true. She made her way back through the forum, followed by the two girls and escorted by the palace warriors on a wave of cheering, applause and shouted blessings.

The tale had run ahead of her. The gate-guard said that her grandfather wanted to see her as soon as she returned. She went to his room with the despairing calm of a walk to the gallows.

I've ruined myself now. I'll be under lock and key in Penarwan's convent till they hand me over to the Englishman. And they'll drag Arianrhod back to her family, to her widower— her death. I've destroyed us both.

Rhun looked angrier than she had ever seen him.

'Have you lost all sense of modesty? How dare you walk the streets? And get into a vulgar brawl?' He stared into her eyes, trying to read her mind. Had she meant to disgrace herself publicly, so that the English prince would refuse to take her?

'What were you doing out there?'

'Redeeming an English war-captive.'

'What?'

She had not planned the lie, but it came as smoothly from her lips as if someone had made it ready for her long ago.

'I know that King Oswald and his family can speak British, but I've little skill in English. I thought it would be gracious to greet them in their own language. I could have asked you to lend me one of your clerks to instruct me, but they're busy men. A maid I can chatter to at all hours— that's the best way for a woman to practise a language.'

Rhun smiled benevolently. 'An excellent idea, child, but still you shouldn't have risked—'

She lifted her beautiful eyes with saintly innocence. 'And then it came to me that if I could free one of their people from slavery, it would be a good-will offering—my own wedding gift to my bridegroom.'

Rhun was deeply touched.

85

'Heaven must have inspired you.'

'So it seems. For I found an English girl of decent manners about to be sold into a—' she lowered her lashes '—a house of ill-fame. I was able to save her from that wickedness.'

'An act of blessed charity.'

'St Paul tells us that Charity is the highest Grace. Oh, that reminds me,' she went on brightly, as if she had just remembered some trifling detail, 'a poor woman came to me, begging. She's quite destitute, and I should like to provide for her before my marriage, on one of my own estates in the south—with your consent, of course.'

'Do whatever you like, my dear. You don't need my permission to do good works. Your estates are your own.'

Rhun was so delighted with her, and so relieved at the pleasant spirit she was now showing towards her English bridegroom, that he would have let her maintain a hundred beggarwomen if she chose.

'I'll tell one of my clerks to draw up a deed of gift and send it to you—you'll have nothing to do but add the name and fix your seal.'

He kissed her forehead.

'I can't tell you how much your help means to me in these sad days. Cumbria will be blessed in its next queen—tender-hearted, gracious, and good to the poor.'

Riemmelth smiled at him virtuously and withdrew. In the colonnade the steward met her to ask if she wanted the new slave sent to the kitchens.

'No, she's to serve in my rooms and run errands for my maids. Enid and Nesta will train her.'

She went on her way, thinking with satisfaction how good deeds reward the doer. *A stranger, who doesn't know our ways and won't see anything odd, whatever we do. A foreigner, not ready with her tongue to gossip. An English girl, who won't find any friends here to coax her to talk. A perfect tool. Grandfather spoke truer than he knew: it was indeed an act of blessed charity.*

Next day the English arrived, and Riemmelth was summoned to meet them. She went shrouded in her deepest mourning, partly for defiance, but mainly to avoid sealing any clear impression of herself on her bridegroom's memory. She murmured her greeting; her eyes were modestly cast down, though alert and wary under her long lashes.

Her first startled view gave her an impression of gigantic size and fairness; even Rhun was dwarfed by them. Oswald was as bright as the summer sun, with yellow hair and calm blue eyes. His face was long, fringed with a rather thin beard, and he had small lips which seemed to rest naturally in a kindly expression. He was very broad-shouldered with hands and arms that were long and showed great strength. He sat as still as a church image, his big hands palm-upwards on his knees in an odd gesture, like the hands of a priest making intercession at Mass.

The other man—*her* man, Heaven help her!—seemed to be slighter, but perhaps that was only because he was more quick to move and his eyes were restless. He was very like his brother in features, with the same strong jutting nose, long cheeks, long upper lip and long jaw, but he kept his beard trimmed short and close, which made his face look harder. He was fairer than Oswald, his hair like silver sand, washed and gleaming from the ebb-tide; she could see the same fair sheen across the backs of his hands and wrists, as if he had just come up sleek from a plunge under the waves. Once she started thinking of him as a sea-creature, she couldn't get the idea out of her mind. It was the effect of his eyes that changed colour as they moved, now harmless blue like Oswald's, now bleakly grey, now green, cool and remote.

Those eyes had moved quickly over Riemmelth and passed on without much interest. She was not at her best; unrelieved black did not suit her and her lithe figure had vanished inside the heavy folds of her robe. With her glossy hair bound under a mourning veil, her face expressionless with downcast eyes, she looked drab and sullen.

Oswy told himself that at least she didn't seem deformed, that anyway he had to take the breeding stock along with the land, and then turned his attention to the Abbess. Penarwan was taking a lively part in the talk between his brother and Bishop Rhun; Oswald was as interested in church affairs as in kingcraft.

There's a pleasant woman, thought Oswy; *she must have been very handsome when she was young; she still is, when you can find her features among her cheeks and chins.*

Behind his eyes he stripped her and was amusing himself imagining what it would feel like to sink down into all that flesh, breasts like cows' udders, billowy buttocks, cushioned thighs. The Abbess turned a remark to him; their eyes met, and he could see that she knew exactly what he was thinking. He smiled at her politely and began to talk to his betrothed about the coming celebrations.

'There won't be any celebrations!'

Riemmelth's eyes flashed blue lightning at him; she was tense and spoke more sharply than she meant.

'Riemmelth!' Rhun tried to get a rebuke into his tone and look; he didn't dare say any more in case she made one of her dreaded outbursts. Oswy noticed this.

She didn't want this marriage; they've fought about it.

'I'm in mourning,' cried Riemmelth desperately. 'My brother's not a fortnight in his grave!'

'Grief must yield to duty.' Rhun's voice was stern. 'Everything will be done with fitting ceremony.'

She found unexpected allies.

'God forbid,' said Oswald, with grave kindness, 'that we should break the repose of the dead with unseemly revelling.'

Her bridegroom grinned at her.

'Don't worry, sweetheart, I won't come drunk to bed.'

She gave him another furious look, but inwardly she was appalled. To have Oswy coming in on her and Arianrhod before they were ready—perhaps, oh, horror! retiring with her, cold sober and taking everything in with those watchful eyes—that would ruin her plan.

'My granddaughter has been practising your language,' said Rhun, to break an awkward silence. 'She saved an English girl from slavery to be her teacher.'

They turned to her, smiling; she felt a tide of goodwill flowing towards her and took her chance to escape on it, murmuring something about bringing the girl to meet them.

Rhun rose and invited Oswald to come and look at his copy of the *Cura Pastoralis* that had come from St Gregory's own scriptorium. They went off happily together. Oswy offered the Abbess his arm, but instead of following the Bishop, she turned into the courtyard garden and strolled leisurely along its path.

In spite of her age and sacred office, Penarwan felt a mild ripple of pleasure at the company and touch of a man from her dead lover's race. She liked his tall body, his fairness and she was not in the least angry at his insolence. It was gratifying that a man should still take the trouble to undress her, even if only with his eyes.

Oswy was highly amused by her company; also he welcomed the chance to find out a few things about his new marriage-kin.

'The princess's mother has been dead for a long time, I think? You are her aunt, perhaps?'

He'd taken about thirty years off her age by the guess, and she sparkled at him, though she knew he was flattering her, and not even expecting to be believed.

'You must look further back than that to find the kinship. I'm the widow of her grandfather's elder brother, Owain ap Urien.'

'She doesn't seem very pleased about her marriage.'

'She's been spoilt. Her father and brother let her have her own way in everything—she thinks she should have been left to pick herself a husband.'

'You mean she's picked herself a lover.'

'Oh no!' Penarwan's hazel eyes were bright with indulgent

affection. 'She's just in love with the heroes of the old British tales who fought against the Romans—and the English. She'd like to rule Cumbria by herself and keep you out.'

They turned at the end of the path and began to stroll back. Penarwan went on with her work.

'She'll need firm handling, especially at the start. There isn't the least harm in her, but she might let herself be used in a way to cause harm. Any Cumbrian noble plotting revolt could use her name as a war-cry.'

She looked up at him, sincere and friendly.

'My advice is that you take her away to Northumbria at once—separate her from her maids and other trouble-makers until she knows her master.'

She went up the steps, smiling, and left him in the colonnade, having made as sure as humanly possible that Riemmelth would be given bit and bridle, and a strong hand on the reins.

8

'Well, that was a very pleasant meeting. This marriage promises happily.'

Oswald had spent an enjoyable hour in the Bishop's library; he was sitting now in the sumptuously furnished guest chamber, poring over a manuscript that Rhun had lent him. Oswy stretched and yawned.

'If Rhun can fix a dispensation, I'd as soon have the Abbess.'

'You must guard your tongue, brother. You'll offend the Cumbrians if they hear you.'

'I can tell you one who wouldn't be offended. She's a grand old warrior from Venus's war-band—she'd have her shield broken and take a man's spear-thrust with the best of them.'

'Oswy! I won't have you talk like that. It's unseemly—and you know how touchy the Welsh can be.'

'Yes, I might be struck by lightning from my loving little thundercloud. At least, it would brighten the gloom!'

The same idea crossed the mind of more than one of Oswy's hearth-companions during the wedding ceremonies next day. Cumbria was very wealthy, and Rhun's sense of dignity and Penarwan's skilful preparations had provided a lavish feast. The great basilica of the palace was brilliant with hangings from Constantinople, the tables were weighted with massed gold and silver dishes, the wine was flowing freely; but for all that, the Northumbrians were finding it a slow and dreary business.

Godric, Oswy's shield-bearer, made another disgusted survey of the wedding party at the High Table. Penarwan had insisted that Riemmelth should leave off her black clothes, and she was sombrely magnificent in dark purple brocade with a pearl coronet like tear drops. She had left her raven hair streaming loose down her back in token of her maidenhood, savouring the bitter jest, telling herself that she could wear this much of black in mourning for her betrayed love; she could go on wearing it till it turned white with age. Then nothing would matter any more.

Godric set her down in his mind as a sulky little lump. He didn't envy Oswy his job tonight; he'd need to have his torch well alight and hold it up for a long time before getting any sort of fire going between her legs. Queen of the Lightning! She was more like a day's drizzle in the Cheviots.

The rest of the wedding group seemed contented enough. Oswald was deep in talk with the old corpse of a bishop—that was all he ever needed to make him happy. Oswy was laughing with the Abbess—now, there was a nice woman, she made you feel welcome, unlike the rest of these Cumbrians. A fine wedding, though, when a seventy-year-old Abbess was the cheeriest thing about it! He wouldn't say it was like a funeral, he'd been to some good funerals.

Godric's face was not expressive, but it could express that much. The Horse-Thane of Northumbria, Cadman Cadwalsson, was watching him, his dark eyes agleam with mockery; he had to choke back his laughter. These two had been friends since they were boys at weapon-training, though Godric was only the son of a churl, whose courage had earned him a place in the prince's war-band. Cadman was one of the old Welsh nobility of Bernicia, fiercely proud. He was truly fond of Godric, but he'd never pick him as envoy to a tricky peace-meeting.

The look on their two faces, the stolid contempt of the Englishman, the Briton's malicious amusement, goaded Idwal into speech.

'Cumbrian feasts aren't usually like this. The princess broke her heart when her brother died; they were very close.'

'Poor lass,' said Godric, good-naturedly, 'she's lucky to get our atheling to warm her bed for her.' Then, with much more interest, 'How did he die?'

Idwal told him; then they all began to swap tales about their own ambushes and escapes which passed the time much better. Idwal thawed and invited them to come back to the guards' quarters after the bride was bedded. There would be ale and mead, they could finish the night properly. Godric brightened, he prayed the bride wouldn't be long about it. No, thank God, she was moving at last.

Nesta and Enid undressed Riemmelth and laid her gently in her bed. She gave them a kiss and dismissed them.

'Off to the hall with you, my dears—drink some good luck to me.'

When they were gone, Arianrhod came to her bedside in a loose black robe and veil.

'I've sent the English girl away—she wanted to watch you in the hall. I told her not to come back till morning. She'll be quite happy talking to her own people.'

She took off her clothes and helped Riemmelth to get into

them, then lay down naked in the bed. Riemmelth saw the
gleam of a silver necklace as she drew up the coverlets. She
put out all the candles except one on the chest at Oswy's side
of the bed. The room was dim, she could hardly see
Arianrhod's face through a sudden mist of tears, as she
touched her cousin's cheek gently with her lips.

'Don't speak if you can help it—let him talk—just
whisper—'

She lit an oil lamp from the candle and glided out to wait
by the outer door.

She was shaking and there was a rushing sound in her
ears. If anything went wrong, it would mean death for
Arianrhod and herself. It might mean the end of Cumbria.
Soon she heard the tramp of feet and men laughing. Oswy
had kept his word not to stay and drink. She heard his voice
outside. 'Right, my lads, you can get back to the feast.'

Somebody seemed to ask a question.

'No, I don't want your help to undress—or anything else!'

A guffaw, feet moving away; the door opened. She held
the lamp away from herself to light his path; he was across
the room in a few strides, she saw his tall figure black in the
chamber doorway, the door closed behind him.

Riemmelth put the lamp on the table and sat down. She
could not bring herself to listen at the door but she was
straining for sounds from the bedroom: Oswy's voice raised
in sharp questions, a bellow of rage, a scream, the door
crashing open. She braced herself, ready to throw herself
between Oswy and Arianrhod, to take the brunt of his anger.
There seemed to be a low murmuring from the inner room
and she tried to make out which of the two was speaking.
Silence. Then a louder sound, Arianrhod's voice raised in
delighted laughter. A man's laugh drowned it. Silence again,
then a sharp cry, but not of fear.

Riemmelth sank back, she no longer needed to hear.
Longing swept over her like a flood, she drowned in it,
screaming silently for Elidir. She made his dark face bend
smiling over her, clutched his arms round her, made his

heart beat against her, felt him inside her body. But memory and moonlight cannot warm the blood, and long before the night ended, she felt corpse-cold.

With the first grey of the dawn, Arianrhod stole out to her. Riemmelth wrapped a cloak round her; though Arianrhod was naked, her skin was warm from her bed and she seemed to be carrying more warmth inside her. The ashy film of bitterness had been brushed away, her cheeks were flushed and her mouth had softened.

Riemmelth had a casket ready with some of her finest jewels, a bag of gold, and a deed of gift of her estate in Gwensteri. Arianrhod smiled.

'You're over-paying me for my hire.'

Her eyes were laughing, but Riemmelth, sunk in her own bitterness, did not notice. She felt that she had wronged Arianrhod by making her spend the night with Oswy, had treated her like a whore. She hurried to make amends.

'Don't talk about hire. It's a gift to a dear, kind friend and kinswoman. We share the same flesh and blood, remember.'

'We do, indeed.' Arianrhod's voice was strangely tender. 'Well, friends exchange gifts at parting. This is all I've got, but it's precious to me. I wouldn't barter it, even when I was starving.'

She had taken off her necklace and held it out. It was a chain with a strange triple pendant: a silver moon-disc flanked by two crescents, waxing and waning. Riemmelth was startled.

'You worship the Goddess—you keep the Old Faith?'

'Don't be alarmed, my Christian cousin. You, too, revere the Queen of Heaven. Besides, it's as well you should wear this. He—noticed it. You are me now, remember, for him.'

Again, there was that strange tone in her voice.

They kissed farewell. Riemmelth had made all the arrangements for Arianrhod's departure: one of her own bailiffs had been in Caer Luel with his wife and would escort the 'widow' to her new home. Arianrhod went to her own room to robe and veil herself while Riemmelth went cat-footed into the bedchamber, slipped off her shift and got cautiously into bed. Oswy, sound asleep, was turned towards her. She held herself as far away from him as possible; she felt like ice, but where Arianrhod had lain it was warm.

9

Riemmelth heard Nesta and Enid moving about; Oswy slept on. She went out to them, to get dressed before he woke. They were red-eyed and catching their breath and she tried to cheer them with a joke.

'Don't cry—marriage isn't so terrible.'

'Oh, my lady, the Abbess told us last night—'

'Why didn't you warn us you were leaving so soon?'

'*Leaving?*'

'Today, she said. The King's taking you back to Northumbria.'

Riemmelth was horrified. She had taken for granted that Oswy would be staying in Cumbria to guard it for her—after all, that was why they had made her marry the creature.

'To Northumbria?'

'Yes, the Abbess told us last night after the feast. And, oh my lady, she says—' Enid's voice choked. 'She says we're not coming with you!' They broke out sobbing.

Riemmelth went storming back to the bedroom where Oswy was awake and stretching.

'Up already, sweetheart? You put me to shame. Come here and rouse me.' He reached out his long arms to pull her on to the bed but she stepped back, her fists clenched, her eyes flashing. Whatever she had been in the night, she was truly Queen of the Lightning now.

'My maids say you mean to set out for Northumbria

today—why wasn't I told?'

'A husband always does mean to bring his bride home.' He grinned. 'You feel it's too soon to go riding again? Don't worry, my love, I'll see you have plenty of chances to lie down on the way.'

'I can't—I won't—travel today! Who do you think you've married—a hill-farmer's daughter to be pulled up on your horse and hustled off to your farm to get on with the baking and the milking the day after the wedding?'

'Listen, my lady, this marriage took us as much unawares as you; your grandfather told us you were in peril and begged us to come at once, and so we did. But both my brother and I left many tasks undone in our own land when we came.'

'Then go attend to them and welcome! There's no call for me to leave Cumbria, and I won't do it!'

'She'd like to rule Cumbria by herself and keep you out.'

Oswy's eyes were grey as the winter sea, but his voice was pleasant.

'There's a call from your kinsfolk. Our sister, Oswald's wife, our cousins, they're all eager to meet you, why should you wish to slight them? And your grandfather thought it would do you good, after your sad loss, to come to your new family for a while.'

He was courteous, he was reasonable—and he was unyielding. She shifted to another battlefield.

'My new family will think it strange to see a princess arrive unattended. It's surely not beyond your power and skill to convey my maids?'

'—separate her from her maids and other trouble-makers till she knows her master.'

'My dear, Bebbanburh and Gefrin are swarming with maidservants. You'll find more than enough to attend you there.'

'And on the journey I fend for myself, I suppose—or will your war-band come to undress me and put me to bed?'

He laughed. 'Trust me, I could do that for you unaided.

But there's no need for you to be in such dire straits. You've got your English bower-woman, Mildred. She's good-tempered and modest—I thought that was why you took her into service, to come with you to England and help you talk English.'

Riemmelth stood baffled and sullen, silently cursing Mildred.

'As to dressing you, I'm happy to do my share. Here's my morning gift to you, sweetheart—and a poor return it is for the treasure you gave me in the night.'

He had put the casket ready on the bedside chest last night and opening its lid he set it in her hands. Riemmelth was rich in jewels, but still she gasped.

The six brooches were gold, divided into bands where strange flat serpents writhed, knotted, coiled, in elaborate patterns. Honeycombed among them were scores of filigree cells—squares, diamonds, triangles, steps—each set with a dark red garnet. The gold shone behind the garnets, so that every brooch seemed to hold living flame at its heart.

The gift was fit for the Empress at Constantinople, it would have been hard to find the right words to thank him even if she had been grateful—even if she had earned the brooches. Mercifully, there was a knock on the outer door and some of his bodyguard tramped in grinning from ear to ear, so she was able to withdraw modestly.

She had ample time to prepare for leaving, while Oswald and Rhun made parting speeches, the bodyguard doused last night's mead fumes out of their heads, and the grooms loaded pack-horses. She played with the idea of shrouding herself in her mourning robes, but her pride revolted at the picture of herself being hauled off in a travelling-waggon like a war-captive, so she dressed in her hunting gear. With a courtesy that was also mostly pride, she added a couple of Oswy's brooches, pinning her plaid at the shoulder, fastening the feather in her cap.

She intended to take her leave of Rhun with the coldest formality, to punish him for sending her away, but he looked so old and frail, and gazed at her so wistfully, when she came to him, that she threw her arms round him and lifted her face to his kiss.

'God's blessing on your happiness, my dear!'

There was a hum of approval from the Northumbrians when she came to the outer courtyard and swung herself lightly up on to Gwylan's tall back. The hunting jerkin and breeches showed up her lithe shape, she'd had something worth the finding hidden under her black wrappings. Oswy had a sleek, satisfied look, you could tell he was pleased with his bargain.

Mildred, her English bower-woman, was riding pillion behind Godric, her cheeks rosy, her grey eyes shining like stars. She was handsomely dressed—Riemmelth could never be petty to her servants—but it wasn't this, or the fact that she was going back to her own people, that made her so happy.

The poor girl had seen her father and brothers hacked to death, her home in Weorf Dale going up in flames over their bodies as she was dragged away by raiders from Dunoding. The man that took her had a jealous shrew for wife who had opened up another hell for Mildred beyond her rape. After a few weeks of screaming and vicious spite, her master had traded her for a hunting dog; some while later—she'd stopped counting days—she was in the slave-booth at Caer Luel with a bawd haggling for her.

Riemmelth had flashed down into this pit of horror and despair like a fiery angel. Mildred had not picked up enough Welsh to follow all the talk, but she saw Riemmelth striking the bawd's hand away, defying the bawd's knife to save her, throwing down the bag of gold to ransom her. There were no fit words to praise her new mistress—how good she'd been to that poor starving widow! And now she had chosen Mildred above all her maids to attend her. King Oswald was very kind, too; he had promised to have her farm rebuilt and stocked, but she thought little of it. She was the princess's bower-woman, it was all she asked.

98

Godric was pleased to have Mildred up against him with her arms round his waist and he told her to hold him tight in case he fell off. Mildred would rather have had Cadman, whose dark looks and lilting accent made him like her lady. However, he and Godric rode together, so she could watch him and listen to his talk.

They rode across Idon bridge and climbed the slope above the river. Riemmelth took a last look back at the red city, glowing under the westering sun, and at the distant mountains guarding her own lost Eskdale, where she had ridden free and laughing with Elidir.

'We've got all our lives to love each other' . . . *'But if I should lose you?'*

Then everything melted into tears. Oswald saw her wet cheeks.

'Whichever way you ride this road now, sister, you'll have a home-coming at the end of it.'

She felt the kindness and she was comforted, as he had meant her to be, by his taking her return to Cumbria as a matter of course. She made an effort to talk to him and point out things by the way, thinking how much easier life would be if she was a war-captive. Then she could just hate them, and plan her escape; now she was struggling to think of polite remarks. She noticed that they attended at once to the least thing she said. Oswald would listen gravely and follow up the point with painstaking courtesy, Oswy would turn it off with a jest. Nevertheless, it was Oswald who caused her the most dreadful pain she suffered that day.

The sun was setting as they came to Uxellodun above the Irthing, where they were to lodge that night with the lord. Across the river, in a ruined Roman fort, St Nynia had consecrated a church with a baptismal shrine at the foot of the cliff. There was a ferry for pilgrims. Oswald had a reverent spirit and, besides, he was eager to show honour to Riemmelth by his respect for her country's saints.

'Shall we keep a vigil, sister, at St Nynia's well?'

Oswy saw her stricken look and shouted with laughter.

'Have mercy, brother, it's only our second night. She's got another kind of vigil to keep.'

Their escort joined in the laugh, but approved when Riemmelth turned her back on them. A well-bred lady shouldn't seem to understand such jokes. Snow on her face, fire under her shift—that's how a decent wife should be.

She hurried through the feast that the lord of Uxellodun gave in their honour and withdrew early, pleading that she was tired and needed her bed. Oswy raised his goblet to that with a will. But a man, even a bridegroom, couldn't run away from the mead-bench like a girl and she had plenty of time to be in bed and asleep by the time he came to her. She lay with closed eyes listening to him tell Mildred to get out, with something that sounded like a kiss; the rustlings and movements as he undressed, humming under his breath. Then the coverlets lifted and she felt a large body looming over her. She lay still, pretending sleep.

'Riemmelth!'

She felt a warm hand on her shoulder, sliding down her breast, and made herself keep breathing evenly and deep, praying he wouldn't feel her heart jump.

'Riemmelth?'

He fingered her body a while longer, but lightly, as if he was brushing his fingertips across harpstrings without trying to pluck out a melody; then he stretched and yawned.

'Oh, well!'

He settled himself down beside her. With the weariness at her heart and the warmth from his body, she was soon really asleep.

She found later that the journey took four days but she only woke up to it at moments. Most of the time she was caught in a dream made up of hills and clouds, a horse's head nodding in front of her, wind brushing the bents and heather, the sound of hoofs . . .

They stopped a night at Ceasterholm, a big farming village among the ruins of a Roman town. There was a bustle to prepare their quarters, and escaping from Mildred's officious care she wandered down to the beck. The water was flowing clear and fast, leaping among the stones, trees grew close to its edge, there were hawthorns still in bloom. Every ripple of the water, every rustle among the leaves, was whispering 'Elidir' to her; her spirit was crying out to him but he seemed to be going further and further away from her, as he had gone in her nightmare. She tried to pull him back, behind her eyes, but he did not come.

Oswy found her tranced and staring at a bush of may bloom.

'Are you saying your vespers to Frea? I thought you needed to wait till moonrise.'

'Frea?'

'That's what we call The Lady in English. I know you've got her silver token on you—and I wasn't too busy to hear you whispering to her for her favour on our wedding night. Did you put that in your confession?'

Riemmelth writhed in spirit but dared not speak. He put his arms round her. 'The mists are rising—it's time we went in. I wouldn't want that warm blood to get chilled now I've taken charge of it.'

She was lonely and desolate for the place was haunting her with her loss. It was something to feel strong arms and warm flesh close to her, to be taken in out of the cold. She went with him passively and let him do as he liked. He was skilful and surprisingly gentle, her mind was far away, and in a while it didn't matter.

Next day, there were the same hills and clouds, Gwylan's head and mane nodding in front of her, the wind sweeping the moors. A pause, with Oswald in prayer under his cross at Heavenfield, his bare head golden in the sunlight. He had set up the cross with his own hands, in the early dawn of that day, seven years before, when his small army had broken the southern invaders, destroyed Cadwallon, sent Penda in retreat from Northumbrian land, and ended the Accursed Year.

Then north from the Wall on to Deira Street, among

higher hills. A road forking north-east. Cloud patterns and sheep on the moorlands, curlews calling, clumps of reed and bog-cotton, black pools among the peat.

At last they came to a river flowing eastwards out of a valley, with a wide plain stretching beyond it to the north, watched by a line of hills. The furthest hill rose in a huge cone, its whole summit crowned with the ruined walls of a great fortress. There was a town at its foot all of wood, one vast hall towering over all the rest. Then faces.

Faces of warriors and grooms. Faces of officials appearing in some ritual order as they made their way through the township, faces with unpronounceable names making speeches in the language she still barely understood. Then she was with Oswy in a large, bright room and the faces staring at her were women's.

There was a face like Oswald's: the long bones, wrapped in a widow's veil, unsoftened by hair or beard, looked like a melancholy but good-tempered horse. A face framed in smooth bands of fair hair, that had the bland expressionless beauty of an ivory Virgin from Constantinople. A vivid, clear-cut face like a handsome boy, under a crown of golden plaits. A small delicate face with big, pale-blue eyes like a kitten's, and an oddly mean little mouth.

Struggling with fatigue and bewilderment, battered with strange names like a cornered fugitive under a hail of stones, she grasped that the horse was Ebbe, Oswy's sister; the ivory image was Cyneburg of Wessex, Oswald's wife; the handsome, boyish young woman was Hild and the kitten was Elfwyn—these two were cousins, mother's kin of the Royal House.

Then Oswy left her, telling her to make haste to be ready for the feast, and she was alone with the women. Maids had brought in spiced ale and cakes, but Ebbe and Hild had served them to her. The royal women stood round, watching her and smiling; their maids and bower-women stood and stared behind them. She realised that they were going to stay and assist her to dress, while they found out what clothes and jewels she had brought from Caer Luel.

Apart from Ebbe, whose black clothes made her look like an abbess, they were all richly and brightly dressed in kirtles and tunics of scarlet, emerald and sapphire, heavily trimmed with wide bands of elaborate embroidery. This flood of colour should have swamped them, but their fair skins and bright hair sailed over it triumphantly. They were loaded with gold—in their hair ribbons, their buckles, their bracelets and rings; many of their brooches flamed with garnets, and ropes of amber were strung across their breasts.

Riemmelth felt uneasy. She had been too bitter about her marriage, and had left Caer Luel in too much of a hurry to care about making herself fine for Oswy, but she did not want to see herself, or her country, belittled now. She wondered anxiously what had been packed for her. The Abbess might have taken a malicious amusement in shaming her with shabbiness and poverty. She need not have worried, for Penarwan was too intelligent, and set too much value on Cumbrian prestige, to take such a vulgar revenge. The humiliations she planned for Owain's last heir were more subtle.

Riemmelth could not, and would not, vie with the Englishwomen in gaudy colours, but she had silks from Constantinople, and jewels that had been in the Cumbrian Royal House while Britain was still in the Empire. She chose a robe of silver tissue, with an over-tunic of silver-brocaded purple and a coronet with pendants of pearls and amethysts falling to her shoulders. Though she had little heart for feasting, it was some satisfaction to feel that she looked like a Roman empress queening it among the Goths.

There was a moment's unpleasantness as they set out for the feast. Riemmelth moved to go first as she had done all her life. The ivory image came suddenly alive.

'I didn't know I was to lose my place,' she said peevishly, 'just because the King's younger brother got married.'

'Our sister was only looking round for the door,' said

Ebbe, firmly. 'She doesn't know her way about yet. Take my arm, dear.'

Riemmelth took her place beside the King's sister, angry with herself at her mistake, bitterly galled to be in the train of a Saxon queen. Elfwyn and Hild walked behind them, followed by the rest of the women.

Having spent most of her life in houses of Roman brick or stone, she was expecting the timber buildings to be like a cattle-chief's hall, thick with smoke and drunken shouting, the floor squalid with stale rushes and bones, fouled by dogs. She found the great palace of Gefrin almost terrifying in its alien splendour. It was high enough for giants, with a windowed gallery at each end. Its walls were plastered a dazzling white, the lower level hung with embroidered cloths and bright shields. There were four great doors, one in the middle of each wall, covered with dyed leather and elaborately worked metal studs. Four aisles led to the great central hearth, between four raised feasting floors carrying long tables and cushioned benches. At the far end, facing the hearth on a dais above a flight of steps, was the 'gift-stool', the throne where Oswald received envoys and gave out rewards. It was empty now. Oswald was at the head of the table to the right, looking down the hall, with Oswy next to him first of a line of nobles. Cyneburg took her place at the head of the left-hand table and Riemmelth sat down on the bench between Ebbe and Hild.

Her eyes and mind were drawn away from Oswy, away from the solemn processions of servers up and down the aisles, even from the display of gold, silver and polished ivory on the table before her, to the hall itself. Every inch of its woodwork—door frames, roof posts and tie-beams—was covered with bands of carving. She thought at first that the bands were endlessly interlaced ribbons, then she noticed that the ribbons had flat heads and bead-like eyes; they were coiling serpents. Her eyes were helplessly caught, she had to follow the coils up and down, through and under; now she saw that there were birds and animals inside the coils, and people doing odd things. There was a man watching a girl turn into a swan—or was it a swan turning into a girl? A jewel-smith was making a goblet—only it was a skull; a queen was wearing a necklace of teeth; someone she didn't want to see too closely was riding a horse with eight legs; two wolves were eating a man's head—only it was the sun . . .

She didn't want to watch the figures, but when she looked away she found she was worrying about what they might be doing out of her sight. She began to feel the serpents slithering over her body, winding her in their coils, dragging her away into their strange world—when a movement on her bench broke the spell.

Cyneburg had risen. She was holding a gold-rimmed drinking horn, which one of the servers was filling from a richly ornamented bucket full of mead. To Riemmelth's amazement, she stepped down from the platform and went across to the King's table to fill the drinkers' goblets. Ebbe was next, carrying her horn to the other end of the King's table; Hild was stirring beside her and she realised that the servers were looking inquiringly towards herself.

She was appalled and furious. At home, she had presented the guest cup to specially honoured visitors, but her spirit revolted at the idea of serving drink to a pack of spearmen, as if she were a bondmaid or a war-captive.

She heard Elfwyn's soft little voice; she was speaking apart to Hild, but it was odd how clearly her tone carried.

'The Welshwoman thinks herself above being courteous to the King's hearth-companions.'

'Riemmelth thinks herself, quite rightly, to be our guest tonight.' Hild smiled at her. 'Of course, you're not expected to greet the gesithas yet—the King's hearth-companions,' she explained to Riemmelth's blank look; then, with the irritating self-mockery of the English when using a British word, his "teulu". Would you like to come round with me and meet some of them?'

Riemmelth went, rather than sit alone and be stared at. Then there were more faces and more names—Wulfstan,

Dunnere, Cenelm, Guthlac—and she smiled at them all till her face felt stiff.

When they were back in their places, a man with a harp had come to the steps of the dais, one of their bards. Mildred had taught her the English word: they were called 'scops'—shapers, creators—because they made images of life. She tried to follow what he was chanting, but the language was difficult, not like their ordinary talk. It seemed to be mostly long speeches and she struggled to make sense of it—this was what she was going to have to listen to in the evenings.

A warrior called Waldere had run away from the king's court with Princess Hildegyth, who was being held hostage. The king was generous and trusted him, but he loved the princess and had promised to take her home. They were trapped now, in a mountain pass, where the royal war-band had caught them. The captain of the war-band, Hagena, was Waldere's dearest sword-friend and sworn brother. Whichever loyalty he followed now would destroy him.

It was an odd story for a bard to tell. There was no magic in it, no shape-shifting, no castle of wonders or fairy-woman out of the Hollow Hills. Just four people who liked and respected each other, who meant no harm, trapped so that whatever they did they would hurt and betray, not an enemy, but a trusting friend.

The story nagged at her mind. She thought of several endings, and wondered what the Princess Hildegyth would feel, watching her lover go out to fight his friend—and hers—for her sake. You could argue about it for hours— what ought they to have done? Then she lost the thread of the long, elaborate speeches.

She stirred restlessly, the bench was getting hard under the cushions. She looked at the English: they were sitting rapt, smiling and nodding approval, sometimes exclaiming, 'Good! Good!'

The scop seemed prepared to go on for hours. She felt that at last she could fully understand Arianrhod's rebellion.

She, too, couldn't believe that this was all that life would offer her, for years, for ever.

10

Next morning started better. She had slept quite late and woke to find Oswy already risen, and a sound of horses and hounds in the courtyard. She jumped up to look. Hild came in at that moment dressed for riding.

'Would you like to come and follow the hunt? You're not too tired?'

'No indeed!'

They hurried out to the stables on the far side, downwind of the Great Hall. About ten feet beyond the door that led to the dais was a curiously carved post with a goat's skull on top; between it and the door was an oval space outlined with small stones. Riemmelth remarked that it looked like a grave.

'It is a grave. That's the Watcher.'

'Who?'

'When Uncle Edwin built the palace he wasn't a Christian. So he put the Watcher in there to keep the marsh demons away at night.'

Riemmelth was about to ask if the Watcher had been alive when he began his watch, then decided it was better not to know. She looked hurriedly away and pointed to the great rampart that stood to the east.

'What's in that fort?'

'That's not a fort, it's a stock pen. They bring the cattle in for tax, and hold fairs at the season's ends.'

'But—' Riemmelth was startled. She turned round to check what her eyes told her. 'Why hasn't the town got any walls—not even a fence?'

'Because it's holy.' Hild looked up to the top of the hill

behind them. 'See those walls on the Gefrin? There was a city up there long before the Romans came. But the country folk say this place was holy ages before that. So it's always been rebuilt, never destroyed. Even when Cadwallon came, he wouldn't touch it. Anyway, most of the people behind the hills are Welsh, so Cadwallon didn't—'

She broke off. Riemmelth saw Elfwyn coming to join them. They went to the stables and got their mounts and hunting spears. Grey Gwylan towered over the Cheviot ponies and Hild patted him admiringly.

'You must love being up on a horse like that!'

'Yes, you can look down on everybody,' said Elfwyn sweetly, 'get a good view of the hunt.'

Riemmelth was not sure enough of her English to know whether the words were meant to be as insulting as they seemed.

She soon forgot her irritation in the joy of movement. They followed a track that circled the Gefrin, the Hill of the Goats. She found herself in a wide, bare land of sweeping moors, hill rising behind hill with the wind flying free across them. The turf was sweet-smelling and springy under Gwylan's hoofs, her blood began to dance and she gave the grey his head in a mad gallop without caring to follow the hunt. Cumbria lay beyond those hills. There was nothing between her and her own country but rock, heather and empty sky and the south-west—the Cumbrian wind—was singing to her. She heard the rush of water and let Gwylan pick his steps down the hill. A beck flowed through the valley with a few stunted trees, alders and thorns, at its brink, and where the hills closed in, the water jumped in cascades down a flight of rocky steps. She let Gwylan drink, and sat down on a smooth boulder, watching the water flow past her. It wasn't Eskdale, but it would serve.

I can come here alone, away from the staring, the strange faces, the foreign tongue, the alien ways. At least my mind is free—they couldn't give that away in marriage! In my mind and in my heart, I can meet Elidir here in peace.

Something dark sped over her head and crashed among the alder boughs. Gwylan started, his hoofs clattering on the loose pebbles. Riemmelth stared at the spear; then jumped up, furious. Elfwyn was trotting her pony along by the stream.

'Riemmelth! Did I startle you?'

'Startle me? You could have killed me, or Gwylan.'

'Oh, no. The spear went over your head.' Elfwyn was smiling. 'I saw something move among the trees.'

'If you always throw your spear at anything that moves, you must have made noble sport amongst King Oswald's sheep—and shepherds!'

'The spear went right over your head.' Elfwyn seemed to think it made everything satisfactory. 'But I'm sorry I frightened you.'

'Angered me.'

'Made you angry because I'd frightened you,' agreed Elfwyn, her kitten's eyes wide and innocent. 'How Oswy will laugh—at me—when you complain how my spear went right over your head.'

Riemmelth mounted Gwylan in silence, fighting down her anger. Elfwyn would make her look faint-hearted and ridiculous; this was clearly what she had planned to do, and Oswy *would* laugh. He laughed at nearly everything Riemmelth said or did, and she hated it.

On this point she was wrong. When Oswy at last heard about it, he did not laugh, but by then it was too late.

They were in a field between two hill-crests; the peaty soil was wet, there were black pools between the rushes and bog-myrtle. The group carrying the bier heard the hoofs splashing, turned and drew together with that immediate suspicion of strangers always shown by peasants. These must be desperately poor; they couldn't afford the wood for a coffin, the corpse was lashed to a hurdle and it was naked, without even a shroud.

Riemmelth turned Gwylan towards them, she meant to give them her cloak for Christian charity and get the name of the dead, so that Oswald's priest could say a prayer. She heard Elfwyn calling, 'Leave them!' but took no notice.

They stared at her with blank eyes as she jumped down. Whatever words of pity and kindness she had been going to say were driven from her lips. The body was a girl's, hardly more than a child. The head had been shaved, the eyes were blindfolded, the thin, tightly-bound limbs were quivering.

'She's alive!'

'Not for long.' One of the men, thick-set and heavy-boned, pointed to a pool of black water. 'Not when she's in there.'

'You can't—'

'Why can't I? She's my woman. She's a whore, she lay with my brother.'

'Then take her to the King for judgement.' Riemmelth was struggling to hold on to her English, she could hardly make out the man's broad speech.

'No need. We've already judged her. If she was a good woman she'd have cried out when my brother took her.'

'Took her? Then it's his crime, he must be charged before King Oswald.'

'The kindred have spoken with my brother. He's agreed to pay wergild for spoiling my goods.' He glanced at another man standing at the hurdle's foot, who nodded. The two men were alike, this could be the brother. She felt sick and angry.

'Then why kill her?'

'Because she's my woman.'

Riemmelth gripped her spear and stood over the girl. She wondered if she should make a jump for Gwylan and charge them down, but they would still have time to put the wretched creature into the pool, and the marsh would soon suck her under. The men growled and stirred threateningly; Elfwyn threw herself in front of them.

'Leave them, Riemmelth! You'll make them mad. Let me talk to them.'

She started a rapid, low-voiced argument with the

peasants. Riemmelth laid her spear handy and bent over the girl, cutting the bonds with her hunting knife. She wanted to get her up on Gwylan's back; if Elfwyn was alert they could all soon be safe away. She pulled off the blindfold, but the poor creature's eyes were still blind with terror, she was beyond helping herself. Riemmelth chafed her limbs, wrapped the cloak round her, tried to hearten her. She was too busy to hear what was passing among the others.

'Put *her* in the pool with the other one and shut her mouth,' said the brother. 'Peatbogs keep their secrets, they don't talk.'

There was a snarl of approval.

'Don't trouble about her,' whispered Elfwyn. 'Her doom's on her already, I've put the spear over her, she belongs to Woden.'

'Then let's give her to him now, why keep him waiting?' asked the husband.

'Not safe, she's the atheling's wife.' Elfwyn was alarmed, too many eyes had seen her ride after Riemmelth; the peasants might vanish into the Cheviot hills, but she could not.

'I reck naught of Oswy, or King Oswald either.' He spat. 'King! He's more than half a woman, I'd say, like those gowned priests he spends his time with. If old King Ethelfrith could come back and see him, he'd deny him for a son—he'd smash his skull with his own axe for some Christian's bastard.'

'Put Oswy's woman in the peatbog,' urged the brother. 'Send her to ask Woden to come back to us, with the gods and the heroes, like old times.'

'The hero's coming, don't worry. A real champion. Woden-born. Let Oswy's woman be, for now. Her time's not long. Listen to the wind when it blows from the south— hear it whisper,' she bent her head towards them and whispered herself '—*Penda*.' She smiled and, in spite of herself, her voice lilted up. 'There's going to be an offering to Woden, I promise you, a much greater offering!'

Riemmelth looked up; she caught the words 'I promise you a much greater offering.' Was Elfwyn buying them off with her brooches? In fairness she ought to give something for the girl's life too. She got to her feet. Elfwyn hurried over to her, smiling.

'All's well, I've talked him round. He was beginning to think better of it anyway, but you made him angry and stubborn.'

'Are you sure he'll treat her decently?'

'Yes, yes, but come away now or you'll spoil everything. Dear Riemmelth, you're so brave and kind, but you're a foreigner, you say the wrong thing without knowing.' She hurried Riemmelth over to Gwylan. 'I understand how they feel, I know how to talk to them.'

As they rode off, Riemmelth turned in the saddle. The group was still standing round the crouching girl. Elfwyn urged her pony to a faster trot.

'Don't look back! They'll think you don't trust them; you'll goad them to do it after all, just to show they don't care for you. Churls are stubborn as mules.'

The men watched the riders out of sight. Then the husband stooped and knotted the severed ropes, which were still long enough. The brother put back the blindfold, and they swung the hurdle between them. The kinsfolk looked on. She was light, the hurdle held up in the muddy water, and it was a while before she sank.

Riemmelth's foot struck against the staves and scattered them as she came out of the bedchamber next morning. Oswy had left early to hear a lawsuit on one of his estates at Coludesburh and she thought at first the things were part of his gear that he had dropped. She gathered them up and studied them, puzzled. They were quite small and signs had been scratched on them, sometimes just a straight mark |; sometimes a pattern ᚾᛏor ᛇ ; sometimes all four together, always in the same order ᛇ| ᚾᛏ. She carried them with her to the queen's hall where

Ebbe was alone, working at an altar cloth.

'Do you know what these are?'

Ebbe glanced at the pieces of wood.

'They're runes.' She looked more closely, caught her breath, then snatched the cross-embroidered kerchief that wrapped her psalter.

'Put them down—here!'

Wondering, Riemmelth obeyed. Ebbe knotted the corners of the kerchief and set the little bundle down on the psalter.

'What are you doing —what are runes?'

'Just letters.' Ebbe spoke hurriedly. 'Where did you find them?'

'In Oswy's hall, lying on the floor. Did you say "letters"? What do they mean?'

'*Night*.' Ebbe tried to smile. Riemmelth thought wickedly that she looked more like a horse than ever—a nervous horse with its ears back and white round its eyeballs. 'One of your servants must be trying to fix a love tryst.'

'Oh, is that all? Well, I wish they wouldn't leave their rough drafts where I'll trip over them. Give them here—I'll put them in the fire.'

'No!' Ebbe put her hand on the bundle. 'Don't worry, I'll—dispose of them. And if you see any more, don't pick them up. Don't touch them.'

Then she talked firmly about other things and wouldn't be led back to runes however hard her sister-in-law pulled. Riemmelth was curious, did Ebbe think one of the maids was sending love messages to Oswy? Could she suspect Mildred?

After a while she went back to her own chamber where Mildred was airing her robes and shaking the folds out. Riemmelth took a strip of linen, then burnt the tip of a piece of firewood into rough charcoal.

'Come here, Mildred.'

Mildred hurried up, eager to be of use.

'Do you know rune letters?'

'Yes, lady.'

Riemmelth handed her the charcoal. 'Write me the word for "night".'

Smiling, Mildred began to draw the same signs that had been on the staves. Then her face changed like Ebbe's, and to Riemmelth's angry astonishment, she crumpled the cloth and pushed it into the neck of her gown, crying, 'I take it on myself! I take it on myself!'

'Have you gone mad? Give that cloth here at once!'

Mildred shrank back, clasping her hands on her breast. She was white with terror, but clearly only force would get the cloth away from her.

'What's the matter with you? It's only a word.'

Mildred shook her head. 'Runes aren't just letters, lady. They're names. Every rune holds the power of its name— whoever takes a rune draws its power on to himself.'

'So what are those names on the cloth? Come along—if you won't tell me, I'll find someone who will.'

'Need, Ice, Hail, Tiw.' Mildred's whisper was almost inaudible.

Riemmelth laughed. 'Someone's sent Oswy a bad journey today, in foul weather! He'll need a stout cloak, with ice and hail coming—and a tue, whatever that is!'

'You don't understand. "Need" is—utter lack: when your sword breaks in the last battle; when your home is burning over your head and no help comes. Ice and hail come from Hel's kingdom, the Corpse-Goddess. And Tiw is the Sword-God. And they all lead to the cold, endless Night. These are death-runes, lady.'

Riemmelth was unimpressed. 'I don't think much of that for a spell! You've only got to destroy the rune to destroy the power.'

'No! You must never do that. When you break or destroy a rune-stave, you set the rune free, let its power loose.'

'Rubbish! Now, give me that cloth, I'm going to put it straight in the fire. I'm having no more of this nonsense.'

Mildred did not budge but then, when Riemmelth took a

threatening step towards her, she suddenly dodged past and threw the cloth into the flames.

'I take it on myself!'

'You English!' said Riemmelth. 'You're all moon-touched, you want your wits!'

Riemmelth had spent much of her life in a man's world. Her father and brother had shared all their plans with her and she had ruled her own lordship. She felt belittled and hemmed in when she found that her place now was in the women's quarters—and not even first place there.

Cyneburg was harmless. She was beautiful, mild apart from rare moments of fretfulness, and she seemed to think of nothing but her embroidery and the growth of her baby son, Athelwold.

Ebbe had been widowed at Heavenfield and she intended to take the veil. She had already built and endowed one convent at her chester south of the Wall; she was busy planning another on an estate Oswy had given her at Coludesburh. She was intelligent and capable as well as devout. Hild was very bookish, for all her love of horses and hunting, and was keenly interested in Ebbe's schemes. Riemmelth enjoyed listening to them, sometimes joining in; it stung her a little to realise they were far more learned than herself. So was Oswy, who spent a fair amount of his leisure in the queen's hall. This was not because he was a doting bridegroom; she could see he had always liked Ebbe and Hild, and relished their talk.

These three had spent much of their exiled youth in the British kingdoms and could speak the language (which they insisted on calling Welsh) though they took it for granted that she would always speak English as far as she could. Oswy showed a surprising knowledge and interest in bardic poetry and music. He liked to hear Riemmelth playing her harp, comparing Welsh melodies to the Irish ones he had heard on Iona. He would whistle a tune to her, then listen smiling as she caught it from him and wove it into patterns of sound as complex as English embroidery.

Cyneburg didn't understand a word, she just went on placidly stitching and smiling. Elfwyn either could not or would not join in, though it was clear she listened. When Oswy had gone, she would make wide-eyed, sharp-clawed little attacks on the Welsh, their poetry and music. Such things, she implied, were not worth the notice of English warrior earls. Goaded by the scratching, Riemmelth said sharply that there was at least one English earl among Elfwyn's own family who found them worthy of note.

'Oh, we all know what Oswy feels about bards!' Elfwyn was grinning as wide as her pinched lips would let her.

'Well, we needn't quarrel about it,' Ebbe put in hastily.

'I'm not quarrelling. I was just telling Riemmelth, when an Irish bard came to Bebbanburh last month, Oswy offered his own hall and bedchamber.'

'That must seem strange to you English,' retorted Riemmelth, 'but among *our* people there's no honour we wouldn't give to a really great bard.'

'Well, Liadan's great, no doubt about it, she must be six foot; but then, Oswy's a big man himself. It must be like Beowulf fighting Grendel's mother at the bottom of the lake, when they're together under the sheet.'

'Don't be silly, Elfwyn,' said Hild firmly. 'Riemmelth might not realise you're only joking.'

Riemmelth realised perfectly well that Elfwyn was not joking, and was quite untroubled. Oswy had the skill that only comes with regular practice; another reason why she did not feel guilty about the wedding-night trick she had played on him. It was only to be expected that Oswy would have mistresses; though it was surprising that he should have picked an Irish ollave—and even more surprising that an Irish ollave should have let herself be picked.

She was thinking about this when they were together in their private chamber behind his hall. Oswy was studying a manuscript and she was studying him. Elfwyn's wicked remark about Beowulf with the hag came back to her and she chuckled. Oswy looked up, saw the laughter shining in her eyes, and asked her, smiling, to share the joke.

'I was thinking about the story of Peredur and the witches of Caer Loyw,' she improvised hastily. 'He heard one of them attacking the night-watchman, so he went out in just his shirt and trousers and beat her over the head till her helmet was as flat as a plate. So then she invited him to come and stay with her while she taught him to fight properly!'

Oswy was amused. 'I never knew the Welsh had waelcyriges.'

'We had what?' She struggled with the unfamiliar word. 'Slaughter—*slain-body-choosers*? Who are they?'

'Witches—only they dress and go into battle like men, so they serve Woden, not Frea. They bring the chosen warriors into the god's presence.'

'You let women do that?'

'We don't. Northumbria's a Christian land, we've got rid of heathen wickedness, as Bishop Aidan calls it.'

'What do *you* call it?'

'Wicked waste. About the only good reason I can see for a battle is the loot you collect when you win. Why destroy useful things and people? But sometimes a king gives his enemies to Woden before the battle; so if he wins, everything has to go.'

'How can he give them to Woden *before* the battle?'

'He throws a spear over their heads.'

Some dark memory brushed her with its wing and flew away again.

'You said they bring the chosen warriors into the god's presence—into a heathen temple, you mean?'

'No. They set them riding Woden's horse.' He smiled at her puzzled face. 'The ash tree. The waelcyriges hang them.'

She swallowed. 'What happens if they don't win—if they're taken by the other side?'

'They're Woden's daughters, so they're sent back to their father.'

'So they get hanged too, in their turn?'

'You don't hang a woman. The king and his war-band put some of their seed into the waelcyrige to take to Woden as an offering, then they send her home by water—put her into a lake or a marsh.'

Riemmelth hurriedly invented some orders she had to go and give Mildred. She had spent enough time in domestic chat for one day.

11

After the Lammas fair the court moved to Bebbanburh, the great fortress capital by the sea. Riemmelth oversaw the packing of Oswy's gear as well as her own. She had the keys of all his chests and jewel caskets, hanging from a golden chain at her belt; he had handed them over to her the morning after her arrival at Gefrin, in what seemed almost a second wedding-rite. The task was a pleasure as well as a duty, for Oswy loved beautiful things and did not stint himself. Mildred took charge as usual and kept the maids bustling, while Riemmelth dawdled over manuscripts and jewel-craft.

At the bottom of the last chest, laid carefully apart wrapped in oiled cloths, she found the armour. It was fit for a prince—indeed, only a prince could ever afford such war-gear: an iron helmet set with elaborately wrought plates of gilded bronze; a byrnie of linked rings; a sword with welded snake-patterns rippling down its blade, the gold hilt and scabbard-chape inset with garnets. It would not be Oswy's armour; it had been made for a much smaller, slighter man and, though it had been carefully repaired and burnished, it had been damaged in some fierce fight.

Riemmelth had the drawn sword across her lap, wondering who had last held it, in what desperate struggle.

Some young prince of Oswald's line, remembered with love and grief. He'd been a Christian for although a gilded boar, tusked and bristling, stood guard on the helmet's crest, there was a cross on the brow.

'You must be out of breath, lady, the way you're hurrying to pack.'

Dunnere had come in and was looking at her sardonically; he was Oswy's oldest retainer, rough and shaggy as a Cheviot sheep-dog, and as loyal. Riemmelth smiled back at him.

'Who owned these?'

'What? Oh, that's Oswy's gear. He's got it stowed ready for his son.' Dunnere winked at her.

'Oswy's? He'd burst it, trying to get it on.'

'He didn't grow to his size overnight. He was as slight as a lass when he marched with Oswald to Heavenfield.'

Riemmelth looked surprised; she had never linked Oswy with the battles where Oswald won his kingdom back, he was ten years the younger. She had imagined him safe on Iona, learning to love Irish—poetry. Dunnere growled a laugh.

'I suppose they told you Oswald just waved his sword and God sent our enemies packing. That's monks' talk—and not much credit to Oswald and the rest of us, I reckon. Cadwallon's Welsh fought like all the demons of hell. It was the worst strait I've ever been in—they broke our shield-wall and had Oswald down, I thought it was the end of us. But Oswy stood over his brother and held them off till we rallied.'

He stooped and fingered the byrnie. 'Ah, I can see him now. We need another lad like that, fit to stand by his dad, you must make haste about it, lady. And if we don't make haste now and get this gear out, we won't see Bebbanburh before night!'

Several times during the day's ride, the vision came behind her eyes: Oswy, young and fair, standing over his brother, holding the slayers at bay. But what was so wonderful about that? She'd never thought that the English wouldn't fight when they had to; as she had told Elidir, they were good dogs to whistle on your enemies.

They saw Bebbanburh well before night, black against the east on its huge cliff between sky and sea. It had the same towering, carved halls as Gefrin, the same richly adorned chambers, roomy stables and space wide enough for the country folk to come in at need with their flocks and herds. There was a deep spring of pure water welling up from the rock; Bebbanburh could face all the war-hosts of Britain and laugh down at the besiegers.

In spite of the mass of solid black rock beneath, the fortress belonged in spirit to the ocean. The sea wind blew over it unresting, the gulls circled and cried, the great lines of breakers came roaring over the sands at its foot. Riemmelth was up on the rampart behind the palisade, clutching her cloak round her, while Ebbe and Hild, with Elfwyn in close attendance as usual, put names on what she saw.

'Those are the Farnes,' said Hild, pointing to a scatter of small islands fronting them. 'And that's Lindisfarne, the holy island,' pointing to the north. 'Bishop Aidan's monastery is over there.'

Riemmelth looked along the shore. 'Those sands look wonderful for a gallop, you can ride straight across.'

'Don't try it!' Ebbe looked alarmed. 'There are rivers flowing out into the channel—Lindisfarne's cut off at high water, the tides are treacherous.'

She turned and went down, followed by Hild. Elfwyn came snuggling up.

'Ebbe clucks like a hen.' Her big, pale eyes were amused and friendly. 'She thinks she's already mother of a convent, but we're not her novices. The sands are perfectly safe, I know the tides. I can tell the grooms to take our horses out, quietly, so Ebbe won't be worried. When would you like to come?'

'Thank you, Elfwyn,' said Riemmelth, coldly. 'As you say, it wouldn't do to worry Ebbe—or slight her, either.'

She went down and joined the others.

Riemmelth was not only concerned to spare Ebbe's feelings. She was never at ease with Elfwyn and would not have relished a ride anywhere in her company; but there was not one of the whole English race that she would have let near her on the pilgrimage she had in mind.

There on the sands to the north, between the dunes and the sea, the tragedy of her House had been played out. Her great-grandfather, King Urien, had united the feuding British lords of the North, out-fought the English and penned them up in Lindisfarne. Then, at the very moment of final victory, Urien had been treacherously murdered by one of his brother-kings, through jealousy of his leadership and his fame.

The horror and pain of that killing still echoed in the bards' laments. They sang how Llywarch, Elidir's grandfather, had hacked off the great king's head, to save that at least from his foes' triumphant mockery; of black ravens settling on the lonely corpse; of the palace silent and desolate, overgrown with briars, the great days of Cumbria dead with Urien.

That was not altogether true, Cumbria had recovered magnificently. But there was never the greatness that might have been.

We could have been ruling now as High Kings in London, she thought bitterly. *Owain ap Urien wouldn't have died before his time, worn out with constant border wars. My father and brother wouldn't have been killed in petty cattle-raids from Dunoding. I could be in Eskdale, in Elidir's arms—not trapped in the Sea-Wolves' lair with one of them bedding beside me!*

These regrets were repeating themselves over and over again as she made her way along the bleak coast at low tide next afternoon, on foot to avoid notice, skirting the dunes, splashing through streams, scrambling over outcrops of rock and slippery weed.

Suddenly her thoughts were broken by a shout from behind her; looking back she saw Oswy riding to overtake her, with a groom and a led horse.

'On your way to the holy island already? Very devout, but you can't make your pilgrimage on foot from this end, you'd never get across the Low. We'll have to go round.'

He jumped down to help her mount the spare horse. Clearly, he meant to come with her. If she'd had a sword, she would have killed him on the spot; she set out to goad him into leaving her.

'I was making my pilgrimage to Aber Lleu—the Low as you call it. We nearly wiped you out, there.'

'And you didn't succeed.' He swung her to the saddle, her skirts already kilted for her walk. 'Well, it's all been over a long time ago. Stop brooding and find something better worth thinking about.' He mounted and rode beside her while the groom kept his distance behind.

'You're a true Englishman, aren't you?—you only care about success. You'd think nothing of a warrior riding out to ·face certain death against hopeless odds!'

'I'd think he was a fool.'

'So "hero" means "fool" in English. I'm surprised you've got a word for honour in your language. Do you ever need to use it?'

'How often do you think Mildred used it, after she was carried off?'

Riemmelth was silenced.

'It's getting dusk, and the tide's on the turn. There's a grange with a guest house for folk waiting to cross to the island. Would you like to spend the night there, or go back to Bebbanburh?'

'You can go back to Bebbanburh as soon as you like. I'm going to walk on the sands.' She jumped to the ground and turned angrily away from him. In a moment, she heard the sound of hoofs receding and looked round hopefully. The groom was taking the horses back along the shore but Oswy was striding after her. He glanced at her furious face.

'There's nothing honourable in making your country a gift to its enemies.' Oswy had taken up the talk where he left off, his voice damnably reasonable. 'If a king can't lead his army to a fairly sure chance of victory, he ought to lead it out of reach as fast as possible. A dead soldier's no use but "he who fights and runs away lives to fight another day".'

'And if he—if even you couldn't find a bolt-hole, what then?'

'Fight.'

'And if you were struck down?'

'Get up again.'

'If they knocked you down again and again? Kicked you as you lay? You'd take it, wouldn't you, just lie there?'

He laughed.

'There's a lot to be said for lying down at the right moment. At the least, you can get your breath back to fight again, while you think of the next move. There's always something. You can sink your teeth in the other man's ankle and topple him—or get him in the privates when he bends over you.'

'It's all a jest to you! Is there anything you don't laugh at?'

'I'll tell you what I do laugh at. People weeping for their country's wrongs, and crying out for deathless revenge—and as soon as they find a king who leads them to victory, they put a knife in his back.'

'And you've good cause to laugh—because when the king's dead, a crew of pirates can come scavenging in and take his land for loot, like mine!'

'Nobody's going to loot Cumbria. That's why I married you, isn't it? I've got your land secure without a blow.'

Riemmelth suddenly screamed with laughter.

'Don't flatter yourself, Oswy. Not without a blow!'

She slashed her hand across his face with all her strength behind it, then turned and raced over the darkening shore towards the water. She wanted to get free, to drown herself, to blot out his eyes, his smile and the sound of his voice.

Her feet were splashing through the wet sands, her skirt hem slopped in the water and hampered her legs. Then she stepped into a hollow and fell sprawling. The current took her, the water was deeper than she had thought. She struck out wildly but her sodden clothes dragged her down; she had been carried some way before she struggled out on the other side and ran on, stumbling and gasping for breath. She felt Oswy's hand grip her shoulder; she turned on him, biting and writhing, and kicked his legs from under him. They both went down into deep water; there was choking, and roaring in her ears, before Oswy pulled her on to a little spit of sand. She was still feebly trying to struggle, so he put his fist in hard under her ribs as the sandspit vanished swirling and the tide rose round their ankles.

Riemmelth came round in a small stone hut, thatched with turf. She was lying by a fire on a pile of bracken, wrapped in a very coarse blanket that scratched her bare skin as she moved. Oswy was wringing their clothes out of the open door and spreading them before the fire.

'Where—what is this place?'

'Waking Rock,' said Oswy, grimly. 'It's just not covered at high tide, so it's used as a refuge. The good monks keep it stocked as a shelter for travellers in danger from the tides—or from raving Welsh.'

He stooped over her and put a leather bottle to her lips; it held barley spirit, harsh and crude, that felt like liquid fire inside her. Oswy drank after her, then stared at her balefully.

'I—am—weary,' he said slowly, 'of your black moods and your grudges. What's your grievance? Who's wronged you?'

'Is it such a little thing—nothing to resent—to tear a woman's life up by the roots, and drag her away from her own people?'

'Tearing and dragging—you talk like a war-captive! Every princess marries outside her land. Cyneburg came more than twice as far as you, with less than half the fuss. My own mother—' He stopped abruptly.

Riemmelth was too weary to argue, most of her strength had been pounded out of her by the sea. She felt her anger ebbing and tried to draw it back into her, for fear she should weep.

Oswy turned to a cupboard at the back of the hut and brought out a couple of crude earthenware mugs and platters, with some oatcakes and smoked fish. He set the food out and filled a mug for her with the raw spirit; then squatted back on his heels, with the firelight playing over his limbs, making the great Cumbrian ruby on his hand shine like a gout of fresh blood. He saw her staring at it.

'Remember our wedding night? When you lifted your arms and drew me down on to you—you said you'd like to draw the moon down out of the sky to keep that night from passing.'

She caught her breath; the wind rattled at the latch as if some lost spirit was trying to come in to them.

'Then you changed, the very next day.' His voice was bitter. 'You're too tired, or you're already asleep, or you submit like a slave girl.'

The ocean-grey eyes stared at her coldly.

'It's because I took you from Cumbria, isn't it? Brought my bride to my hall to meet my kin. That's the great wrong I did you, that you punish me for, every night.'

She suddenly felt afraid, and dreadfully helpless, trapped in the little hut out among the wild tides, without the protection of her women and household, without even her clothes. Bebbanburh lorded over the sea; this rock where she was lying was part of the sea itself; all through their talk she could hear the crash and foam of the breakers reaching nearer and nearer, feel the fingers of wind searching for crannies in the walls. Kneeling by the fire in the smoke and wavering flame-light, Oswy's tall form seemed to fill the hut, like some merman who had just jumped out of the waves, his pale hair like silver foam round his head and shoulders, gleaming like spray across the gold of his body.

'It all happened so suddenly,' she stammered. 'I'd never expected—I'd thought—taken it for granted you'd stay there with me, we'd help my grandfather rule Cumbria.'

'So your life didn't go just as you'd planned! How many of us ever get just what we want?'

He stared past her, through the walls of the hut, as if he was looking out across the sea, far away. He was silent for a while, then looked down at her.

'That's no good reason for refusing to take what pleasures life does offer, though it seems to be the Welsh way. You've all got some everlasting quarrel with life.'

He laughed, and offered her the plate of fish and oatcakes.

'This isn't exactly a feast in Caer Luel—we can even do a bit better in Bebbanburh—but we've got fire, food and bed. Let's enjoy them.'

She still had enough spirit to aim a blow at him. 'That's all you ask from life to make you happy!'

The sea-lights glimmered in his eyes. 'You wouldn't last long without them. But if you're determined to spend the rest of your life in mourning, then mourn for me as well. You didn't want to marry me, I didn't want to marry you. Your king told you to do it, my king told me to do it—and by the way, it was your folk that made the first offer. If anyone's been trapped or wronged, it seems to me that I should be doing the complaining.'

'For all that, it goes without saying that I should be the one to give up my own home and my own language—to be called "Welshwoman", foreigner, while you English put your name on my land!'

'I'll talk Welsh to you if you like, my lady. Let me tell you a Welsh story to pass the time for us, about some Welsh warriors—or British warriors, if you prefer it. They'd gone overseas to Gaul, to fight for the Emperor Maxen; they saw Armorica and liked the look of it, so they took it. They bedded Armorican girls, then slit their tongues, so their children would grow up hearing nothing but Wel—British. That's why the land's now called Brittany.'

He smiled at her sympathetically. 'Yes, it's tiresome, isn't it—an Englishman who understands Welsh as well. When we don't know, we're ignorant savages; and when we do know, we answer back!'

She wanted to snap at him but found she was laughing, perhaps it was the whisky doing its work. Oswy reached his hands to her and clasped her slender waist, lifting her to his knees.

'You've got a lovely body, Riemmelth—colour and line and touch blending in it like notes in music. Enjoy it, it was made for pleasure, like a harp, not sullen dumbness or shrieking discords.'

He laid her body gently across his thighs and deliberately set himself to play on it. His mouth and fingers had the delicacy and sureness of a skilled musician, her flesh answered like an instrument to his touch. Her skin glowed, there was soft warmth between her thighs, her limbs were tingling with life. At first, she let herself float on the stream of enjoyable sensations, with neither love nor hate to torment her, murmuring drowsily with closed eyes. Then zest roused in her for Oswy's body, its strong beauty of rippling muscles and hard flesh. He guided her hands; soon she began to explore him for herself, laughing delightedly. At last, he lay back, she lifted over him on a great wave of pleasure and their bodies flowed together with the beat of the tide, while outside the sea beat against their rock and the wind went crying past them shorewards to the west.

In the morning Riemmelth stood at the door of the hut, looking with growing suspicion at the few yards of shell and weed and rock pools that lay between the islet and Lindisfarne. They had certainly been undersea, but she wondered how soon and how deeply they had been covered yesterday evening when Oswy had carried her unconscious on to the islet.

A heavy hand clapped her shoulder.

'There's the last stage of our pilgrimage—the monastery's just beyond that slope. Fold your veil round your head—and try to look more saintly, you've kept vigil all night.'

12

Riemmelth found she was more at ease with Oswy; it would have been hard to stay cold and distant after a night like that. He talked to her more about statecraft, too; telling her about Oswald's plans for Northumbria, asking her about her own country. She followed his advice about taking pleasures as they came and it worked quite well. She seemed to divide in two: her heart and her dreams with Elidir, her body making agreeable use of Oswy. Where his heart and dreams were, if he had any, only God and Oswy knew.

Winter came, with shrieking north-easterly gales and suffocating flurries of snow, then pale sunshine and air like crystal. Oswald and Cyneburg had gone south to Gatesheafod to celebrate the Nativity. Oswy was lord of the feast in Bebbanburh, and a merry time he made of it.

The warriors built a fort of snow in the courtyard and pelted the maids as they went to and fro. Riemmelth thought that Englishmen played like children, but as her practice with the hunting spear had taught her to throw hard and straight, she led the girls in a counter-attack and drove the men off.

They dragged up sled-loads of greenery to deck the halls, holly for the men and ivy for the women, insulting each other's sex as they did so. The girls made themselves ivy crowns and blocked the doors of the hall; the men marched up waving sprigs of holly and singing:

> 'Nay, nay Ivy!
> Never be so bold;
> Holly shall take the lordship
> To have and to hold.'

The girls retorted:

> 'Ivy's fresh and bright of hue,
> Against all bale, she is bliss;
> Well is he that may her reach,
> Ivy queen of trees she is—'

but when they got to 'Well is he that may her reach', the men tried to prick them with the holly twigs and they broke back into the hall, giggling and screaming, with the warriors after them.

Inside the hall, the great Yule logs were blazing on the hearth to keep the sun warm till he got his strength back in the New Year. The servers brought in succulent joints of meat, with a great boar roasted whole, the tusks snarling in its open jaws, in honour of the Frey, the Lord of Life who shines in midwinter's darkness.

After the feast, they had songs, stories and riddle poems, passing the harp from one to another, as each took it in turn to entertain the company. Godric challenged Mildred to answer his riddle:

> 'I'm a strange creature, for I satisfy women,
> a service to the neighbours! No one suffers
> at my hands except for my slayer.
> I grow very tall, erect in a bed,
> I'm hairy underneath. From time to time
> a beautiful girl, the brave daughter
> of some churl dares to hold me,
> grips my russet skin, robs me of my head
> and puts me in the pantry. At once that girl
> with plaited hair who has confined me
> remembers our meeting. Her eye moistens.

Mildred refused to answer; her cheeks were pink when Godric told her it was 'An onion', and went even pinker when Cadman asked her politely what she'd thought it was.

Riemmelth watched the harp coming her way with some nervousness. The English wouldn't understand her stories without long explanations; the language of her songs would be meaningless; their complex, jewelled beauty would be lost if she tried to translate them. But she didn't want to be the only one to fail the company. Then the green garlands, and the holly and ivy games they had been playing, reminded her of a simple tale.

Everyone settled quiet and expectant as she took the harp and played a rippling prelude, like leaves rustling in a summer wood. She told them how Trystan took King March's pretty young wife for a walk in Calidon Forest, and after they'd been in there a month or so, her husband complained to King Arthur.

Menacing chords. Clapping from the listeners and cries of, 'A nice little stroll!', 'Did their legs ache?'

'Arthur's horsemen surrounded the wood,' she made the notes gallop, 'and Essyllt trembled in Trystan's arms,' a succession of shivering scales.

'King Arthur summoned the three to appear before him.' She made them hear horns calling. 'And as neither man would agree to give Essyllt up, he said they should have her for half a year each: one when the leaves were on the trees, the other when the trees were bare, and the husband had the right to first choice.'

A contest of cheers and booing from the married and single men.

'So March said he would have her in winter, when the trees are bare, because that's when the nights are longest.'

Oswy led the cheering and stamping. Riemmelth made Essyllt's laughter ring from her harp.

> 'Three trees are good-natured:
> The holly, the ivy, the yew
> wear their leaves all year—
> So Trystan's got me for good!'

She ended with a mocking little phrase and a triumphant chord.

They loved it; roaring and slapping each other on the back, explaining the point to each other in case anyone had missed it. Elfwyn said, very clearly, 'That's a real Welsh trick!' smiling to show she was only joking.

'True!' shouted Oswy. 'The Welsh have wit in their heads, music in their tongues and witchcraft in their fingers.' He kissed Riemmelth's hand as it rested on the harp. He was a bit drunk, she knew he would keep the revelry going in bed long after the feasting hall was dark. Well, it was Watch Night.

She sighed. Elidir was far away; Urien's bones lay lost on the shore, under the sand and the sea-winds. His last heir slept with an Englishman, and told the love story of Trystan and Essyllt as a jest to make the English laugh.

The pale sun had time to gather its strength by the late morning. Ebbe had taken the chance to work in its light and was bending over her embroidery when Riemmelth stormed in, her black hair streaming round her shoulders, blue lightning flashing from her eyes.

'That Elfwyn! She must be married off at once! I'll not endure her sneers and her insults any longer! Get her a husband, in God's name, and get her out of my sight!'

Ebbe laid down her needle. 'That's impossible, Riemmelth.'

Riemmelth laughed savagely. 'I can understand that men aren't fighting for her hand, but surely there must be some English warrior brave enough to take her with a dowry to sweeten her—she's the King's cousin, after all.'

'It can't be done.'

'Well, if the Royal House of Northumbria can't afford to buy a husband for a kinswoman, I can. Cumbria's rich, and it'll be money well spent. I'll write to tell Oswald that I'll provide the marriage-portion if he'll choose the hero.'

Ebbe shook her head. 'Oswald would never allow it. Elfwyn is a Deiran, like Hild.'

Riemmelth looked blank.

'Sit down, my dear, and listen. I see you don't know the story of our House.'

Riemmelth had never troubled to find out.

'Northumbria is two kingdoms. We—my brothers and I—belong to the north, Bernicia; Deira lies to the south, round Eoforwic. Our grandfather conquered it and killed their king; he would have killed Prince Edwin too, only his nurse got him away. But he took the Princess Acha and made her marry our father, to unite the two kingdoms.'

Riemmelth heard Oswy's voice say '*My own mother—*', then stop. What had that marriage been like?

'Edwin came back when he was a man, and killed our father; we had to flee into exile. So Edwin ruled the two kingdoms till Cadwallon of Gwynedd killed him and laid the land waste. Then Oswald came back from exile and won all that our father had ruled, and more. Edwin's sons died in childhood, but Hild and Elfwyn are his great-nieces. Their husbands or sons could claim Deira from us in their name. So Oswald keeps them here in his court.'

'You mean they're hostages?'

'Hild will take the veil quite soon now.'

'Hild!'

Riemmelth was horrified. She liked Hild most of all her marriage-kin; it was dreadful to think of that warm, vivid nature shut away from life. She recalled Rhun's grim face and voice: '*No, of course you wouldn't be forced to take the veil without a vocation. You'd just stay in your cell till you found one.*'

'Oswald couldn't be so cruel! As if Hild would ever act against him. I'll speak to him myself when he comes back— I'll find her a safe husband in the west, some great Cumbrian noble worthy of her—'

Ebbe was smiling. 'My dear child, you'd break Hild's heart if you tried to do that. Bishop Aidan says he's never known such a strong vocation. She's preparing herself now, in her own time and her own way—talking statecraft with my brothers, riding far and wide among the hills. An abbess has to be a ruler and a farmer as much as a woman of God—and where, outside the Church, could Hild find a fit use for all her book-learning?'

The smile faded. 'Elfwyn is—different. She has no vocation, but she'll never be allowed to marry outside the Royal House. We thought once that Oswy might—but then—'

'—but then he was offered a better bargain.'

'A much better bargain,' said Ebbe calmly, 'and a much better wife. You can talk to him, you share his taste for music and poetry; she doesn't. It's a pity, of course, that you can't love Oswy—'

Riemmelth looked up, startled. Ebbe was watching her kindly.

'You talk with your eyes, my dear. When Elfwyn told you there was a woman loved Oswy, you didn't look jealous, you didn't even look annoyed. You were surprised.'

Riemmelth went disconsolately back to her own apartments. She would miss Hild, but it seemed she was saddled with Elfwyn for ever. The burden of her presence grew more wearisome as the weeks passed. There was a lot of rain that spring; not hearty downpours that left a blue sky and a clean-washed world, but foggy drizzle that swathed Bebbanburh like a sodden blanket and kept her in her bower for days on end. Oswy was away much of the time; Ebbe and Hild were deep in their own affairs, but Elfwyn haunted her company, nearly driving her to madness.

One wet day, Riemmelth was trying to embroider a silk border for her dress and realising that Mildred could have done it much better. She would have liked to take her harp, but Elfwyn had got it and was striking odd notes and jarring little discords. Riemmelth wanted to tell her sharply to play it or leave it alone, but she fought the words back and struggled on with her needle and coloured threads. She didn't realise that Elfwyn had begun singing; her voice was very quiet, hardly more than a murmur. Then, bit by bit the

words wove themselves among her stitches and she began to
listen:

> '—the day was wet; and I wept with it,
> my mind wandering far to my Wulf;
> One of the war-lords wrapped me in his arms
> then I loved what I loathed.
> Wulf, my Wulf, I'm wasted with wanting,
> starving to see you—'

Elfwyn's voice choked; Riemmelth looked at her, blinking
through her own tears. She remembered what Ebbe had told
her about the girl's fate. If Elfwyn loved somebody, and
knew there was nothing to come but empty years and
hopeless longing, no wonder she was bitter. She dropped her
embroidery, hurried across the room and took the girl's
hand; another moment and she would have kissed her.
Elfwyn snatched her hand away.

'Don't you pity me!'

Riemmelth shook her head; Elfwyn looked at her sharply,
then smiled. She reached out her hand again and with cat-
like delicacy brushed the tears on Riemmelth's cheeks,
looking at the drops on her fingertips.

'You're crying for yourself, aren't you? Well, thank you
for your fellow-feeling. It'll be comforting to know, as I lie
on my pillow, that you aren't laughing in your bed.'

Something burst in Riemmelth's brain.

'It'll be comforting to me to know that at least you've got a
pillow to lie with—and I *shall* be laughing in bed, believe
me!'

'You bitch! You Welsh don't need daggers while you can
use words.'

'You showed me the weapon, Elfwyn, and God knows
you've spent long enough teaching me how to use it.'

'Then make the most of your time—you don't know how
long you've got!'

Elfwyn turned abruptly and rushed out. Riemmelth sat
down, stunned, and hating herself.

What's happened to me? I was loving once, and generous—
where's it gone?

She bowed her head; her black hair tumbled over her face,
shrouding her. Mildred came in and scolded her tenderly for
tiring her eyes with stitching.

13

The weather cleared at last and her spirits lifted. At Easter,
she knew she was pregnant. She thought about it, and
decided she was pleased. Urien's blood was safe, she had an
heir for Cumbria. She would teach him to know his
ancestors and be proud of his ancient race.

She didn't tell Oswy at once, because the secret gave her
an advantage over him. He'd notice soon enough, of course.
She made up her mind that she would tell him when she
chose, either to take him aback, or to reward him if he
pleased her, she hadn't decided which.

After Easter, they moved south to join Oswald, then went
on all together to Eoforwic, for his crown-wearing at
Pentecost. Riemmelth enjoyed the ride in fine weather
through the rich eastern plains, asking herself wryly every
time she dressed in her jerkin and breeches how much longer
she would be able to wear them.

When they passed the Deiran border, Elfwyn began to
boast and swagger a little, pointing out the fertile lands and
rich townships as if she was the heir showing the country to
visiting savages from the North. Her temper seemed to be
sweetened by the southern air; she was merry and gracious
with the Deiran thanes who came to show their duty to their
Bernician overlords. Often, she made herself into a shield
between the two sides, helping Riemmelth to ward off some
unpleasant moments. She gave signs of taking charge, but
Riemmelth let her preen unchecked; she could pity Elfwyn,

who was really little better that a high-born bondmaid. Her own life, when she looked at it coolly, was so much richer.

I shall be Queen of Cumbria, she told herself, *I'm carrying the heir; my life counts for something. I'm helping to hold two great realms in freedom and peace. As Oswy said, no princess weds to please herself and I can't say I've been unlucky. The husband I was given is good-humoured and courteous—book-learned, too; and yet he can hold his own as a warrior, so they say. He can certainly hold his own in bed—* That thought recalled Elidir. But how could she have forgotten him? How long was it since she last fell asleep to dream of him and waken into yearning?

It must be the child growing in me. The future destroys the past. I have to make Cumbria strong for him, to hold against Northumbria when Oswy and I are gone—But if little Athelwold dies, or proves unfit for war and council, my son might come to hold both kingdoms. My son, ruling the lands where Urien died! King of the North!

She smiled wryly.

I'm getting to think like Rhun or Penarwan... My youth's passing; I'm in my twentieth year. Soon, my love will be no more than an old tale, like Essyllt's, sung by a bard on a summer's evening. 'Once upon a time there was a princess of Cumbria, who loved a young huntsman...' Girls will sigh, listening to my love and grief. But then they'll see faces smiling at them, across the torchlit hall, as I saw Elidir's—and they'll slip out to meet their loves, as once I stole out to mine in the greenwood. And the harp will fall silent, and I shall be forgotten...

She sighed, then shook her head as if midges were pestering her, and asked Elfwyn to tell her the name of the river they were just going to ford.

She was as impressed by Eoforwic as even Elfwyn could wish. It had been the Roman capital of the North and still kept something of its former imperial state. The Deiran palace was in the old principia, where Riemmelth felt more at home than she had ever been since she came to Northumbria. She had to admit that even Caer Luel had nothing to compare with the walls of Eoforwic and their massive towers. It was the towers that held her notice.

'Do you think we should build towers at Caer Luel?' she asked Oswy, who seeing her interest, had taken her up on to the walls. He was struck by the idea; he was also struck by the fact that she had said 'we'.

'You could say the whole of Caer Luel's a tower already, set up on that sheer cliff. Eoforwic's low down among the marshes, as you can see.' He pointed to the wide fens around them. 'The Ouse is tidal, they can bring seagoing ships right into the heart of the city; where merchants can come, pirates can follow. Caer Luel hasn't got that worry—still, a tower might be a good idea down by the South Gate where the ground's lower. We'll have a look when we get there, then talk about it again.'

She looked at him, her eyes shining.

'We're going to Caer Luel?'

'It's high time we went. Your grandfather will be wanting younger hands to hold the reins for him. I must meet the Cumbrian nobles; you'll have to tell me how to deal with them and whom to trust. As soon as Oswald has finished his business here, we'll be off.'

Her spirits went soaring above the clouds. She felt very kindly towards Oswy and decided that he deserved to know about her child, the heir of Cumbria; she would tell him tonight. It seemed to her that tomorrow would start a new chapter in her life and in the history of the North. It did.

Oswald rose first, he always heard Mass at earliest dawn. Then he set off with his attendants to visit one of the Deiran thanes on his estate outside Eoforwic. They had affairs to discuss and afterwards there would be hawking in the marshes along by the Foss.

Elfwyn was also stirring early. She took a bag of Frankish coins and went out, followed by two of the palace servants, Deirans who thought of her as their own princess. Today was one of the great horse-fairs for which Eoforwic was famous. She needed plenty of money and plenty of time; she was looking for a mount of particular quality and it was a while before she found one to her mind.

Oswy was much later, he came out of his bedroom in a rush to catch up with Oswald. Mildred was waiting in the ante-room to attend her lady and beaming at her he tweaked one of her plaits.

'You're a good lass. Buy yourself a fairing.'

He strode out, leaving Mildred staring at the gold in her palm, and hurried to the mews to choose his falcon. Godric was swearing over a frayed border on his best shirt which one of the maids had promised to mend for him and then forgotten.

'You should get yourself a wife,' said Oswy, cheerfully. 'What about Mildred? She's a good-humoured, sensible girl with land of her own—and I'll add to her dowry, she's served my lady well.'

Godric made a sour mouth.

'You're not bothered about that misfortune she had? Forget it. Bad luck isn't a fault and, if it doesn't make a woman bitter, she's not any the worse. Isn't Mildred fair enough for you?'

'She's got the prettiest back to her head that ever I saw.'

Oswy raised his eyebrows.

'It's forever turned, looking at Cadman—for all the good that'll do her. You know what the Welsh are about high birth and blood.'

'I do indeed. Well, it was just a thought. Come on, or we'll spend all day hunting Oswald, not the water-fowl.'

Riemmelth was the last to get up. Her pregnancy was beginning to make her lazy; besides, with one thing and another, she hadn't slept much in the night. She broke her fast very leisurely, then decided that she would ride out towards the Foss where perhaps she would get a sight of the hawking. She strolled down to the stables, and saw Elfwyn coming in followed by two servants leading horses. One was a magnificent bay stallion with black points, the other was the most exquisite little grey mare she had ever seen.

Elfwyn came up, glowing. 'Look, I've got fairings for you and Oswy, a present from Deira to remember us by and speed you on your way home. Do you like them?'

'They're beautiful.' Riemmelth was touched by the gift, for of course Elfwyn must have heard she was going back to Cumbria (for good, Riemmelth hoped) and was trying to make up for her spitefulness before they parted.

'Where's Oswy?' Elfwyn looked eagerly round. 'I want to see his face when I tell him the stallion's his.'

'I'm afraid he's gone—he wanted to catch up with Oswald.'

Elfwyn had already made sure of that but outwardly she drooped like a disappointed child. 'Oh dear, it'll spoil my surprise. Someone's sure to tell him first—I was so looking forward to it!'

Riemmelth felt sorry, so much had been spoilt for Elfwyn.

'Suppose we ride them and go to meet him? We can show off their paces and Oswy will ask where we got them. Then you can tell him they're your presents.'

'What a good idea!' Elfwyn paused, then said with a careless laugh that didn't ring quite true, 'Of course, you'll want to be up on the great horse.'

Riemmelth hesitated. She couldn't imagine how Elfwyn would handle the stallion but she remembered that bitter little sneer, '*You can look down on everybody*', at the beginning of their first ride together. She did not want any more hostilities just when everything was going so pleasantly. She'd stay close beside Elfwyn, to pick her up if she took a toss.

'Oh, not for anything. I can't wait to try my lovely mare!'

The radiant smile in Elfwyn's eyes told her she had made the right choice. They mounted and set off for the marshes.

Mildred was strolling through the great market down by the Ouse, enjoying every moment. She was happy to be free, she had never quite got over the wonder of that. As a Deiran, she was pleased to visit her royal city. Best of all, she had Oswy's gold, so now at last she could make her dear lady a fitting gift to show her gratitude.

It was difficult to make a choice among all the rare goods that poured into Eoforwic from the ships crowding the quays: furs and amber from the Baltic, gold, jewels and brocaded silk that had come stage by stage from Constantinople, glass from the Rhineland, Frankish ivories next to jet from the Deiran coast. She would have liked to gather up the whole fair and lay it at Riemmelth's feet.

After all her heart-searching, the gift she chose at last was English work: a casket of whale bone, carved with the story of Wayland and the swan-maid. It had the whale's own words in runes round the edge, saying how foolish he had been to get washed up on shore, but that he was glad his bones would give joy to some fair woman. Mildred thought with satisfaction that the casket was very beautiful, that it would be just the thing for her lady's jewels, and that she could spend a long, happy time telling what it was all about; Riemmelth had been curious about runes.

The merchant gave her some silver pieces in exchange for her Frankish gold. She decided to get herself some hair ribbons but sat down first to rest on a bench by an ale-house. Voices chattered all around her and she listened idly.

'Let me pay for the ale.'

'What's the matter with you, then—aren't you well?'

'Very well, thank you. I'm just off—sold all my stock.'

'What, the grey mare and all? You must have caught a blind lackwit.'

'I caught a woman—it's the same thing in horse-trading.'

'No wonder you're making a quick getaway. You could be on a manslaughter charge.'

'No fear. She was a soft, pampered-looking little thing, the sort that never rides alone. Her man'll pick her up, and then give her a good beating for throwing his gold away.'

'How d'you know she's got a man?'

'Because she bought the bay stallion as well. No

unmarried girl would be let spend that much of her father's gold.'

'Only a thane would have that much gold to spend on his woman. You watch it, you could be in bad trouble.'

'There's nothing wrong with that mare if she isn't startled.'

'By someone calling, or a dog barking, or a horn blowing, or a baby crying, or a bird flying over her or a twig snapping under her—cheer up, it may never happen! That mare's a rogue and you know it.'

'Isn't that just life for you? The prettiest bit of horse-flesh I ever saw, and she had to have the devil in her.'

'Aye, they're like women.'

Mildred was amused for a moment, then forgot about it when she went to choose her ribbons. She came back to the palace, put the casket on top of a chest in Riemmelth's room where she would see it at once, and then went to find her lady. Like Elfwyn, she wanted to enjoy the effect of her surprise. One of the maids told her that Riemmelth had gone riding with Elfwyn a short while ago, to join the hawking party down by the Foss.

'They wanted the atheling to see their horses.'

'Oswy's seen their horses often enough.'

'Oh no, the two Lady Elfwyn bought this morning at the fair. Such beauties, a great bay stallion for Oswy and the prettiest little grey mare—'

Mildred was already racing to the stables. Cadman was there, just mounting in a hurry and a very bad temper. As Horse-Thane, he'd had to stay and settle a fight between two of the warriors, so missing most of the day's hawking. It had been an idiotic quarrel, and hawking was his favourite sport. The frown deepened on his black brows when Mildred came panting up with a request to him to find her lady and ride with her.

'The princess should have made it clear to you, Mildred, when she took you into service. You're her bower-woman, not her nurse.'

'You don't understand! I heard the horse trader talking down at the fair. The grey's a rogue—if it bolts with Elfwyn, my lady might be hurt—kicked—trying to catch it!'

'Elfwyn's not riding the grey,' put in one of his grooms. 'I saw them go off. Elfwyn was up on the stallion, and a right fool she looked. Lady Riemmelth was riding the mare.'

Mildred shrieked, Cadman swore and galloped off, shouting to his grooms to follow and bring some rope. Mildred kilted up her skirts, scrambled on to a pony and rode after them. Folk scattered from under their hooves as they went for the Foss gate like a cavalry charge.

When they got to the marshy ground, they drew rein; it was not safe to go fast and they did not know where to look for Elfwyn and Riemmelth. Oswald had gone to an estate northwards, up the river, so the hawking party would be returning from that direction; but it was impossible to guess how far they had come, or what track the women had taken to meet them.

Much of the district was marsh and standing pools, thick with reeds; some of it was only under water at flood-times, so there were clumps of alder and willow. Here and there, on patches of rising land, cottars had their huts, living by fishing and fowling. The few tracks clung to the firmer ground, hidden among the reeds and osier withies, always slippery and often treacherous.

They listened, nothing but the whispering of reeds and willow leaves, the buzzing of flies. The marsh was oddly silent. Cadman looked up and saw why: his sharp eyes picked out a black dot, a peregrine sailing high above. Suddenly there was movement and a clatter from the middle of a pool, a heron rose from a stump, making frantically for the shelter of some alders, its big grey wings flapping heavily, its legs trailing. The peregrine stooped like lightning, there was a cry and a plash of hooves beyond the thicket; then a high dreadful screaming like mad laughter.

Elfwyn appeared at the turn of the track ahead, tiny on the stallion's back, her mouth gaping with her shrieks. She stopped when she saw them, shock and terror on her face, her hands clawing at the reins.

'Riemmelth's been thrown!' she shouted. 'Must get help!'

Then the bay stretched his neck, and it seemed Elfwyn could not hold him, she was hurtled past them back towards Eoforwic. The others hurried on. They could hear flounderings and splashings among the reeds but no voice called. Then they stopped, appalled.

The ground melted into a reach of mud and black water. Some way out was the grey mare. She had been struggling, the water rippled round her and the mud was churned, but for the moment she was still with terror. The mud lay thick and deep; sunk to her belly the mare was settling fast.

Riemmelth was lying on her face a little way beyond the mare, her head and one arm held by a patch of muddy ground among the reeds, her feet and legs dragging down into the marsh. She was making no effort to help herself, stunned by the fall or by a kick from the struggling mare or perhaps smothering in the mud. Her body seemed to be slipping backwards.

Cadman kicked off his boots and tied an end of rope round his waist.

'You can't swim in there, lord, you'll be sucked down by the mud.'

Feet plashed behind them; two cottars were hurrying up with a length of withy fencing.

'Get this out to her!'

They pushed the hurdle across. It was barely long enough to reach but they managed to jam one corner on the muddy ground among the reeds. Cadman began to crawl along, but when he was halfway across the corner of the hurdle was pulled away by his weight and the whole end sank under him. They dragged him back by the rope but the churned mud pulled Riemmelth further down. The other men looked at each other; they were sorry for the lady but they weren't going out there to be choked to death for her.

'Give me the rope!'

143

Mildred had torn off her clothes so that nothing would add to her weight or catch in the mud. She was muttering as Cadman looped the rope round her; he thought she was praying but could only hear her say over and over again, 'I take it on myself, I take it on myself.'

The men pushed the hurdle out again, stretching as far as they dared, and got the end back on the mud patch. Mildred lay flat and inched her way along, trying not to jolt her frail bridge. It dipped a little as she reached the end but still held. The men watched her turn gently on her side, untie the rope and stretch out warily to pass it under Riemmelth's body. She got the end round, knotted it, then, rising quickly to her knees, she lifted Riemmelth till she was lying across the hurdle as far as her waist. The hurdle dipped and sank under the weight of two bodies; Mildred gripped her mistress with one hand, the hurdle with the other and screamed, '*Pull!*' The men backed, hauling with all their strength; for a second or two the women were ducked head under, but Mildred held firm and they got to solid ground. Cadman knelt, feeling Riemmelth's heart.

'There's a fire in my hut,' said one of the cottars.

'Carry her there and get her dry and warm.' Cadman turned to the grooms. 'Go back to the palace, Sigeric, and fetch a litter; Alfgar, ride on north and see if you can find Oswy.'

'What about the other brave lass?'

Cadman looked down at Mildred, shivering and half-fainting at his feet, her fair skin and hair blotched with mud. She was too dazed even to tend her lady.

'I'll see to her.'

He wrapped his cloak round her, and carried her after the others.

Riemmelth was at the bottom of the peatbog, buried in black mud. They had roped her to a hurdle, so she couldn't move. The peasant's wife lay beside her, naked and blindfold, and there were countless others. So many had been given to

144

Woden, through countless years, lying still in the mud but alive. They put you into the mud alive when they give you to Woden. So they were whispering, lying still in the black mud, whispering.

'You lost your child, Riemmelth, can you feel the blood oozing down your legs? You lost your hold on it in the marsh where I sent you. Your child, Riemmelth, the royal blood of Cumbria and Bernicia, just a little clot of bloody gristle voided out and thrown into the privy. I know all about losing babies, Riemmelth, I've seen it happen before. It happened to my mother when Cadwallon's men came. She'd hidden me under the bed and told me to keep quiet; she begged them by the Virgin Mary to spare her for the child she carried. But they laid her on the floor and did it; then they slit her, Riemmelth, and cut the child out of her.'

Riemmelth tried to turn her head away, but she was roped to the hurdle and the mud was thick about her. The whispering went on.

'I screamed and they found me. I was ten years old. I'd never harmed them but they took me away. I couldn't understand why they were so cruel, I'd look at them and wait for someone to comfort me, and they'd laugh and do it. Then Oswald came and cut them to pieces, and Oswy found me. He said, "Poor little cousin, don't cry"; then he kissed me and took me home. I was sure that when I was a woman he'd marry me. But your people bought him to be your husband and he brought you here. And I said, "That's the second time the Welsh have come to destroy me, but I won't let her!" So I've given you to Woden, Riemmelth, and it doesn't matter if they pull your body out, because the marsh has got you and it's going to kill you, kill you, kill you—' The voice changed, it spoke aloud, heart-breakingly tender and melting into sobs. 'Oh, my poor Riemmelth, that it should be a gift from me that had to kill you!'

Another voice, low but impatient.

'Stop crying, Elfwyn, you're not helping anybody.'

Mildred's voice; if Mildred knew she was lying close by,

just under the mud, she'd come and save her.

'She's been like this for three days!' cried Elfwyn, all anguish and concern. 'I've been watching her for hours now and she never stirs. The marsh demons have taken her spirit, it's only her body lying here.'

Riemmelth made a dreadful struggle to drag her eyelids apart, to call out to Mildred.

'Look, she's coming back!'

She was drawn up out of the mud and got her eyes open at last. Her head was against Mildred's shoulder and she was in her bed in the palace of Eoforwic, with the sunlight slanting in on her and a scent of roses. She lay back panting in Mildred's arms, trying to find herself, to collect her memories: a heron flapped across her path, the little mare turned into a fighting demon, Elfwyn screamed.

The rest was a nightmare, born of her shock and terror, taking shape, as the Night Mare always did, from the scraps of memory and fear it found in your own brain.

It must have been a nightmare, out of her own brain. How else would she have heard Elfwyn talking Welsh?

14

It took some time for Riemmelth to recover her strength after her miscarriage and the ordeal of near-drowning. She rested in her bedchamber while a stream of visitors and gifts flowed in. Elfwyn was loud in love, grief and self-blame that still, to Riemmelth's weakened spirits, felt like an attack.

'I took the stallion, I thought she could handle the little mare!'

When she went, Riemmelth tossed fretfully on her pillows. 'Oh, for God's sake, tell her to be quiet and keep her away from me!'

Oswy looked stern. 'It's not fair to blame Elfwyn. She meant to do us a kindness; she feels bad enough about what happened without you turning against her. Ill luck is nobody's fault, it does no good to punish other people for it. What's done is past, you can't change it.'

He saw the misery in her eyes and said more gently, 'You're sorry about the child, my dear, but try not to waste your strength with grieving. We're both young and healthy, there'll be more. When you're well, I'll take you back to your home. You'll be leading the Harvest Dance all round the palace at Caer Luel in a month or two.'

Riemmelth tried to smile.

'In the meantime, as you can't travel to other lands, I've brought other lands to your bed. Look here, what I've got for you, it came from Rome.'

He sat down on the bed beside her and opened a book; it was Virgil's *Eclogues*—Penarwan had driven enough Latin into her unwilling head for her to be able to make that out. Every poem had a picture, bright as an enamelled brooch: country scenes under a sky of intense blue, shepherds piping while their white flocks grazed, vines loaded with grapes, girls bringing baskets of flowers or dancing with little goat-men.

Oswy had his arm round her shoulders, he was turning over the pages for her, pointing out details he liked. Hild came in and took a stool by him; she began to read some of the poetry aloud and argue with Oswy about favourite lines. Riemmelth leant back against him, feasting her eyes on the colours, carried away as he had meant her to be into the Arcadian world, yet enjoying the strength of his supporting arm. She didn't love Oswy, but he was a good shield-friend. As Dunnere said, he would stand over you when you were down.

Mildred brought wine for them, beaming to see her lady looking so bright. She was tiptoeing out again, but Riemmelth caught her hand and made her sit on the other side of the bed so that she, too, could see the pictures.

Elfwyn came to the open door and looked at them. Nobody noticed her; in a while she went away again.

A group of Deiran thanes came to ask after Riemmelth, bringing gifts and good wishes for her return to health. But she was still too weak and tired to face the ordeal of sitting up when they came to her room, listening and replying to their long speeches, presiding over their refreshment. Hild was with her at the time, Ebbe was at her prayers, Cyneburg placidly disinclined to a task that would take her from her son and her embroidery frame, so when he had received them with his usual grave kindness Oswald gratefully handed them over to Elfwyn's care, to be Lady of the Hall. He bade her, smiling, take Riemmelth's place and speak her thanks for her.

Elfwyn was willing and dutiful. She led the visitors to her own apartments, saw them supplied with wine, mead or ale to their taste, dismissed her attendants and set about quietening their fears about Riemmelth.

'—oh yes, the child's gone, don't worry.'

'And is she dying, herself?' asked one of the thanes, eagerly. 'I'd heard—'

'Not this time, I think. A pity, but nothing to spoil our plans. The main point's gained: there's no son to bind Cumbria to Oswald's side; she won't start another child this while. We can get rid of her the next chance that comes— when they stop hanging over her day and night. Leave that to me. Without her son, Oswald won't have Cumbria at his back when Penda comes. As soon as Rhun dies—and you can count his life in weeks now, he wrote to Oswy himself, but they've kept it from *her*—there'll be a revolt in Cumbria against Oswy's rule. That'll get him out of Deira; if the Cumbrians don't finish him Penda will, as soon as he's destroyed Oswald.'

'But is Penda coming? We've heard that every year since Heavenfield.'

'Soon. I've had word since I arrived, from Helmstan on

148

the southern marches. Cynric and Hewald, who work here, were born on his lands; they carry messages. It'll be at harvest time, when Oswald's war-host are busy on their lands. Tell our people to be ready to rise.'

'They're ready. Too long we've been waiting to see the Bernician vermin chased back down their holes.'

Elfwyn laughed. 'They won't find safety even there. I've got friends in Bernicia. They're our own blood and stock too, remember; they want what we want—to get that Christian dung swept out on to the midden and to call back the true Gods to our land.'

Her eyes were cat-slits, she nearly spat.

'Forgive your enemies! Turn the other cheek when you're struck! Did you ever hear such filth?'

Time stood still for Riemmelth during the long summer days, but her strength was coming back. June passed into July. Messages came from Cumbria and Oswy broke the news to her gently. Rhun had died in his sleep. He had known his earthly life was ending and sent them his blessing. The Cumbrian Council had accepted Oswy as king by right of his wife. As soon as she was ready to travel they would go to Caer Luel.

Ebbe and Hild took a loving farewell of her. Ebbe was going north to her new foundation at Coludesburh; she would take the veil from Bishop Aidan. Hild was going down to East Anglia. Her elder sister, Hereswith, had married the king in Edwin's time. He was a mild man and a Christian, who would never have let himself be embroiled in the quarrels of the Northumbrian dynasty. Oswald made no objection when Hild asked to stay with her kin for a while before going on to Frankland to continue her studies.

A week later an embassy arrived from Powys with a friendly greeting to the new King of Cumbria and his British Queen—and a friendly warning. It had been learned in Powys that there was unrest among some of the Cumbrian nobles at the idea of an Englishman as king. A revolt was brewing: a plan to offer the crown to one of the Dunoding clan. The envoys suggested that King Oswy and Queen Riemmelth should come across to Caer Legion on their road to Cumbria and take counsel with the lords of Powys before they went north.

They sounded worried. Oswald and Oswy questioned them closely about the dangers they suspected and they gave convincing details. There was a long, friendly conference.

Arthgal trod warily down the colonnade, trying to look at ease. If anyone questioned him, he'd say he had lost his way. He hated these places, with their inward-looking rooms and their columns like trees turned to stone. One thing, though, he had discovered in Glannaventa and Caer Luel: all Roman buildings followed much the same plan. Yes, here was the courtyard, with its grass-plot and rose bushes. He paused, glancing round cautiously. The place seemed deserted; the girl standing among the roses was so still that at first he didn't see her. She was staring at him.

'Lovely roses,' he said, coming smiling up to her, 'but the prettiest flower of all isn't growing on a bush!'

She was a pretty little thing, too, with her curls and big, pale-blue eyes.

'Do you want anything?' she asked quietly.

Arthgal gave her an admiring look. 'Ah, we can't always have what we want!'

The girl smiled. Arthgal judged he had got her into the right mood.

'Apart from anything else, I wanted a word with the Queen of Cumbria.'

'There I can't help you. She's unwell.'

'Not badly, I hope?' Arthgal was alarmed, that would spoil the whole plan.

'Oh no, just a woman's ailment.' She lowered her eyes modestly. 'It's the curse of all our sex, we have to bear it. She'll be all right in a few days.' She was smiling again. 'Would you like me to take a message?'

'I'd be grateful if you'd take her this letter.' He took out the little roll of parchment, heavily sealed, that the monk had prepared in case they couldn't speak to her alone. 'It's from the Prince of Powys—he's her cousin, you know.'

'I didn't know.'

'It's not about anything important—something about a ruby ring old Bishop Rhun had, that belonged to Powys, or had been promised to Powys. King Oswy won't have heard of it, but she'll know what it's all about.'

'I'll take it in to her at once. Will you be waiting for her answer—or where else shall I bring it?'

'The Prince said there was no answer needed, it was just to remind her about the ring. Many thanks to you, maiden, you're as kind as you're beautiful.'

'I'm happy to help you,' said Elfwyn, sweetly.

She took the letter to her room and broke the seals, peering suspiciously at the strange black marks on the parchment, wondering how best to hurt or annoy Riemmelth. She could hand it to Oswald or Oswy—but Oswald would certainly send it straight back with a polite apology; Oswy would most likely bring it himself and read it with her—his arm round her shoulders, talking and laughing with her about it. In the end she decided just to destroy it. She rolled it up again and tied it round a pebble; the next time she went riding, she dropped it in the marshes down by the Foss.

'Are you sure he's taken the bait?'

The Powys envoys were riding west over the plain of Eoforwic. The Roman road was rising in front of them to climb across the dusky swells of moorland to Manceinion.

'There's no reason why he should refuse it,' said Congair. 'His brother's as concerned to know what's happening in Dunoding as he is. And she'll tell him they ought to go—you're sure she got the letter?'

'I saw her maid taking it in to her.'

'That's all right, then. We'll get them in the hill-country

151

south of Caer Legion as they come down towards Pengwern.'

'It could be a bit hard for the Queen, going with the man who's just killed her husband,' said Arthgal, thoughtfully.

'She won't mind that!'

'No, but the priests might. And it's just the sort of thing a bard could put into a satire.'

'It's all arranged. We won't kill Oswy—that's Penda's job. Then we arrive, rescue the Queen and make straight for Caer Luel.'

'There'll be war with Northumbria.'

'That's all arranged too. There won't be any tell-tales left alive from Oswy's war-band and Oswald won't be expecting to hear from his brother till he's in Caer Luel. While we're on our way to Cumbria, Penda's going to take his men north up the Long Hills and sack Oswald's palace—Gefrin, they call it. That'll get Oswald racing back north to Bernicia, and there'll be a revolt in Deira as soon as his back's turned.'

'It's a lovely plot,' said Arthgal, appreciatively.

'It ought to be. Elidir's been working on it long enough.'

When the last speeches had been made and the parting cup passed round with many good wishes for the envoys' journey back to Powys, Oswald went to his private room. Oswy followed him. He was restless, pacing about, stopping to stare out into the courtyard, picking up Oswald's psalter and turning the pages without reading, then putting it down again. Oswald sat still as usual, his upturned palms resting on his knees. Finally he spoke.

'What are you going to do?'

'What they asked—meet them, find out what they've got to tell, make some agreement with them—then get up into Cumbria before the trouble starts. Powys wants our help against Gwynedd, of course; that's what this friendship is all about, but I want to know their exact terms. Riemmelth can come up and join me later; perhaps you can see her on her way as far as Corabryg, then she can come along the Wall to Caer Luel.'

'You won't take her with you?'

'She's not well enough to make a long journey yet—and if there really is trouble in Dunoding I might have some hard riding on my way north.'

'It's a pity you should leave her while she's still weak and in low spirits; besides, do you think Cumbria will rally to you without her?'

'I shall have to find that out when I get there.'

'I think it's too great a risk. It's because you're an Englishman that the trouble is starting. Wait till she's stronger, and go together.'

'Delay's a risk as well. Besides, I've got to keep this link with Powys, it's too useful to throw away.'

'The link with Powys is just as important to me as to you, brother. I'll go to meet them. By the time I come back, Riemmelth will be stronger, and I'll have shortened the journey for her. She can ride into Caer Luel at your side.'

Mildred put down the ivory comb and began to braid the dark tresses showering down her mistress's back. She always marvelled at Riemmelth's hair, the black waves, the silkiness and raven-sheen, the living warmth. She loved to handle it, to comb it tangle-free, braid it, planning new ways to loop and pin it. Today she was taking special pride in her task, for it was Riemmelth's first appearance at a feast as Queen of Cumbria.

It was not a very splendid occasion: Oswald was away with all his hearth-companions, Ebbe and Hild were gone, the Deiran thanes had scattered to their own estates to oversee their harvests and tax-gathering.

Riemmelth had little heart for feasting; she was in mourning for Rhun, whose death had saddened her more than she thought possible. *I should have been there beside him, giving him my love to light him on his way. I would have been in Caer Luel now, if it hadn't been for that accursed ride. If Elfwyn had really wanted to offer my life to Woden and Hel, as I dreamt, she could hardly have hurt me more.*

Grief gripped her hardest when her mind followed Oswald over the moors, west and south to Powys. Was Elidir still there with his uncle, or had he gone back to Manau? Did he look east across the sea to Glannaventa at nightfall and watch the mountains above Eskdale fading into the dusk?

If only I hadn't ridden that mare; if only Pascen hadn't died; if only I'd run away like Arianrhod; if only—if only—

She was heavy-hearted indeed, though darkly splendid in her purple robe, with the pearl-drops of her coronet like tears on her black hair. She left her room at last and walked slowly along the colonnade. She was feeling so little joy in her queenship, that when she came face to face with Cyneburg, who was looking peevish and resentful at having another queen in the family, she bowed her head graciously and glided quietly into second place. Cyneburg almost visibly smoothed her ruffled feathers as she went up to the Queen's seat.

Riemmelth's thoughts were still dwelling more away in the west than in the feast before her. The main meal was over, and she had followed Cyneburg with her drinking horn to the King's table, when the palace herald appeared at the door and beckoned to Liodwald the Dish-Thane. They spoke together, then Liodwald hurried up towards Oswy.

Her mind had been so much in the past all day, it wasn't strange to hear Elidir's voice beside her, calling for the tale of Blodeuedd; the knocking at her palace door; Meirion the usher speaking to Drutwas the gate-warden, then hurrying up to her on the dais. It almost seemed that the two times were one: this message that Liodwald was bringing had been on its way to her even then. Every step she had taken since had brought her to stand there in Eoforwic, waiting for it. She strained to listen, but could not hear much.

'. . . Westerfalc, thane of Deawesbyrig . . . been set upon . . . king's errand . . . in the waggon . . . speak to him yourself.'

'Oh, bring him in,' said Oswy, impatiently.

There was a stir at the door and a group of men came slowly in. Talk died along the benches as folk turned to look. The well-dressed man with greying fair hair must be Thane Westerfalc, three of his retainers behind him. At his side, with a hand on his shoulder, so that he seemed to be using the thane's sturdy body as a crutch, moving like a sleepwalker, was Godwin, Horse-Thane of Oswald's warband. A fortnight ago he had ridden west out of Eoforwic at Oswald's side.

He was clean and kempt, his loose robe and mantle were not travel-stained. Someone, probably Westerfalc, had provided them for they were not the clothes he had worn to ride with Oswald, and he was without his weapons. He walked steadily enough, his right hand on the thane's shoulder, his left muffled inside his mantle, clutching it across his body. His tanned face was calm.

Oswy was watching Godwin intently, and Riemmelth, standing by the king's table with her drinking horn, saw that he was very still, his eyes grey and bleak. When the newcomers were barely half-way up the hall, he rose and went to sit on the gift-stool, as if they were coming up for judgement. He waited for them to draw near, while the silence grew thick all round him, then said very quietly with his eyes on Godwin's face:

'He's dead.'

Godwin's white lips moved to form, 'Yes.'

Another second's quiet. Then the silence was ripped by a scream from Cyneburg, followed by an outburst of sobbing and wild calling on Oswald's name. Riemmelth signed to Mildred and Elfwyn to attend her, and there was a confused swirl and scuffle as the women were got out of the hall. Riemmelth came to Oswy's side. Now that she was closer to Godwin she could see that under his tan he was corpse-colour. His eyes were blank, his lips seemed to be bleached out, the hand clutching Westerfalc's shoulder showed bluish nails. He and Oswy were holding glances like a wrestler's lock.

155

'How and where?'

'There was a message waiting for us at Chester, saying the King of Powys was on his way from Pengwern; he'd be in his hunting-lodge at Cogwy that night, about twenty-five miles to the south, and he'd give us the meeting next day in Chester—unless we'd like to honour him by being his guests at the lodge. Of course, Oswald sent word that he would—'

'Of course.'

'Osmund rode out with his answer. We never saw him again.' Godwin's voice was quite matter-of-fact, he might have been describing an ordinary morning's ride.

'They'd sent guides for us. In the morning we followed the Roman road south for some ten miles; when the road turned easterly, we still kept south on a track past Bancornaburh.'

That name struck chill. Oswald's father had slaughtered the monks of Bangor-is-y-Coed before the battle of Chester.

'We still kept south; the land was rising steeply to the west. We forded a river—the Pever, they called it, and the guides said the lodge was close at hand. They rode ahead fast, to see that the Welshmen were ready to greet us; they told us to follow. No one came back. The land was still as sleep. Then, to the west, I caught the glint of spears among the trees where they were waiting for us.'

Godwin paused, he was growing breathless and his chest was labouring. The hand on Westerfalc's shoulder gripped desperately, but he still kept himself upright.

'If they had come for us at once, I think we might have ridden up to them in greeting, since we were thinking no harm. But they held their place, and we knew what they were waiting for. There was an old fort, bramble-grown, on top of a hill and we rode for it. We'd no hope of holding out; we hadn't the numbers to man the ramparts, but we would have been well placed above them for a last stand. They'd planned for that, they had troops up there ready to greet us.'

'Trust the Welsh.' There was wormwood in Oswy's voice.

Godwin shook his head; it seemed to be heavy on his neck.

'Not the Welsh. Even if he'd tied his calves to the back of his thighs and fought down on his knees, you couldn't mistake him.'

'Penda.' Oswy was not asking a question.

'He threw the spear over us. The others were coming up behind, we knew we were trapped. We dismounted and drove our horses at them while we made our shield-wall. It didn't last long, they broke us by weight of numbers. At the end—when his shield was smashed and his sword-wrist broken—he lifted his arms and prayed for us—"God have mercy on their souls"—then I was struck—they trod me down in the last rush—'

Riemmelth saw him sway and she lifted the drinking horn to him, but his eyes were shut though he remained standing. She glanced at Oswy, expecting him to tell Godwin to rest, but Oswy's face was cold. The ghost-voice went on.

'When I saw and heard again, there were Welsh on the hill. They were looking for something among the bodies— they weren't knifing wounded or stripping armour, or they'd have seen I wasn't dead. Whatever it was, they didn't find it; they had high words with the Mercians, then they went. Then the Mercians went. They'd put us under the spear so they left us as we were, for the wolf and raven. I waited till dusk. One of our horses came to me in the woods and I worked my way through the hill-country north-west of the Peak—'

'And got safe away.'

'My lord, he'd nearly bled white when I came on him,' said Westerfalc, uneasily. 'He's been in a swoon most of the time in the waggon.'

Oswy ignored him. 'Had the Mercians found an ash tree to hang your king's body, or didn't you stop to look?'

'I stopped to look. They'd put his head on a spear. And they'd cut off his arms and bound them to spears as well, one on either side, with the hands upward, as he held them when he prayed.'

'And you live and tell me.'

'And I lived to tell you. You can choose what you do about it. I told him before I left, I wouldn't stay long behind him.'

He dragged his hands out of the folds of his mantle and threw what he had been holding on to the floor between himself and Oswy. It was a little piece of turf, the grass withered and stained brown but with a fresh sticky patch of red on it. With his last strength, Godwin took his hand off Westerfalc's shoulder and stepped forward. He managed to get his foot on the turf before he died, and kept his warrior's honour by falling on the spot where his lord was slain.

A sob tore Riemmelth's throat. Oswy swung round and saw her.

'You shouldn't be here, my lady.'

He gripped her arm and led her to the door. The colonnade was still rosy with sunset.

'Go and calm the women. We can't keep the death a secret now, with Cyneburg screaming her head off. The news'll be on its way across Eoforwic, but we might be able to pass it off for a while as a riding accident, for a day or two at least until they realise his war-band isn't coming back with the body. Tell Mildred to get your things—and mine—together and be ready to travel the moment I give word.'

The sunset faded into dusk; lights shone for a while in the palace and then went out one by one, leaving just the cressets at the ends of the colonnades to light the night-guards. Riemmelth sat on the end of her bed, staring into a blackness where no light shone, where there was no sound but a dead man whispering '*—there were Welsh on the hill*'.

A war-band from Gwynedd, of course; they'd always fought alongside the Mercians. But Cogwy was in Powys, a royal hunting-lodge—what were Gwynedd warriors doing there?

'*—they were looking for something among the bodies—*'

A clan of moorland cattle-raiders, come scavenging behind the Mercian war-band, on the look-out for spoils.

'*—they weren't knifing wounded or stripping armour—*'

What—or who—were they looking for? Elidir wouldn't—he's a warrior of royal blood, not a bandit—

158

*Elidir's a huntsman. It's no sin or disgrace to decoy your prey
into a trap.*

But if that were true—I've killed Oswald—

*No! It was a war-band from Gwynedd, keeping up the old
alliance. It was cattle-thieves, taking the chance to loot.*

Outside, the torches faded into the coming dawn. Still
Riemmelth sat on the end of her bed, staring out into the
courtyard but seeing nothing, even when the pillars and rose
bushes took shape out of the greyness.

She was seeing another dawn: mist drifted between the
oak trees down by the Petteril; there was a scent of hawthorn
blossom; a darkly handsome face stared at her, lips drawn
back from strong white teeth; a low, musical voice hardened
to a snarl:

'If anyone tried to take you from me now, I'd kill him.'

15

'Well, that's settled.'

Oswy had come striding into the room. He took in the
neatly stacked chests and leather bags with one swift glance,
and came over to the still figure on the bed.

'You've never waited up all night for me? That wasn't my
meaning, sweetheart. Where's Mildred?'

'With Cyneburg.'

Oswy turned back the coverlet. 'Well, off with your gown
and shoes, lie down in your shift. Try to get some sleep, we
won't be riding for an hour or two.'

'Riding?'

'Back to Bebbanburh. Trouble's coming, and I want to
have Bernicia firm and ready at my back when it comes. I'll
send Cadman and half the war-band with you; he'll warn the
ealdormen to be on the alert for word to call out the fyrd.'

'Aren't you coming?'

'In a while. I'm just going to bring Oswald home.'

She stared at him, thinking she had misheard. He spoke in a flat, almost absent-minded tone, as if he had left a book in another room and it hadn't been packed.

'But—Cogwy—it's in Powys—close by the Mercian border—you can't—'

'I can, you know.'

'Oh, don't you see, you fool!' She jumped up and screamed in his face. 'It wasn't Oswald they wanted to kill, they didn't know he was coming. The message was for you—and me. They were going to take us on our way to Cumbria—'

She stopped, terrified of what she might say next. Oswy's face was grim.

'Oh, yes—Cumbria. There's some objection to my rule, it seems. They're thinking of calling in your family's blood-foes in my place, and then you won't be queen after all. That would be a shame, no wonder you haven't slept all night for worrying. Well, if you can just spare me a few days, while I stop my brother's body being fouled by heathens, I'll get back to my marriage duties, don't fret.'

Oswy had not raised his voice above its usually pleasant tone, but Riemmelth felt as if he had spat in her face. What could she say?

She sank down on the bed; her shock and despair must have shown on her face. Oswy lifted his hand and touched her cheek.

'This hasn't been the happiest summer in either of our lives, has it, my dear? We're neither of us at our best.'

'Have you thought what will happen,' she said dully, 'if you meet Penda with only half your war-band?'

'Oh, yes. I'll be one of his Welsh friends from Powys, of course. And if I meet any of your loving fellow countrymen, I'm one of their loyal Mercian allies. I doubt very much if I'll meet either though. I'll be travelling by night—and, you know, avoiding battle is one of my greatest skills.'

He was trying to make her smile, but she could not.

'There could be Mercians with the men of Powys. And you don't look like—one of my people.'

'Well thought. Then I'll be Irish—bringing a band of footloose warriors looking for war service and amusement at one of the Welsh courts. There's one thing to be said for exile—you learn tongues!'

'How would you explain to Mercians that an Irish warband was travelling east?'

He startled her by laughing outright. 'That would be easiest of all. Our devout Penda is a heathen. He pays his own devotions to Woden, of course, but he's a broad-minded man, all the Old Gods are honoured behind his broad shield. There's a great shrine to The Lady just south of the Peak—Arnemeton. She's been there since men lived in this island, perhaps before. Her worshippers come from far beyond Mercia, especially now, when their own holy groves have been given to the saints. She doesn't mind where they come from or what they call her – Frea, Rhiannon, Hecate, She's still the same, and her priestesses make themselves willing altars for any man who comes to worship her.'

He grinned. 'I've heard there's a well-beaten road all the way out of Wales, where the grass never has time to grow. If anyone asks us what we're doing heading east out of Powys, we're a little flock of St Patrick's straying lambs!'

In spite of the tumult of her own feelings Riemmelth had been listening, her quick mind testing the story for weak places. As far as one could trust such a crazy scheme at all, it sounded quite hopeful, and if anybody could dodge or lie his way out of danger, Oswy was that man—apart from one thing.

'Setting out will be the hardest,' she said slowly. 'If you slip away from Eoforwic by night, I couldn't hide it. If the Deirans aren't all to be trusted, the news could be out and racing to Mercia and Powys before you get there. But if you leave us on the way north, that will be seen as well.'

'I'll leave you on the way north—unfinished business in Deira. It's an undeserved slight to you, my lady, but I'll be off on a love-errand. Could you do your beauty that great wrong, and pass that lie for Oswald?'

At last she smiled back at him.

'Why not, if you can tell that truth for Oswald?'

For a while there was much to do and no time for brooding, as they tried to clear the palace and leave Eoforwic as quickly as possible without it looking like a panic-stricken retreat. She tried to comfort and help Cyneburg; the widowed queen was going to the nunnery at Heruteu with her little boy. Riemmelth was shocked to see that as well as her grief, Cyneburg was stricken with terror—not of Penda and the Welsh but of Oswy and herself. It was unbelievable. Then she remembered Ebbe telling her how their grandfather had won Deira: '—*killed their king; he would have killed Prince Edwin, too, only his nurse got him away*—'

They started for the North. Riemmelth helped Oswy to get away as best she might, taking public leave of him with cold ceremony when he set off with laughing apologies and a grinning escort on his 'urgent business' with the thane of Hrypum. She listened, clearly bored and scornful, while Cadman, who was in on the secret, talked pointedly about the thane's hospitality and what his daughter Edyth would do for her father's guests. They both hoped they had covered Oswy's real purpose closely enough.

Then, as they held their way north and the Long Hills marched with them at their left shoulder, mile after mile, she had time enough to think. They passed Catraeth, and the road that went up over the roof of the hills and down to Penrhyd. Twenty miles more of arrow-straight road through the oaks of Inglewood; then the Petteril and the Caldew came in to join hands with the Idon round Caer Luel on its rock. Riemmelth's mind went racing to her city. Her body ought to be there too, holding her land against rebels and raiders if Oswy never came back from Powys—and the odds were heavily against him.

Now that she could not hear his cool, amused voice explaining his plan to her, or see him smiling as he spoke, she had no defence as the foolhardiness of the exploit struck her—to ride through Mercia and Powys with a handful of men and bring back a corpse. If he wasn't a corpse himself at this moment, he soon would be.

She was surprised at the pang that thought gave her. But if you live close to someone for over a year on fairly good terms, of course they leave an empty space when they go. God knows, she grieved for Oswald, too; she'd break her heart, now, if she lost Mildred. As a husband—a foreigner, an Englishman—she could not say that Oswy had been bad to her; they'd shared laughter and pleasure together. She was already thinking of him in the past.

This is the fate Rhun dreaded for me when Pascen died—a woman alone, with greedy hands reaching to seize me and tear my land apart. And now there's no Rhun to protect us, no Oswald at our backs. If Northumbria falls to pieces, I won't have a mile of borderland safe, except Strathclyde, perhaps. But I can't see help coming from Alclud, they owe us nothing. There's one who would help, if he knew how I'm beset—if he still remembers me—if he's free of other ties.

The thought of Elidir made her heart seem to lurch—she couldn't tell if it were hope or fear—she felt giddy, had to shut her eyes for a second as she clutched the reins to steady herself.

I tried to tell Rhun when Pascen died, but he wouldn't hear me. Elidir was sent to take Pascen's place. Together, we could hold Cumbria. If only I could get to Caer Luel and send to him for help. Godwin's dead voice came whispering inside her head, reminding her that she might not have to send; the helper might be in Caer Luel already, waiting for her.

'*. . . there were Welsh on the hill . . . they were looking for something . . .*'

She shut her mind to it. Elidir was in Manau, of course; a fast ship would soon take him word and bring him back to her. A widow could not be coy like a maiden. If she did not choose a husband, and marry him quickly, she'd likely be claimed by some cattle-raiding kinsman from Dunoding soon after she crossed the Northumbrian border.

Who would rule Northumbria, if Oswy never came back? Not Oswald's little boy. Doubtless there were nobles who had some royal blood, who would fight it out; there might be someone of Edwin's line to seize Deira—with Elfwyn as his queen? Elfwyn would love that! She glanced at Elfwyn, riding companionably at her side as usual. Since the mishap by the Foss, Elfwyn had hovered over her with a protective tenderness that hardly left work for Mildred.

Then, as she remembered what Elfwyn's lot had been, for the first time she felt real terror for herself.

She had no claim to Northumbria, but suppose they held her, to see if she had any lately conceived child of Oswy in her womb? There wasn't, Oswy had not slept with her since her miscarriage. Forcing himself on a sick, low-spirited woman was not one of his sports. And when they saw there was no child, what if they still kept her, handed her over to one of their nobles to bind Cumbria fast; bundled her into one of their nunneries; made her stay, like Elfwyn, a barren hostage at the court while Urien's line withered and died in her body?

Now she was wild to get away; but her escort would not follow her to Caer Luel without Oswy's orders, or let her ride off alone. Without the protection of Oswald or Oswy, without the comforting presence of Ebbe and Hild, the English suddenly seemed as alien and dangerous as when she had first come to their land. She was lost and lonely among strangers. And once she was on the sheer sea-rock of Bebbanburh, she would never get out. Her mind worked away frantically at the bars of the trap, and at last she made her decision.

They had forded the Alne when she told them she was going to Gefrin.

If Oswy comes back, I can welcome him at Gefrin as well as in Bebbanburh. And if he doesn't, then I can be in Caer Luel in a day and a night, with Gwylan under me. There's nothing I can do for Northumbria; my duty's where my heart is, in the west. I'm the last of our House.

Cadman looked ready to object.

'You've got to garrison the fortress and send word to the ealdormen that they might have to call out the local levies. Whatever we do, we must not give the idea that we're expecting to be besieged in Bebbanburh. Otherwise, every man will stay where he is to guard his own lands. If I stop in Gefrin for a day or two with just a handful of folk, while Mildred goes ahead to get my bower ready, that will show there's no panic.'

Cadman nodded, it made sense. At the parting of the ways he went off toward the coast, taking most of the servants and the baggage under his escort. Riemmelth saw with pleasure that Mildred was riding at his side. Elfwyn had moved to ride with them but Riemmelth called her back. For a second, Elfwyn's eyes were as wide as a startled kitten's, she opened her mouth to protest, then closed it on one of her tight little smiles: Riemmelth would meet some unexpected guests at Gefrin, to help her time pass quickly, but these guests would not harm *her*, and what happened there would be amusing to watch.

'The King told us to go to Bebbanburh.' She made her voice carry to the ears of Cadman's warriors, 'And I, for one, don't mean to disobey his orders.'

'The Queen tells you to come to Gefrin. I want your company there, while Mildred is busy.' *And not meddling with her in Bebbanburh, reminding her sweetly in Cadman's hearing how grateful she must be that I took her out of a slave-booth.*

'If that is what you want me to do,' said Elfwyn, very clearly, 'but I would have gone to Bebbanburh.'

Having made sure that everybody within earshot would remember her innocence, Elfwyn went with Riemmelth meekly and made no more difficulties. When Riemmelth came out of her bower into the late afternoon sun and strolled up the slope at the foot of the Gefrin, Elfwyn turned a beaming face to her. She had been deep in talk with one of the hill-farmers.

'Look!' she cried, holding up a neatly-made rush basket. 'Beorn heard you'd been poorly in Eoforwic, and he's brought you some goats' milk cheese. Goats' milk is very strengthening.'

Riemmelth turned to smile her thanks at the hill-farmer, a thick-set, heavy-boned man in a sheepskin cloak. She tried to still the shiver of distaste that went through her when she saw it was the man she had stopped from drowning his wife in a peatbog.

'My thanks to you—Beorn; and to your wife. I suppose she made the cheese. I hope she's well.'

'She's dead, lady. Lung disease.'

'I'm sorry to hear it.'

She crossed herself and walked on, nodding to the man but not caring to say any more. Elfwyn stayed for a few more words.

'—the track west of the Cheviots, coming from the south along the burn. It's dark of the moon, they'll need guiding. Have them in place before dawn but tell them not to attack till full light. No one must get away.'

'If anyone does, he won't get far.'

Smiling, Eflwyn ran to overtake Riemmelth.

Next dawn was bright, too bright with a blood-red eastern sky and a smell of rain on the south-west wind over the Cheviots. Riemmelth decided to have her ride at once, and got into her leather jerkin and breeches. She was at the door of Oswy's hall—she'd had no heart to move into Cyneburg's quarters in the royal palace—when the war-band came.

At first she thought they'd been sent over from Bebbanburh and felt a spurt of rage at Cadman's officiousness. She stood for a second watching Edgar fall with a red stream starting to flow out of him; Ashferth and

Wermund racing towards the gates of the great cattle-fold, shouting to everyone to make for it; Siegerun the hen-wife screaming and vomiting on the point of a spear—as if it were all some unforeseen morning's work they were busy about. Then she turned and went back to the inner chamber, straight to the chest at her bedside.

I ordered them to come here. They could all be safe in Bebbanburh, but for me. Mother of God, what have I brought on poor Elfwyn! I can't save them, but at least I can strike a blow for them. I'll pay my blood-debt for their deaths.

She moved fast, because she didn't want them to come on her unprepared, but her hands were steady and her mind was clear. The mail-shirt fitted quite well over her leather jerkin, the boar-crested helmet was a shade too wide and loose and she wrapped her hair round her head to fill the space, buckling the cheekguards as tight as possible. She passed the sword-belt through the scabbard and buckled it round her, checking that the sword moved easily in its sheath, the hilt ready to her hand. She lifted Oswy's light boy's shield on her left arm; it felt heavy enough to her, but she wouldn't live long enough to be tired. There was no war-spear in the place, so she took a hunting spear from the rack as she went back through the hall.

A figure sprang into the doorway, yelling; the hall was dusky after the light outside and Riemmelth's spearpoint took him in the mouth before he was aware of her. She held the shaft steady and let him kill himself by his own rush, as if he had been a boar. There was a jarring shock along her arm, metal grated against bone, the yell was cut off on a choke, there was a weight on the end of her spear. She pulled the point free, stepped over the body and came out on to the porch.

The folk of Gefrin had stopped screaming; a few still shapes were lying huddled or sprawled in the courtyard; there was a hideous outburst from the stables, of horses whinnying and threshing in agonised terror; shouted calls and answers; the thud of axes on timber; a drift of smoke in

167

the air; figures running towards her.

The raiders paused when they saw her step out beyond the shadow of the porch, a young atheling in princely armour, spearpoint crimsoned with blood. They shouted. Riemmelth raised her head proudly. She would be dead in seconds after they rushed her; she could take one more with her, two if she had time to draw her sword.

But there was no rush. The warriors stayed where they were, pointing at her and talking excitedly. Then they drew aside; someone came slowly towards her, monstrous in height and breadth, an oak tree walking.

'Even if he tied his calves to the back of his thighs and fought down on his knees you couldn't mistake him.'

Penda.

He had no spear or shield with him; he had his great sword in his hand, swinging it a little as he walked, blood running down the blade. His men kept their place, he meant to give her single combat. Well, they wouldn't have much doubt of the result, but she'd make them wait for it; she'd give them something to watch. It was better than being trampled and hacked to death in a general brawl. She was smiling a little as she stepped to meet him.

She moved as if she meant to come in close with a spear-thrust, then changed her grip and hurled the weapon with all her force at his face. If it struck home, it would kill him or blind him while she leaped to finish him with her sword.

He moved with amazing speed for his size, stepped aside, flung out a huge arm and caught the spear in flight. She had given him her weapon—and his reach must be twice her own.

Penda waved the spear at her with a shout of laughter, held the shaft in front of his foot, stepped on it, broke it like a dead twig and kicked the pieces aside. Then he came for her with his sword. The only way she excelled him was speed, and that would not help her long. The warriors had made a circle round them; she couldn't break and run for it, she couldn't even get back to the hall to hold the doorway against them. If she kept on running from his sword strokes, he would tire her out; she didn't want to die scuttling like a frightened rabbit in the last standing corn at harvest. She made as if to run, doubled with lightning speed and dived in under his left arm, driving her sword-point in a dagger-thrust to his unshielded side.

He brought his arm down like a crashing bough; she jumped aside just in time to keep her skull or shoulder from being smashed, but even the glancing blow made her stagger and trip, wrenching her ankle cruelly. The loose helmet tilted askew, her hair tumbled down to her knees. The watchers shouted.

'A waelcyrige!'

Penda raised his sword in salute, she saw his teeth as he called, 'He—y, Woden's daughter! Take my greetings to the Ash-Rider!'

Now she was terrified. She knew the way she would go— *'they send them home by water'*—but it wasn't the thought of black peat-mud choking her that made her lungs labour now, and her eyes misty. *'The king and his war-band put some of their seed into the waelcyrige to take back to Woden for an offering.'*

Penda seemed to have grown taller, to blot out the sky; the sunlight had gone. The circle had drawn closer, they were clashing their spears against their shields and chanting, a heavy-beating chant that got into her head and dragged her sword down to keep time with it—'Ravens croak, keen for the carrion'—she hurled herself at Penda, trying to goad him with a shower of blows to kill her—'the grim wolf, the grey wold-dweller'—he brought his sword-blade down on hers, jarring and numbing her arm so that she dropped her weapon—'seize the shield-maiden, slit her with man-spear'—she threw her shield down and tried to run on his sword but he stepped back laughing. Then hands were everywhere on her, clutching and pulling at her limbs.

Now she forgot all pride, shieking, writhing, kicking, snapping with her teeth, knowing nothing but the horror of

169

being a woman helpless under the man-pack: the laughter, the force, the stench of sweat. Then the silence, the ruthless grip on her wrists and ankles, the cobble-stones hard under her back and her spread-eagled limbs, cold air with a drift of rain in it on her bare flesh. Huge legs straddling, knotted with muscle, furred like a bear. '*The king and his war-band ... some of their seed ... take to Woden ...*'

The peatbog was merciful, black and deep. She closed her eyes and willed herself towards it with all the power of the death-runes.

Night.

Penda came into her like the King Bull at stud; but her spirit tore free of him and went out into the darkness.

Elfwyn had meant to greet the raiders, to stand by Penda's side when they dragged Riemmelth out, to watch her cringing at their feet, begging for mercy while they roped her to the hurdle. She had gloated over it so long, preparing her words and smiles. And then—when they came and the first man was cut down and the first woman writhed on a spearpoint like a broken crane-fly, and the screaming started—then she was ten years old again; they had just done something dreadful to her mother and they were coming to take her away.

She ran up into the lofted gallery of the Great Hall and crouched by one of the windows, too dazed with terror to throw herself out. No one came; Gefrin had been given to Woden, there was no looting. When everything that moved had been hacked to death, the raiders piled kindling against the timbers in the path of the south-west wind and set torches blazing there.

Elfwyn saw the slim figure in the boar-crowned helmet step proudly out of Oswy's hall; Oswy's young self as he had come to save her after Heavenfield. She watched the fight, saw the raven tresses under the helmet and knew now that Oswy was Riemmelth—or Riemmelth was Oswy. She could not take her eyes away, though the crackling of flames was louder behind her and the smoke had begun to coil upwards.

She saw Riemmelth disarmed and the men crouching over her. She knew what they would be doing. In a while, they all left, carrying something.

The fire was spreading.

16

It was dark of the moon, but the sky was clear and brilliant with stars. There was a cool wind from the mountains, the woods were whispering and astir with shadows. One of the shadows stepped out from under the trees and paused where the turfy ramparts rose up, wave after wave.

'Stay with the troop, lord, in case we're surprised. I'll go up.'

Oswy shook his head and began to climb. Godric followed, then Wulfstan and Guthlac. As he went up, soft-footed on the short upland turf, Oswy tried to harden himself for what he was going to see and touch. He had seen corpses in plenty, including his eldest brother some time after Cadwallon had finished with him, had made a fair number himself. But this was Oswald, and his body had been chopped to pieces to make morsels for a heathen god.

His eyes were well used to the dark; he moved surely, threading his way through the gorse clumps and the stunted thorn trees. At the top he paused and listened, straining his eyes and ears for movement. The birds would have roosted but the wolves could still be feasting. But there was no gleam of green eyes, and the darker shapes on the turf did not stir. The stars were so thick, the three stakes stood out quite clearly against the sky. He braced himself and went forward, ready for the horror. It was more than two weeks since Oswald's head had been lifted to the ravens. Oswy placed himself in front of the mid-most spear and stared his brother in the face.

Oswald had been dead before they hacked his body apart and he had died in an act of charity, praying for the souls of his men. His eyes gazed tranquilly at the wide sky, his hands upraised in blessing, as they had so often been in life. No carrion bird had touched him, his flesh had not started to rot. It could be said—sceptically, he himself would have said if he had read of it in a saint's life—that the cool dry air had halted decay; that the upraised hands and wind-stirred hair had scared the birds. But face to face with him, Oswy knew that some greater power than nature was working through that quiet flesh.

Godric was half snarling, half sobbing with fury.

'Rot the heathen swine! He must be boasting about his courage—striking a dead enemy!'

'Penda was afraid of him,' said Oswy, calmly. 'He saw Oswald praying at the last; he thought he was a priest. He offered the body to Woden, because he'd vowed to do it but he didn't want to offend whatever god my brother worshipped. So he broke the body to stop the magic, but he left him praying to his god.'

He laughed. The others stared at him puzzled and alarmed, it was an eerie sound among the corpses.

'The idiot! He couldn't even remember what happens when you break a rune-stave! He's let Oswald's power loose—and it's in our hands, the holiest relic in Britain!'

Before they took Oswald away, Oswy knelt and said a prayer for his brother's war-band, who had been granted the warriors' chosen death-bed—the field where their lord was slain. Then he went down the hill, light-footed and light-hearted. Before dawn broke, they were well on their way to the North.

Two days later they were watching the dawn come up from a fold in the moors above Manceinion. Eastwards the Roman road lifted over the slopes of the Long Hills to Elmet and Eoforwic. They would be able to travel by daylight now;

Oswy had let them rest for a few hours and they were expecting him to give word for mounting. He was staring thoughtfully towards the North.

'Shall we be keeping to the road now, lord?' Dunnere was impatient to be off.

'I wonder.' Oswy sounded preoccupied.

'You think they're after us?' Godric sounded surprised. He'd been on the watch and seen no sign of pursuit.

'I think they might be before us.'

'What do you mean?'

'It was a decoy, that ambush where Oswald died. What I'd like to know is who was being decoyed, and from where? If we had died at Cogwy—which is what was meant—Oswald would have come down here to avenge us. Meanwhile, an attack would have been made—where? Cumbria or Northumbria?'

'What would you say, lord?'

'Cumbria, I believe,' said Oswy slowly. He was not completely sure. 'It's more open to attack from this quarter. Anyway, I think we'll go up and take a look on our way back to Bebbanburh, just to make sure all's well. Or our proud Welsh lady will say I lost her land, which would be a pity since she married me to hold it for her.'

Godric looked up sharply; there had been an odd note in Oswy's voice, but he was smiling.

The Northumbrians made a wary circuit round Manceinion and took the road to the North. The fine weather had broken at last, there were squalls of rain on the south-westerly wind.

Abbess Penarwan woke up to a feeling of oppression. *Well, that's no wonder, at my age and with my bulk*, she thought wryly, staring at the guest-chamber ceiling. She was trying to will herself into heaving up from her pillow, it seemed to take more effort every morning. *I'll be on my way after Rhun any time now; I've had my notice served.*

She accepted it calmly; that wasn't the weight that bore

173

down on her heart and lungs. She had already felt anxiety stir, sitting holding Rhun's hand while he drifted off to sleep.

Oswy should be here, with his war-band behind him, ready to take over. He should have been here all these months, learning whom to trust.

Since Rhun's death she had grown more and more uneasy. She had always had an instinct for statecraft and now she felt an undercurrent of unrest in the land. Also, some monks from Kentigern's foundation at Llanelwy had visited her, on their way to the saint's shrine at Glasgu. Bound by loyalty to Kentigern's own people, they had warned her of trouble brewing in the south, of invitations sent to Dunoding.

Riemmelth could have held Cumbria. Well, who saw to it that she isn't here? Who made sure that anything she said about ruling Cumbria would go unheard? It's time to set aside old hatreds now, and make my confession before I ask for the Viaticum.

She made her effort of will and hauled herself up to sit on the side of the bed, dizzy and gasping. She had to rest for a while before she tried to stand. She could not dress now without help from one of her novices, so she wrapped her cloak round her before she sat down to her writing desk. Her hands were shaking slightly, but her beautiful clerkly script was as clear and even as ever.

She wrote it all down: her adultery, her lover's death at the hands of Owain ap Urien, her forced entry into religion. Then she went on to the decoying of Elidir, Guriat's murder, what she knew of the plotted rebellion. She ended with urgent advice to Oswy that he should bring Riemmelth back to Cumbria at once, and trust her judgement. She folded the parchment, sealed it heavily, stamped it with her signet and directed it on the outside:

'Domino glorioso Osuio regi Cumbriae.'

I'll send it as soon as I get back to Caer Luel, she thought; then, with a little spurt of laughter: *There's one thing about choosing Oswy as confessor, he'll know what I'm talking about and he won't be shocked.*

174

She had one more effort to make that day for her dead husband's kingdom, which was why she had dragged herself all the way down to Penrhyd. Rhun had given a magnificent processional cross to the church there but had died before he could present it. Penarwan had come in his stead. She had promised him to see it safely delivered; she also wanted to use what authority she had (which was considerable) as abbess and former wife of the great King Owain ap Urien, to call up the loyalty of the surrounding districts. Penrhyd and Llwyvennydd were important, they controlled the Idon valley with the roads to Deira and the south.

The church stood, remote and secret, in a great loop of the Eamot. There were caves in the cliff beyond the river; the place had reminded Nynia of those caves above the Loire at Tours, where his revered master St Martin had his retreat. This is why Nynia had built his own church opposite the Eamot caves and had withdrawn there to meditate; it was now a very holy place.

It was nearly three miles out of Penrhyd; she went most of the way in a travelling cart; when the track to the church left the Roman road, she had to walk. She came at the head of the procession, carrying the cross, slowly and painfully but with great dignity. Crowds had already gathered in the meadow around the church. They were all in high spirits, craning and watching with interest as the sound of chanting came nearer and the head of the procession came into view, the jewelled cross blazing in the morning sun.

Also watching with interest, in the woods beyond the meadow, were Eobba, Penda's brother, and his war-band. After Oswald had been killed, they should have gone back into Mercia, while Penda set out for his raid on Gefrin, and the Welsh went up to Cumbria. But the Welsh had been displeased, for some reason that Eobba could not understand, since the killing had been honestly carried out as asked. Still, there was no accounting for Welsh; they had gone off to their mountains, so Eobba had made up his mind to come up to Cumbria himself and see if there were any

175

pickings; he wondered what the Welsh had been after. He could see it now: the Christians were having some feast for their god. That meant vessels of gold, jewelled candlesticks—and folk who had left their weapons at home. He waited until the end of the procession had come into the meadow, then headed a charge towards it.

A woman at the edge of the crowd saw them and shrieked. Heads turned, the chanting faltered and drowned in a torrent of screaming, there was a panic-stricken stampede. The raiders were between them and the shelter of the woods; in their terror it seemed as if a whole war-host was on them. Some plunged into the Eamot and struggled across to the cliffs; others, hampered with children, fought on the brink against being pushed into the water; they clawed and trampled each other. A few got to the church and barred themselves in.

Penarwan remained standing, still clutching her cross. There was a strange, growling noise in her chest, then her voice broke out into a deep roar, a sound such as those who knew her had never heard before. Rhun would have known it, but there was no one in the meadow old enough to recognise the tones of her father, Lord Garmon of Caer Voran, cursing at the head of his cavalry.

'Damn you, you heathen bastards, get off my land!'

She started towards them.

The Mercians stopped, amazed; then shouted with laughter. A fat old woman was lurching towards them, lumbering like a clumsy cow. Her veil had slipped backwards, showing close-cropped white curls round a bulging red face like an angry baby's. She was waving one of those cross-headed sticks the Christians set such store by; she was coming to attack them.

They had never seen anything so funny; they roared, beat their thighs, punched each other's shoulders. Eobba had to drag the back of his hand across his eyes to see her clearly. She halted a few feet away, gasping; took a grip of her cross with both hands and whacked him across the face with it,

176

cutting his cheek open. She was a stout-hearted old cow. He was still chuckling as he brought his axe down on her skull.

The Cumbrians by the river saw nothing of this, no fat old woman waving a stick and lumbering like a cow. They saw the one-time Queen of Cumbria, their noble Abbess, going alone against the heathen, the Holy Cross raised in her venerable hands, brutally struck down and mocked.

There was a shout, not a war-cry but a scream of fury; then they hurled themselves on the Mercians. A good many of them were killed, as they had no body armour and no weapons but their knives, stones and their bare hands. They took no heed of wounds or death, for the bare sark fury was on them. They threw themselves recklessly on to spears and swords to clog and weigh them down, while others clawed eyeballs or hung on to arms and shoulders till they were broken or dragged out of their sockets. The eerie horror of it broke the raiders' spirit; those who could fight their way out left their honour with their leader's body, trampled and torn to bloody rags, and fled for the southern road. They met Oswy; none of them got back to Mercia.

At Penrhyd, they brought him Penarwan's letter, handling it like a holy relic. Oswy read it, alone in the guest chamber; then he burned it in the brazier, carefully breaking up the ashes. He went out and rode back along the way that the procession had taken that morning, to the church in the hidden meadow, where she was lying.

They had washed her and fitted back the broken bits of skull, binding them tight under her wimple and veil. In death, her handsome features stood out more clearly from the fat; she looked stern, with her hands folded over the crucifix on her breast like the hilt of a sword.

Oswy took his place beside the Abbot of Whithorn, who had come for the presentation, and stared down at her. He thought she looked neither like a holy abbess, nor the jolly old whore he had once thought her. She was like some great king of the old days, Beowulf or Scyld Scefing, with his weapons around him after his last battle. She should have been lying in her mound, while her warriors rode round it speaking her praise. He spoke it for her.

'She was a very brave woman.'

'She is a saint,' said the Abbot, firmly.

Oswy said nothing.

After that, Caer Luel was easy. The Abbess's death drew the nobles together, angry and proud, ready to defy all southern invaders, and quite ready, for the moment, to accept Oswy's leadership. The fact that he had arrived just at the moment of danger and wiped out what was left of Eobba's war-band made him seem like a deliverer: he was the man who had avenged the Abbess. He played up to this for all it was worth; then hurried off to Bebbanburh to fetch Riemmelth back to her city.

He went up Liddesdale for speed; they were over the Cheviots and fording Oxnam Water when a terrified hill-farmer, making off with his family and stock, gave him the news of Gefrin.

They pushed on as fast as possible. Oswy was grim. A raid so deep into his land was an insult and threat worse even than the sack of the royal city itself. He was thankful that the absence of the court meant that there would be fewer captives and little spoil; Riemmelth was safe in Bebbanburh, nothing could get at her there.

They came into the valley of the Glein; the Gefrin towered ahead. There was a hill-shepherd sitting on an outcrop of rock, looking north across the plain, a stocky, broad-shouldered figure in a sheepskin cloak. They hailed him but he did not turn his head.

'They're gone,' he said as they rode up.

'The raiders? How long since—which way did they go?'

'All gone now—the kings and the long-robed priests and the fine ladies with gold ribbons in their hair. They went to Woden—but he doesn't want 'em, I reckon.'

He hawked and spat.

'They keep coming back, looking for their feasting hall.

I've heard 'em down there.'

Oswy gripped his arm. 'You damned stupid brute, you heard someone left alive there, calling for help and did nothing?'

Beorn shook his head. 'Nay, there's none alive down there. I can tell they're dead—I hear 'em laughing.'

Oswy's men felt cold down their backs; some crossed themselves or made the sign of Thunor's hammer. Oswy kicked his horse forward, the rest followed. Beorn sat staring northwards, where the ravens flapped, settled, croaked. They moved off, cursing, as the horsemen rode in, but only a little way. Then they waited; feasting had made them bold.

Gefrin looked like a town in a madman's nightmare. The south-west wind had been blowing when the fires were kindled, but the seasoned oak timbers were stout and rain had come before they were well alight. Most of the larger buildings were only half consumed, all on the same side, as if a fire-breathing dragon had taken bites out of them as it flew past. On some, the roof timbers had slipped forward, the thatch looking like drunken churls' straw hats. The stables were a stinking horror; the horses had been hacked savagely, but some had still been alive when the fire came. The folk of Gefrin lay here and there, the fires had got to some of them, crows and other carrion-seekers had got to all. There were paw-marks in the mud, and bones had been dragged away.

The place was worse than a battlefield; evil hung over it like a pall, it smothered a man's courage. They stood still, hearing the wind sigh and the burn tinkling down to meet the Glein. The ravens croaked at them to go; the flies buzzed in clouds over the unmoving heaps. Then the laughing started.

They nearly broke and ran, but Oswy went forward into the courtyard between the palace and his own hall, so they had to follow. There, the one who laughed and revelled in Gefrin beckoned to welcome them.

The thatch on the porch had broken Elfwyn's fall, but her

left hip had been shattered and she could only crawl, her leg dragging useless. She had found some tubs of ale and mead that had not been stove in, as the raiders had left them for the fire; she had passed the hours of her agony partly in a stupor, partly chattering to the crows and to herself with shrieks of drunken laughter. The soft-footed, green-eyed things that came by night left her alone; they did not go hungry in Gefrin, and she scared them.

She had fouled her dress, and torn it as she crawled; her hands and limbs were grazed from clawing at the ground, the wounds had begun to suppurate. Oswy ran and stooped over her, touching her gently, trying to find where she was hurt, making soothing noises.

'My poor lass, it's all right, we're here. You're safe.'

He called to the others. 'If you can find any buckets, get me some clean water—or else use your helmets. And a bit of fencing to rig up a litter, or make one with your spears and cloaks. Gather anything we can use to help her. Hurry!'

They scattered and he turned back to Elfwyn. He'd seen enough hunting mishaps, to say nothing of war; he could deal with smashed bones or keep a fever at bay till the leech or cunning-woman got to her. He eased her poor body and raised her gently so that she could rest against him. She lifted her head and looked at him; her eyes were thick with rheum, there were sores on her lips.

'I've been waiting for you, Oswy. It was very wrong of you to make me wait so long.'

'I'm here.' He stroked her filthy, tangled curls away from her face. 'It's all right now.'

'All right now,' agreed Elfwyn. 'Riemmelth went away.'

'Riemmelth's in Bebbanburh. We're going to take you there. She and Mildred will nurse you—we'll soon make you well.'

'Riemmelth went to Woden. I gave her to him. I put the spear over her head when she came here first. I'd meant to send her to him in the marsh at Eoforwic, but Woden chose otherwise.'

Oswy's hands had stopped stroking.

'He called her back here, where the spear had gone over her head. He called, and so she came and made herself a waelcyrige for him—'

'No!'

'Oh yes, she had to come; she belonged to him. She made herself a waelcyrige in your old armour, and fought Penda. Then they all worshipped Woden on her and sent her home by water.'

She shook her head at him reproachfully. 'I'd meant to send you, too, for slighting me so, a princess of Deira. But she's gone, and you've come back to me, so I'm going to forgive you. I'll let you rule Deira with me. I'll make you a great king, Oswy.'

She snuggled against his arm. Oswy looked down at her with sea-cold eyes. She should be dragged before the Witan and denounced for her treachery to the land; for what she had brought upon Riemmelth no torture could atone. But she was of the royal blood of Deira, his mother's kin; he did not want to dishonour that name. He was King of Northumbria—what she'd left of it for him—and the powers of judgement and death were in his hands.

He raised her gently against his left shoulder and got his other hand free. She opened her eyes and smiled at him.

'You picked me up,' she said tenderly, 'and then you said, "Poor little cousin, don't cry."'

She lifted her face towards him.

'Kiss me.'

Very lightly, he brushed his mouth across her scabbed lips. Elfwyn closed her eyes. He put his long fingers round her throat and pressed.

Godric panted up with two slopping buckets.

'Sorry I took so long. There were—things—in the burn, I had to go down to the Glein.'

Oswy neither turned nor spoke. Godric saw that he was staring down at a heap covered by his cloak.

'It's a pity,' he said awkwardly, trying to think of some

comfort. 'I don't think we could have got her back to Bebbanburh alive, anyway.'

There was no answer. Godric looked anxiously at Oswy's face. He was taking this harder than Oswald's death.

Well, it was worse, really, when it happened to a woman—they being so weak and harmless.

Five days later, Godric looked more than anxious, he was nearly desperate.

Mildred came into Oswy's hall at Bebbanburh, as she had done so many times before. Her eyes were red and hollow from sleepless weeping, but her hair was neatly braided and she was not in mourning. As usual, she was carrying wine and food; as usual she set it before the still figure in the High Seat. As usual, he took no notice.

'Some roast beef, my lord? Would you take a little wine?'

Oswy nodded, and went on staring at nothing. Mildred looked hopelessly at Godric, standing at Oswy's shoulder; at Dunnere sitting hunched on the steps of the dais. Oswy's body was clean and kempt; it got up, washed and dressed itself; sometimes it ate or drank a mouthful, without interest; but it neither spoke nor listened.

Cadman had stopped his restless pacing to watch whether Oswy noticed Mildred; he beat his hand against one of the hall pillars.

'I'll call out the war-host in his name; steal the ring off his finger if need be. He'll never see me do it!'

Cadman had spent the most harassing time of his life: the weary days of futile hunting for the raiders in the wilds of Cheviot; messages to alert the ealdormen and thanes without giving away too much of the humiliating defeat; trying to hide Oswy's state for as long as possible for fear of rebellion.

'Deira's going, if it hasn't gone already.' His voice was grim. 'We'll lose the whole country if we stay here doing nothing.'

'It's shameful!' Godric looked bewildered and angry. '"Better for a man to avenge his dead than mourn for them."'

I hadn't thought Oswy so lacking in spirit.'

'The marsh demons have taken his soul away!' wailed Mildred.

Dunnere looked up indignantly.

'He didn't lack spirit when he stood over Oswald at Heavenfield; or when he rode down into the South to bring his body home. He laughed when he took his brother's head from the stake, thinking what he would do to Penda.'

He looked at Oswy's stony face. 'This is the Welshwoman's doing. She took the heart out of his breast to play on, like her harpstrings. Now she's lost, he'll never get it back.'

'But what are we to do?' asked Mildred.

As if in answer, there was a clatter of hoofs on the cobbles outside, and a soft chiming of bells. They looked towards the doorway; Mildred gasped with shock and fright to see what was coming in.

The woman was very tall; the long cloak of speckled birds' feathers swirling round her seemed to make her larger and more than human. The autumn sun blazed on her mass of copper-red hair, she was crowned with fire. One of her attendants carried a golden branch set with silver bells, the other had a harp in a bag of otter-skin.

Liadan swept up to the dais without a word to anyone. Dunnere stepped aside; Mildred stayed crouching at Oswy's feet, too startled to move. Liadan seated herself on the top step of the dais, the attendant handed her the harp, she tuned it and began to play.

It was a melody of such haunting sweetness, such aching regret, that each listener felt wells of sorrow opened up inside the heart, depths of grief they hardly dared look into, for fear they drown. Oswy had not once looked at Liadan, but he suddenly bowed his head on his hands, broken and defeated.

'What are you doing, woman?' shouted Godric. 'You call yourself his lover, and then come and drive a spear into him when he can't defend himself!'

'He was speared days ago,' said Liadan, calmly, while the harp still wept under her fingers, 'and the wound has festered. It must be opened and cleaned before it can heal— salt water's best for that.'

She began to sing a lament for Riemmelth: her beauty, her courage, her anger that was like the summer lightning, her generous heart, her laughter; and the pride of the ancient race that had ended with her, the great palace of Caer Luel empty and desolate for ever, wanting her bright spirit.

Oswy was sobbing helplessly; Godric could not bear the disgrace.

'Stop it, you damned witch! You're shaming him!'

He started towards Liadan to drag the harp away. Cadman caught him by the shoulders; Mildred threw herself in front of him.

'I never cried,' she said, 'when the Welsh killed my father and I was dragged away and raped.' Cadman stared at her. 'But when my dear lady came and saved me and took me into her home—then I cried all night. Let her alone, Godric; she's a wise-woman.'

Liadan was singing in Irish, for Oswy's ears; to her other listeners, the words took the language of their own grief: Welsh or English, it was all one.

Dunnere saw the faces of friends who were young with him, who would never be old with him because their bones were quiet under the earth from Pictland to Mercia. Mildred saw her father, that steadfast, quiet man, hacked down as he tried to defend her. Cadman saw three hundred young warriors, brilliant in their armour and gold torcs, ride laughing to their deaths. Godric saw the burial mounds on the wolf-slopes and windy headlands above the sea.

'Where is the horse, where the hero? Where the gold-giver?
Where is the feast-hall, where are the festivals?
Alas for the gleaming goblets, the gold-armed warriors!
Alas, the prince's glory! How that time has passed,
Shrouded under night's shadow, as if it had never been!'

When Oswy was quiet at last, Liadan stopped singing; her fingers played a drowsy tune and slowly stilled. She gave the harp to her servant, took Oswy's hand and led him back into the bedchamber. The door closed behind them. The two attendants, with the harp and the bell-branch, silently took their places in front of it, to guard the peace-spell that Liadan had made.

17

Riemmelth came back to her body unwilling, loathing and terrified. It was dark, her bruised flesh was being roughly jolted. In her first horror, she thought she was bound and blindfold on a hurdle, being carried to the marsh. She struggled, her limbs moved freely, caught by nothing more than a coverlet; she lifted her hand and brushed it across her eyes. Now she could make out chinks of lighter grey, and dragging herself up she reached for them. Her fingers touched leather and thongs, she swept her hands lower and touched wood. She was in a noblewoman's travelling waggon, its leather curtains drawn and laced over the iron hoops. She knelt up and put her eyes to a chink, but could see nothing except the greyness of dusk or dawn and a glimpse of leaves.

She sank back. There was a mattress under her and a pillow; she had been covered in something soft and woollen, a cloak or a blanket. Mazed and scared as she was, this gave her no comfort. She knew nothing of the rites of Woden, but it was likely that one of his daughters, carrying a king's offerings inside her body, would be sent off with more honour than a churl's wife being killed for adultery. They were taking her to the marsh, to the cold blackness, the soft sucking horror. She remembered enough about the banks of the Foss to know how it would be, dying.

Then the deep bruising of her loins and thighs recalled her to that other part of the rite that had already taken place in her. If the marsh had opened up before her then, she would have jumped in and willed herself to sink. To blot out the memory, blot out the feel of her naked flesh pawed and clutched by sweaty hands, exposed to gloating eyes, the huge legs straddling her, the invasion.

She went down into shame blacker than a Cheviot peatbog. What else could she do but die—thankful that none of her proud kin would ever know how the last Queen of Cumbria had been thrown down and befouled?

'*Get up again.*'

She had thought only of her kin, of the shock and rage it would have been to Pascen, Rhun and Elidir to know that she had been disgraced for ever. Yet it was Oswy's voice she heard; the long-jawed, strong Northumbrian face with sea-coloured eyes smiled at her.

It's all very well for you to smile, Oswy! she raged at him. *You'd laugh on the other side of your face if you'd lain in the dirt, like me.*

'*There's a lot to be said for lying down at the right moment. At the least, you can get your breath back to fight again . . .*'

I can't fight. I'm beaten, destroyed. There's nothing more I can do.

'*There's always something. You can sink your teeth in the other man's ankle and topple him . . .*'

Much good that would do against Penda. I'd like to see you try!

She saw it then: it was like someone lying down beside the biggest oak in Inglewood and starting to chew. Before she knew it, she was laughing; she tried to stop, to think of the wrong she had suffered, the black shame, the hideous death to come. She was furious with Oswy for dragging her up into life again, as he had dragged her out of the tide at Lindisfarne.

Anger and laughter warm the blood. Her head was up and

her eyes were brilliant with life when the waggon stopped
jolting, the leather flaps were pulled back, and Penda
stepped in.

The light showed her the bed where she was lying, a chest
and some bundles, the man who had mastered her. She had
her spirit back. She could stare full at him without being
browbeaten, though her flesh shuddered.

During her desperate battle, and the horror afterwards, he
had seemed like an Otherworld monster, half-giant, half-
brute. Seen steadily, there was nothing monstrous about
Penda but his size; his huge brown limbs were shapely and
there was nothing bestial in his face. His forehead was low
but very broad, his features big and rugged but not
misshapen. He had thick, curly brown hair and beard, large
grey-brown eyes under thick brows. If he had been an oak
tree or a bull, one could have called him beautiful.

He was carrying a mug of ale and a platter; he put them on
the chest, then stared at her sombrely.

'Why did you pretend to be a waelcyrige?'

Because her mind had just laughed at him, she was able to
laugh again.

'You can't complain I cheated you! You must have known
as soon as we crossed swords that I wasn't a warrior!'

He shook his head.

'You fought very well,' he said seriously. 'You're fast and
clever, but you haven't the reach or the weight. Anyway, the
man doesn't live who can match me.'

He wasn't boasting, just stating a fact.

'No, I knew as soon as I took you. The waelcyrian have to
be virgins. But no whore would fight like that to keep herself
from a great king and his warriors.'

He looked gloomy. 'So then I knew you were a decent
wife, fighting for her man's honour.'

Riemmelth was startled; she had never thought of that.

'You're a lovely woman with a good spirit; you'll breed
fine sons. My wife died some months ago—I'll marry you.'

She stared at him.

187

'But you know—you've just said—I'm a wife.'

'You're a widow. We killed every man there.'

'Oh, but—' she decided not to tell her name yet, it could be a bargaining counter—'my man wasn't there.'

'Where is he then? Off on a woman-hunt with Oswy's pack, or holed up in Bebbanburh?'

So Oswy hadn't been caught in Powys, and Bebbanburh still stood.

'Anyway, you're mine now—I won you. Tell me his name and I'll send him your bride-price.'

'I shan't tell you.'

'No matter. When we get to Tomeworthig, I'll send my scops abroad to all the courts to give your likeness and say how much I'm willing to pay for you. The whole land'll know, in a month or two.'

'He wouldn't take any price—it would be dishonour.'

'Then he'll know where to come, to fight me for you.'

She looked at Penda and knew he could beat Oswy—if Oswy should be willing to fight for her—as he could beat any man in the land. Penda knew it too.

'You might as well take me now.'

'That is not what Christians do.'

'So your man's a Christian. You're better off without him, then, they're all women. And what dishonour is it to you, to be taken by the best warrior?' He scowled at her. 'Why do you bother to talk like a Christian, when you bear Frea's sign on your breast?'

He stepped out of the waggon and then turned back, pointing to the bundles.

'There's women's gear, and jewels in the chest. Anything else you want, ask.'

The leather flap dropped and he was gone.

Riemmelth sat stunned. After a while, she made herself take some of the bread, meat and ale he had brought. Then she followed Oswy's advice and lay down while she thought out the next move. She wondered what Oswy would do. Even if she refused to tell Penda her name, everyone would

188

know who she was when Penda's bards recited the tale. Any king—any man—who left his wife in captivity rather than come and fight for her would be dishonoured. Oswy wouldn't let a little thing like that worry him—'*There's nothing honourable in making your country a gift to its enemies.*' He'd told her that a man who went out to face certain death was a fool.

He went out to bring Oswald home. But that had been a stealthy raid, needing furtive speed or impudent lying, and for those she would back Oswy against all Britain. Against Penda with a sword, he wouldn't have a chance.

She thought Oswy probably would come for her, though, there was too much to lose if he did not. He would be killed. Then the whole North would fall into the power of a savage—brave, generous, honourable even, but a heathen savage. She was not going to let that happen, either to herself or to Cumbria.

She thought about escape. It would not be difficult to get out of the waggon; she could trust to her woodcraft to elude any hunter. But where would she go, not even knowing where she was? How long had she been unconscious? They could have got well to the south—and perhaps all Deira was now in the power of the Mercians. If she tried to cross the hills westwards, to her own land, she might find herself in Dunoding. And if she did win through to Caer Luel—she winced, then rolled over, burying her face on the pillow, shaking her hair round her like a pall. A fine state she was in, to arrive there as their queen! Rather than show herself to the Cumbrians, rather than think of Elidir hearing her story, she'd let herself starve out on the moors. Let the ravens pick her carcass clean of the soiled flesh, let her bones lie lost and nameless under the sun and rain.

Then she threw her hair back impatiently, sneering at herself. It was a mad-woman's dream to imagine reaching Cumbria.

Penda's war-band would camp round the waggon all night—and if she did get out and elude them for a while, how far would she get in the forest, in women's clothes, without even a knife? The thought of being caught, of being dragged back by those hands, flung down at Penda's feet before all those gloating faces, brought the full horror of her rape back into her flesh. She faced the fact that there her courage had been broken, perhaps for ever; she could never face that again. She would do anything else: kill herself, marry Penda—

Why had Penda decided to marry her?

He'd praised her beauty and her courage but she wasn't the only brave and beautiful woman who had been taken by force. Nobody had married Mildred. Why didn't he just keep her as one of his women if he fancied her? He had no Christian regard for the marriage-tie to stop him.

'Why do you bother to talk like a Christian when you bear Frea's sign on your breast?'

Her hand went to her breast as she remembered the words; her fingers touched the moon-disc and crescents of Arianrhod's necklace. Then light came to her, bright as the moon itself.

Penda thought he had raped one of the Goddess's women, tried to offer her to the man's War-God. No wonder he was afraid!

Riemmelth had been brought up as an orthodox Christian under Bishop Rhun's stern eyes; but the Lady of the Moon rode through the bards' stories in many guises, under many names: Rhiannon, Olwen, Luned. And there had been other tales, whispered by maidservants and farm-girls, between giggling and terror. There were other holy places, even in Cumbria, besides the churches; Riemmelth had some idea what went on there. She knew well enough what The Lady could do to a man who offended her, if he was not protected by the cross and holy water.

The Lady could call down rain upon a battle-line, driving the wind into warriors' faces, making their spears and arrows fall short or awry. She could hide a boar or king stag in a thicket and then trip or entangle a huntsman as it charged to gore or rip him. Most terrible of all, the cold dread that lurked in every man's heart, She could strike at his manhood, make him incapable of taking a woman or getting a son. And this dread Goddess had her chief shrine in Penda's own land.

I'll make him take me there; I'll threaten to put the Cold Curse on him in her name if he refuses. And once I'm in the shrine, I'll claim sanctuary; they may be heathen, but at least they're women. I'll even worship her if that's their price—Arianrhod called her the Queen of Heaven—I can name Mary in my mind—Our Lady would let women save me from Woden—

Suddenly a picture drew itself on the dusk inside the waggon, a story began to tell itself: an Irish traveller coming to worship at the shrine; wary, sea-green eyes under the shadow of a cloak; Oswy, wily and reckless, coming to seek her out and spirit her away. Her heart quickened—but it was impossible, of course. Not even a scop would dare to make up such a tale. Yet it was a good tale for all that, and comforting to tell herself, alone in the dark. And at any rate, there was no man—not even Penda—who would dare to come to the shrine and take her from the Goddess by force.

She fondled her necklace and smiled. She had her weapon now and she would use it with all the trickery and ruthlessness that life had taught her. She would fight like Oswy in a corner.

Riemmelth had time to plan her campaign as the waggon carried her south. She talked it out with Oswy during her long hours alone, argued with him over details and possibilities, lost her temper and swore at him. Her mind was too busy to stop and wonder why there was no pain or shame linked with the thought of meeting him again. She worded the story of how she outwitted Penda; she heard him laughing as he listened to her, praising her cunning and skill as a liar.

She had no idea where she was. The woodlands stretched unbroken at the foot of the Long Hills, all the way to Mercia. When they stopped, the waggon was always drawn up near some spring or stream among thickly growing bushes, where she could ease herself, then bathe. She never saw Penda's warriors at such times and did not think they spied on her. The man who brought her food showed her respect and even awe, calling her 'lady' when he spoke.

'If ever any one of them shows scorn of me,' she told herself savagely, 'I'll put such a curse on him in the name of the Goddess, his prick will faint with fright every time he goes near a woman so long as he lives!'

What she saw when she left the waggon told her little. Always the same thickly crowding tree trunks, tangled briars and fern, dappling leaf shadows—and glimpses at evening of the waxing moon among the boughs.

On the eighth evening Penda came to her again. She was dressed in the richest of the robes he had saved from Gefrin, choosing green for the Goddess and leaving her dark hair unbraided. Her shift was unlaced at the neck, where the moon-silver glinted against her skin.

'I want to speak to you,' she said haughtily. 'You may sit and eat with me.' She was sitting at the end of the chest and she pointed to a corner of her straw mattress, putting him in a lower place.

Penda gave her a long look under his heavy brows, but he unpinned his cloak, threw it under him and sat down. She held the silence till he stirred restlessly and spoke.

'You're content—you're glad now I chose you and took you from your Christian.' He sounded satisfied.

She raised her winged brows.

'We who follow The Lady take our men as we choose. Woden or the White Christ—what odds to us which you serve? *She* swaddled them both and held them to her breast.'

'I'm the better man. You ought to take the best, to honour her.'

'I have to honour her myself before I can think of that. It will be full moon in a week. And before I can honour her I need to be purified—you best know why.'

She stared at him, putting as much menace into her eyes as

possible. Penda looked uneasy.

'What do you want?'

'The Lady has a great shrine in your land—Arnemeton. I want to go there and see the Chief Priestess, she will do what I need.'

Penda was looking at her as if trying to read her thoughts.

'I'll fetch a priestess to you,' he said slowly. 'She'll come in good time, don't worry.'

'I must go to the shrine!' Her voice was getting sharp; she fought to keep it calm, to show no doubt that he would obey her.

'When you're handfast to me in front of my lords and warriors, I'll take you to Frea's house myself.'

'There'll be no handfasting till I'm purified!'

'You can be purified anywhere there's running water and a priestess. I'll see you have both.'

'And I'll see that the priestess knows—and Frea—how you honour her!' she threatened.

'They know already. There's no other kingdom south of the Forth where the shrines are safe and the folk can worship openly. Behind my shield.'

Penda might fear to offend the Goddess, but her priestess would not care to offend the King of Mercia. Riemmelth felt that her weapon had broken in her hand.

He stood up, flinging his cloak around him, and picked up his great shoulder-brooch. She stared at it greedily and he held it out to her.

'You never saw a jewel like that in Northumbria. It came to me from my forefather, Offa of Angeln.'

However the brooch had come to the kings of the Iceling House, it had been made in Scythia a thousand years before. Riemmelth had indeed never seen a jewel like it in all the North, but it was the pin that caught her notice. It was as long and sharp as a dagger; whoever put it on was wearing at least one death.

'Will you take it as a betrothal gift—an honour-pledge between us?'

She hardly paused for a heartbeat. What honour could there be between a woman and the man who raped her—and what would Oswy do, if an enemy made him a present of a sword?

She smiled at Penda. He pinned the great brooch to her shoulder, like a man setting his seal on some property he had gained after a little vexing delay.

A week later, Riemmelth was standing inside the waggon-hood, clenching and unclenching her hands in growing terror as she waited for whoever was coming to her through the forest. The waggon had been unhitched in a glade that opened out among huge, gnarled trunks; there was a stream nearby, she could hear water rippling. She had no sense of the Mercian warriors at hand; the forest seemed empty of men, but a tide of exultant life was rising all round her, drawn up from the whispering ferns and the trees lifting their boughs to the clear sky, where a ghostly full moon was growing brighter.

Though she had tricked Penda into thinking she worshipped Frea, this priestess would know at once that she did not. I can only appeal to her as a woman, she thought. As Mildred did to me—and how close I was to rejecting her!

She felt cold and dry-mouthed as the three came from the forest shadows and moved silently towards her. There were always three, for the Virgin, Harlot and Hag who was the Great Mother of all creatures. They stepped up into the waggon. Two stayed by the entry and stretched up to hang garlands from the open curtain flaps: ivy stems decked with white flowers for the Lady of the Full Moon, meadowsweet, daisies, yarrow, black nightshade, fairy flax. They laid others on the steps, backing out as they did so, their arms and movements showing youthful grace. Riemmelth heard them singing outside, they seemed to be circling the waggon. She had a feeling that a wall was being raised between her and the rest of the world that not even Penda could break down.

The third figure never moved, shrouded in its cloak. She saw a glitter of eyes in the darkness under the hood. It was the Hag, then, who had come; the face that the Goddess turned to her was death. Then the figure threw back its hood, and the face was Arianrhod's.

They were hugging each other; Riemmelth was crying and laughing at once. Arianrhod said gently, 'Hush, my dear, sh-h-h!' and made her sit down on the mattress.

'How did you know I was here? Is everyone talking about me—is my name down on the dungheap?'

'Never fear. Your name hasn't even been whispered. But when word came to The Lady's House of a woman from Oswy's palace who fought Penda sword to sword and had a moon-necklace at her throat, the riddle wasn't hard for me to read.'

'But what brought you there? What happened to the estate I gave you? Did they cheat you out of it? I thought I'd provided for you—'

'So you did, nobly. I had fair dealing from everyone. The lord of Gwensteri asked me to take his son, a fine young man. But I couldn't settle—and there isn't the man unwed in Britain who could satisfy me.'

Her slate-blue eyes stared into remote distance.

'So I made over my lands to the lord of Gwensteri, I told him I was going into a sisterhood—which was true! I came to The Lady's House, to be one of her white-robed moons and welcome any man who comes to me with silver.'

She smiled. 'What is it you want from us?'

Riemmelth gave a hopeless sigh. 'Everything's gone wrong. I asked Penda to take me to the shrine—I thought I could beg for sanctuary, and then make my way back to Deira.'

'Why haven't you told your name? Penda would take ransom, surely?'

'Penda wants to marry me. He says he'll pay my man a bride-price, or fight him for me. If Oswy took the gold, or did nothing, he'd be dishonoured. If he fights Penda, he'll be killed.'

'You've no high opinion of Oswy as a fighter?'

'I don't believe he could fight one of the wild white bulls with his bare hands, or tear up an oak out of Inglewood. That's not because he's a weakling or a coward, it's just impossible.'

'What are you going to do, then?'

'Could you help me to get out of here, or send private word to Oswy to try and steal me away?'

'Penda would hunt you across Britain and kill Oswy when he found you.'

Riemmelth's face was stony with despair. 'I must die, then.' She gripped Arianrhod's arm. 'Kill me now, cleanly, for the Goddess—not that Woden filth.'

Arianrhod's brows twitched.

'What would the Christians say when they heard you'd given yourself to the Goddess?'

'At least I'd be dying as a true wife—they could see me as a martyr.'

She laughed bitterly; Arianrhod gave her a keen glance.

'*Will* you be dying as Oswy's faithful Christian wife?'

Riemmelth paused over that.

'I'll be dying,' she said slowly, 'as Riemmelth.'

'There's no need. I'm going to take your place again.'

Riemmelth stared at her in horror. 'You believe I'd ask that of you?'

'You don't have to ask. The first time we met, I came begging. You called me "kinswoman" and gave me a gift richer than all my dreams. This time, I'm offering.'

'To let Penda kill you?'

'Penda won't touch me. Remember, I really am a priestess.'

Riemmelth's eyes brightened.

'Penda hardly knows me. Apart from the—the fight, when I was screaming mad, he's only spoken with me twice, here in the waggon, in the half-light.' She laughed, breathlessly. 'He's a great king, Arianrhod—and the finest warrior that will ever be born in these islands, I do believe. He's noble too, in his way, and very generous. You both worship the Old Gods, he'll honour you as a priestess, you'll rule with him. You'll be a great queen—do you remember the story you told yourself on the road to Caer Luel? Some great lord would make you his lover, there'd be music and laughter and bright robes. Now it's all coming true!'

Arianrhod smiled rather sadly. While Riemmelth chattered, she had unwrapped her heavy cloak. Underneath, she was dressed as a hunter, in shirt and breeches, with thonged boots, leather jerkin and cap. She changed clothes with Riemmelth, tying thongs and fastening buckles for her like a careful mother, finally braiding the heavy black tresses and coiling them under her cap. Riemmelth put her hands to her throat.

'You must take your necklace.'

'No, it's already passed from me to you. And you'll need it, it will be your token, to take you safe on your way.'

'He'll notice—'

'He'll think I offered it to The Lady, to take back to her shrine.' She wrapped the heavy cloak round Riemmelth, then turned to some things she had brought with her: a hunting knife, a flint strike-a-light, a leather bottle and scrip.

'These are for your journey.'

'A knife cuts friendship, you must take something from me in return.'

She picked up the great Iceling brooch.

'This was his betrothal gift to me, so he must see you wearing it—but it is mine now, to give.' She laughed. 'If all else failed, I'd meant to kill him with it, and then myself. But now it will be truly a bride-gift.'

Arianrhod smiled back at her. 'All the good things in my life have come to me through your hands. I'll wear this over my heart.' She kissed Riemmelth. 'May the Mother smile on you, and the moon light your way. You must go now.'

197

'May Our Lady bless you for your charity to me.'

Arianrhod took Riemmelth's arm and helped her to step down from the waggon without disturbing the garlands that barred the entrance. Outside, the full moon was riding high in the clear sky over the glade. The two priestesses came silently to either hand and the three of them melted like shadows back into the silvery woods.

Arianrhod watched them vanish, then looked up to the moon. Her mind was drawn up out of her body and flew across the silent country, hovering over the revels that were now taking place, at the circles and standing stones on the moors, in forest glades and beside springs. Her blood danced with the revellers, and with the night-flying owls and moths, with the furred hunting creatures, with the fish swimming up as the high tides flowed inshore.

I was born at the dark of the moon, she thought. I believed the Goddess had turned her face away from me, that I'd be dark and barren for ever. And it wasn't true. She accepted me, gave me joy of my body, took my service—now she's taking me back to herself. There's no such thing as death, only a little sleep.

She went inside the waggon, leaving the flap open behind her, so that the moonlight could come in. She lay down on the bed, staring into the shadows, and made Oswy come to her. She saw his dark shape as he had stooped over her, the bedside candle making silver lights in his hair. She raised her arms, as she had done then, to draw him down into her. The great gold brooch gleamed faintly in the moonlight. The pin went straight to her heart.

18

The track was narrow and wound through the bracken but the priestesses trod it surely and silently. For a long while, Riemmelth was straining her ears for pursuit, but Penda's men were keeping well away from the waggon with its dangerous passenger and uncanny guests. They had no wish to draw Frea's angry eyes upon them; they had already done enough to make her blight their seed if she chose.

The three walked on through the strange silver world, hearing nothing but the brushing of their cloaks among the bracken, an owl calling, the scream of a vixen. The Swan, the Dragon and the Chariot were wheeling round the Pole Star. The women were going north.

At last the trees drew back and left a grassy glade, as if they were keeping well away from the great standing stone that blocked the way, shining faintly in the eerie light. Its shadow pointed like a black finger to where the ground swelled up. A dead-mound, one of the Hollow Hills. The priestess who was leading passed into its shadow and vanished. Riemmelth froze in terror, but the other woman took her elbow and gently urged her on. A hand reached out of the darkness and took hers; she was guided down some rough steps, feeling stones and tree roots under her soles. A bramble twig clawed her; she cried out and someone said, 'Hush!' the warm breath brushing her neck. Folds of hide fell behind her, she felt she was under the earth, and was led blindly for half a dozen groping steps. Then another curtain was pulled back, there was smoke and firelight. Shapes moved towards her, black to her dazzled eyes. Her knees buckled, hands lowered her to a couch of bracken and skins. A cup was put to her lips; she drank fire, honey and sleep.

When she woke up, the earth-house was empty except for one old woman, skinny and smoke-dried, crouching over the hearth. The skin curtains had been looped aside, and some light and air filtered down into the living-place; at the end of the passage she could see bramble sprays in sunshine. She looked round for her guides.

'They went on the night before last,' said the old woman. 'They had to make a wide cast on the way back to The Lady's House, in case the men came after them.'

'The night before last?'

'You slept all the rest of that night, and a day and a night after that. You'll be well and rested for your journey.'

She gave Riemmelth some oatcakes and thin ale to break her fast, then handed her scrip and leather bottle, both full. 'That will see you through till evening.'

She led the way outside, holding back the brambles that hung over the entrance, and went deasil on the sun's path round the standing stone.

'There's your way. Keep northwards all the time. About ten miles ahead you'll come to two arms of a river joining and flowing east. That's the Dierne, the Secret One, on her way to join the Dana, the Mother's own river. There are stepping-stones across to the angle between the streams; go there, you'll find three rowans and a flat stone in the middle. Take water in your hands and sprinkle the stone, then pluck a twig from each tree and lay them there. Someone will come and ask you what you want. Say "Alms from The Lady's table". Now go, and the sun on your path, my daughter.'

'May the moon smile on you, mother.'

It was pleasant, at first, walking as free as air in the sunlight and dappling leaf shadows. The woods were golden and the air was warm. She took her nooning by a little stream, finishing off with some blackberries; rested a little, then followed the track again.

As the afternoon wore on she began to tire. She had spent days in the waggon without walking; before that, there had been the violence at Gefrin, and it had been months since she had a day's hunting. It would be some time before she was as much at home in the wilds as the fox, the wolf and the raven. She began to long for human company.

The sun was westering as she came to a quiet river gliding east, crossed the stepping-stones and came to the three rowans. She did as the old woman had told her, then waited. There was silence, not even a bird called. Then a voice said quietly, 'What do you want?'

Riemmelth spun round; a very young girl, hardly more than a child, barefoot and in a cottar's coarse shift, was standing behind her.

'Alms from The Lady's table.'

The girl nodded and beckoned. Riemmelth followed, north-west up the other branch of the stream. Not far off, they came to a tiny hut of wattles, hardly more than a thatched screen. The girl served her with oatcakes, cheese and goats' milk; then made up a bed for her with fresh bracken and a couple of skins. Riemmelth stretched out thankfully and was soon asleep.

She woke in the morning sun. The hut was empty and no one else seemed to have slept there, but she had hardly stood up when the girl came back with more food and fresh goats' milk. She had also refilled the scrip and bottle.

When Riemmelth had finished the scanty breakfast the girl signed to her to follow and led her a little way northward. The ground was rising as they went further from the river and they came to a well-marked track.

'Keep north,' said her strange hostess, 'and hold to the crown of the ridge. If you go downhill, you'll lose your way and get into the marshes. About fourteen miles north the ground will slope down and you'll see the Kelder to the west and the Roman road to the east, both heading for the Yr. There's an ale-house at the crossing; go there and speak to the wife for a lodging. Say, "If I walk late, I've the moon to guide me," and show her what you've got at your neck. She'll set you on your way tomorrow.' She turned and went down among the trees towards the river.

Riemmelth set off along the track. It was easy enough to follow and she tried to keep up a good pace, but she was tiring faster than on the day before and had to stop more often to rest. It was almost dusk when she came to the end of the ridge and made her way down to the Roman road, a mile or so south of Ceasterford. The firm, straight track under her feet and the prospect of food and shelter gave her a last spurt of energy.

At last the trees ended and Ceasterford was in front of her. It had once been a Roman fort, and its useful position at the ford on the road to Eoforwic meant that someone had always patched up a home and lived there. The ale-house by the ford did good trade with merchants and travellers on the North Road.

So no one took much notice of the thin, dark youth in hunter's dress who came plodding wearily up the road from the south and headed for the steading with the bush of greenery on top of a pole by the entrance. There was an hour to sunset, so the door had not been shut. A red glow came from the hearth inside, a smell of greasy stew, a growl of deep voices and laughter. A figure blocked the doorway, then a man lurched out and made off round the corner, fumbling at his breeches. There was a plash of water against the wall. The dark youth pulled his cloak tighter, turned, waded across the ford and hurried into the trees on the other side.

Riemmelth ran till her lungs nearly burst and her legs became dead weights. She had gone blindly off the road in her need to hide herself; twigs whipped at her face, brambles clawed her, roots stretched out to trip her. She was thrown at last, fell hard and lay sobbing. After a while, the cold damp ground chilled her so much that she quietened and sat up shivering, ashamed of her panic, yet forced to swallow the bitter truth of it.

Since her rape, she had been kept apart under Penda's fearsome guard, or in the care of Frea's women. Now she had to go in alone among a crowd of men with only her huntsman's clothes and her knife to keep them off her—and she could not do it. The loathing and the terror were too great. It was no good dressing as a hunter; she was one of the hunted now, one blood with the rabbits, does and pigeons.

She dragged herself up, found a patch of drier ground among some bushes and piled some twigs to make a fire. It would be company as well as warmth. Then she missed her strike-a-light; it must have been torn from her belt while she broke through the undergrowth. She could have cried, but what was the use? She ate the little that was left of her food and wrapped herself in her cloak to sit out the night.

She was not altogether hopeless yet, because she knew now that Eoforwic was little more than twenty miles away. She would get back to the road tomorrow and follow its line, keeping among the trees if she heard travellers. During the day, while the men were out in the fields, she could risk calling at a homestead and begging food from the woman of the house, showing her necklace if need be. The brakes were full of blackberries and hazel-nuts, there were streams of fresh water. She could be in the palace at Eoforwic before nightfall, enjoying a warm bath, feasting, lying in her soft bed. She fixed her mind on these comforts and got to sleep at last.

Next day the horror came. The marsh-fog had risen in the night, and she woke to find herself muffled in a thick white shroud, damp and chilled to the bone. She waited in the hope that it would lift, but there was neither sun nor breath of air. The cold seemed to be touching her heart; if she stayed there she would die.

The ground sloped downwards, getting softer and wetter, and her feet began to sink; there were pools of black water between the tree roots. A dread came on her, worse than Penda and all living men. The spear had gone over her head; she belonged to Woden, he would never let her go. He would take her, wrapped in his mist-cloak, down under the marshes. She began to flounder, scrabbling wildly to keep to patches of higher ground, calling for help and feeling her voice sucked down by the fog. Once she heard Elfwyn laughing, then knew it was herself.

There were times—moments that stretched into hours—when she crouched in brushwood tangles, clutching the twigs as a drowning sailor clutches the wreckage of his boat; or stood rigid, pressing her back into a tree trunk, while the rest of the world melted around her and she felt herself going with it. Then she would break away and the floundering and scrabbling would start again.

Time had stopped; she was in Hel's kingdom where there were no more days. It was strange she should be alone, there are so many dead. Then she saw them, watching her. They were standing quite still, with their arms stretched out to catch her. If they caught her, they would eat her soul. And there were the others, the ones she knew, who drifted towards her, brushed her with their cold fingers, then glided away before she could catch their hands and beg them to stay with her. Rhun was there, his face like a skull with hollow eye-sockets; Arianrhod smiled at her, but kept her hands folded over her heart. Pascen opened his mouth but could not speak, fingering the arrow in his throat. There was a great king with silver hair, and a jagged line round his neck where it had been hacked.

At last, something shone out behind the waiting black shapes with outstretched arms and the floating ghosts. A young warrior in rich armour came striding towards her, the ravens flying on the shield at his shoulder, war-spear in his hand.

Like the rays of the dawn his whetted spears.

Though he had died forty years before her birth, she knew him.

Owain ap Urien smiled at her; he tore the curtains of mist apart with his spearpoint and sent a beam of light along the track towards the steading.

Teleri found her lying there when she came out at first light to milk the cows. She thought it was some starved tramp, or outlaw from the forest come to raid the hen-roost;

204

she had her knife ready for the stranger's throat when the sunlight glinted on the silver necklace. She took one look and stirred herself to get some of the warm new milk down Riemmelth's throat, then to pull her inside by the hearth.

'Where are you bound?' she asked, when the stranger had been dried, warmed and fed.

'Eoforwic. I lost the track in the fog.'

'Eoforwic? You're not a Deiran, you talk British—you're one of us. Where do you come from?'

'I came down from the North.' Riemmelth was wary. There had been bad blood in the past between Elmet and Cumbria; how much of it lingered since Elmet had been conquered by Deira she couldn't be sure.

'If you're a Bernician you should keep clear of Eoforwic. There's trouble in Deira since the King died.'

'Oswy's dead?'

'No, Oswald. The brother's taken himself off up north. Deira won't have him, they say. I don't know. We Elmet folk don't deal much with Deirans.'

'How can I get back to Bernicia then?' Riemmelth felt near to despair. She had been counting on Eoforwic as her refuge, the end of this dreadful lonely struggle. But if Deira had risen against Oswy, she risked capture and worse at every step of her road to the North. It was well over a hundred miles from Eoforwic to Bebbanburh, and she had already been at the point of death.

Teleri laughed. 'The same way as we go, over the Long Hills. My brother-in-law's a shepherd at Ben Rhydding above the Weorf. We'll see you on your way there, and he'll take you the next stage.'

She saw Riemmelth's face.

'Don't worry. You speak British, you wear that,' she touched the necklace, 'and you're our guest. You wouldn't be any safer with the High King's war-host.'

Teleri was as good as her word. Next day, Riemmelth set off on her journey along the high roof-pole of Britain, that took her across great sweeps of purple moorland and grey rocks, dropping down into well-watered valleys. Sometimes she travelled on foot, pacing the short, springy turf with a shepherd and his dogs; rarely, she had a ride in a farm cart; usually she was on the back of one of the tireless, sure-footed Dales ponies.

She made slow progress. She could be delayed for days by rain or hill fogs, or she would have to wait till a man could be spared to guide her. One thing never changed—the unfailing kindness of her hosts. She felt perfectly safe, even when she was alone for hours on a desolate moor with some tough hill-farmer or silent shepherd.

A farmer's wife in Allendale, rosy and wrinkled like a well-stored apple, offered to exchange her worn, stinking hunter's gear for a clean smock and kirtle. Riemmelth was grateful but refused. The housewife smiled.

'You've nothing to fear, they all know you're a woman. Besides—' she took Riemmelth's hand and patted it. 'I've had seven children, I've delivered five of my grandchildren, I know the signs, even as soon as this. It's lucky you're near your journey's end, lass, and then you'll be willing to take those breeches off!'

Riemmelth had time to think that over during the day's ride north to the Wall. She counted back to her last monthly flow; that had been in July, and now it was well into October. She tried to think of any other signs, but life had been hitting her so hard in the last weeks that any weariness or sickness was only natural.

A week or so back, when it had seemed that the worst was over and she was going to win back to Bebbanburh, she had begun to think what she would say about her life since Gefrin went up in flames. She felt a dreadful relief that Penda had given it to Woden; that there would be no one alive who had seen what was done to her. She had prepared her story and worked over the details:

'I fought my way out, but they were between me and the North. I couldn't get far enough ahead of them at first; I was driven south like a hind before the beaters. I thought you'd be coming up from Deira, and I'd meet you and warn you what had happened. I had to go far into the Long Hills before I could work my way back. There'd been treachery—I didn't know who to trust or ask for help.'

It sounded believable, for her return journey it was mostly true, Oswy's folk would believe it. If she claimed that she had been carrying Oswy's child at the time of the sack, they would accept her word; it would give another reason for her desperate bid for freedom. But Oswy would know that the child could not possibly be his.

What would he do to her, when she came to him with Penda's bastard inside her? She remembered Penarwan's amused smile, mocking her childish pride and innocence.

'Whatever else happens to a king who's taken in war—including gelding or rape—he can't be got with a bastard heir by the victor.'

And the man who got this heir was his brother's murderer. Was there any king—any husband—who would take a wife back on those terms?

Oswy might. She remembered him saying more than once that ill luck was no one's fault, that what was done was past. He'd laughed at Cadman often enough, and damned his stupidity for letting what he called Mildred's misfortune bar him from a brave and lovely girl, with land and stock of her her own, too.

She decided that she would tell her prepared story in front of all the folk; then confide in Oswy secretly and beg his help. The more she thought about it, the more certain she became that he would help. When she crested the ridge below Caer Rhos and saw the sea to the east, and the rock of Bebbanburh, she felt like a battered ship that had made harbour at last.

She dismounted at the foot of the rock and gave her pony back to the boy who had come across the hills with her. Slowly, she climbed towards the gate.

'Be off with you!' snapped the gate-warden, Hunwald. 'The King's already gone into the hall. You'll have to account for yourself to the reeve tomorrow, you're not from these parts. See you do it or I'll—'

Riemmelth put back her hood.

'Mother of God!'

She caught his wrist. 'Don't say a word to anyone till I've seen the King! Take me to him at once!'

Hunwald shouted to a man in the guardhouse to take his place, gripped Riemmelth's arm and helped her across the courtyard; she had drawn her cloak across her face again. At the door, Hunwald spoke to Weybrand, the Dish-Thane. Whatever he said, it was enough to persuade Weybrand to let them in and lead them up the hall. Twice Riemmelth had heard the talk die down along the feasting tables as a stranger came in with a fateful message. This third time, it was her own turn to end the revels.

It was so long since she had been in a king's feasting hall that for a moment she was dazed by the flames of hearth and torches, the fierce colours of robes and jewels, the blaze of gold and silver vessels on the tables. The feasters were just a blur; she blinked and looked towards the Royal Seat.

Oswy was richly dressed, and his broad shoulders and fair head rose above the other feasters, but not all of them. The woman at his side was nearly as tall as he was, and her great crown of coppery-red hair made her look taller. She was a flame of a woman, radiant and queenly. She had been laughing with Oswy; the smile was still on her lips as she turned with the others to look at the thin ragged youth Hunwald was leading up to the dais.

Riemmelth had been practising her story for a long time. She heard her voice obediently reciting it.

'I fought my way out, but they were between me and the North. I couldn't get far enough ahead of them at first; I was driven south like a hind before the beaters.'

The man in the Royal Seat was standing up; he towered in front of her, silvery-fair and sleek as if he had just risen out of the dark water at the foot of the cliff in Eskdale.

'I thought you'd be coming up from Deira, and I'd meet

you and warn you... I had to go far into the Long Hills
before I could work my way back...'

The water was pouring straight down to where the
whirlpool swirled over jagged stones. She stared down into
the falling water; she was losing her hold on the words.

'There'd been treachery; I didn't know who to trust or ask
for help... I didn't know ... who to trust ... who to
trust...'

Her eyes blurred. Her feet were slipping on the edge of the
cliff. Beyond the black gulf, where there was warmth and
light and life, Oswy sat and laughed with a woman like the
midsummer sun at noon. He had no thought for Riemmelth.
There was no help anywhere in the world.

'*Need is—utter lack ...*'

It was not a nightmare so there was no point in struggling,
because she would not wake out of it. A tall shadow loomed
and stooped over her; she let herself fall.

19

Liadan came out of the bedchamber and nearly tripped over
the figure crouching at the door. Mildred clutched her
knees, sobbing.

'How is she? What have you done to her, why are you
keeping me out? I should be in there, tending her—'

The tall Irishwoman stooped and laid her hands on the
girl's head.

'So you shall. So you must, for she'll need long nursing
and it's you'll have to nurse her when I'm gone. She'll want
all the love and care you can give her.'

Mildred had steadied under the strong, sure hands;
Liadan raised her.

'She's quiet now, I've woven a sleep charm over her. Go

and rest, get a cheerful face ready to show her when she wakes.'

She smiled into Mildred's anxious eyes. 'You called me a wise-woman. Trust me.'

Mildred went off obediently. Liadan watched her out of sight before locking the door. She took the key, and went to find Oswy.

The bedchamber was clean, bright, warm. Everything that could give comfort or pleasure to the senses had been gathered round her. The floor was carpeted with fresh rushes, scattered with herbs and flower-heads. The walls and bed were hung with bright embroidery, the sheets had been sprinkled with distilled sweetbriar. Her richest robe had been spread out to air for her; the whalebone jewel casket was at hand on the bedside chest, beside a bowl of rosy apples that had been polished till they shone, and a dish of ripe blackberries, carefully covered with dock leaves.

A blowfly had blundered in and was going crazy among all these delights, buzzing round and round from the flowerheads among the rushes, to the dock leaves hiding the blackberries, to the embroidered flowers on the wall. Round and round.

Riemmelth's thoughts had been going round and round with it ever since she woke up, washed, combed and scented, in the sweet-smelling bed. Anger was building up in her like thunderclouds massing before the storm broke.

The latch rattled, the door opened and Oswy came in, carrying a richly jewelled golden goblet. He saw that her eyes were open and that she was looking at him.

'Wassail, my lady! As I can't drink to you at the feast yet, in front of all the war-band, I've brought the loving-cup to your bedside. When the Queen's the hero, it's only right that the King should pour the wine for her!'

He was smiling; she hated him. He'd had plenty to smile about, these past months, swilling and guzzling in the hall by day, and rolling in bed with his red-haired Irishwoman by night, while she'd been suffering and struggling back to him. Now he'd smile even more, while he boasted to his men about the devotion of his brave and faithful queen. To take that smile off his face was the first object of her life.

'Penda took me.' She threw the words at him like a spear.

He stopped smiling, but his voice was quiet and pleasant.

'I know.'

She gasped.

'How?'

'Elfwyn told me.'

Her lips twisted. 'She must have enjoyed that!'

'I think she did,' he said calmly. 'She was laughing when she spoke.'

Jagged flashes of rage were striking inside her head.

'I'm with child.'

'I know.'

'Elfwyn told you that, too?'

She felt sick with rage and shame, picturing what might have been done to her, said over her, while she lay senseless and helpless in the hall—was it yesterday? Elfwyn's big, pale eyes gloating, her soft, clear little voice pitched to earshot of Oswy's household.

'No. Liadan. She's had the tending of you—we let no one else come near you, not even Mildred. Liadan sat with you all night, and today.'

'That was good of her. And it was good of you, too, to give up all that time she could have been whoring in your bed.'

Oswy put the goblet down on her bedside chest. Her sword had got past his shield and struck home that time. His voice and face stayed calm but his hand shook; the wine slopped on the polished wood like drops of blood. The blowfly circled round, then settled, buzzing ecstatically.

'Liadan is my friend.' He was speaking very carefully. 'She came to me in my need, like a sword-friend coming to stand over a man when he's beaten down in battle. Yes, she's lent me her body; as she'd lend me a manuscript, or make a song for me, or give me food if I was hungry. Because she's

211

my friend and such things are in her gift.'

'And you can lend her your bed, and the Queen's seat in the hall. Because she's your friend, and such things are in your gift—and because you can whistle her here the minute I'm gone.'

'Liadan is an ollave—a pencerdd. It's an Irish bard's privilege to sit next to the King. And because she's a bard, she walks her own road; she comes and goes as she chooses.'

'While I'm only your wife, and your claim to Cumbria. Your property. I can't come and go as I choose.'

'It seems you chose to come back to me.'

'What choice had I got?' she asked bitterly, and waited for his answer. He said nothing; the room was deathly quiet, even the fly had stopped buzzing. Riemmelth was as tired as when she fought Penda, but she could still strike a blow. 'What will you do with my child?'

He must have been ready for that attack for he countered at once.

'Did Penda have you often?'

'Once.'

'August. Then it could be mine. As far as the rest of the world ever knows it, it will be mine. I'll send you to Ebbe's convent to wait for the birth; you'll need the quiet and care that the sisters can give.'

'And then?'

'If it's a girl, Ebbe can take it to bring up as a nun. We'll say you vowed to offer it to God if you escaped from the hands of the heathen. If it's a boy, it will be sickly, and die almost as soon as born.'

She shook her head, speechless.

'There'll be no reproach to you. Any woman could have a dead child after all you've been through.'

She said in a voice as calm as his, 'Can you bear to look at my son, lying dead under your hands?'

'Can you bear to look at Penda's son, growing up in my halls? You're a proud woman, Riemmelth, you know you couldn't endure it. To see the father in his face, and see the

212

knowledge of it in the faces of all my men? And how would *he* bear it—with your blood and Penda's in him—to see himself passed over for a younger brother? For I'll not give Northumbria to Penda's seed, you can be quite sure of that. And so, being Penda's seed, he'd make civil war. Best let such a child die before it knows it's alive.'

She felt very weary; there was no way of avoiding the appalling truths he was throwing at her like spears. She said, coldly, 'Have you thought how you'll explain to the midwives why they should destroy the heir you so badly need? Will you give them my story? How much will you need to pay them to hold their tongues—or will you just drown them in a peatbog?'

'There will be no need to do either. I shall come to Coludesburh for the birth.'

She stared at his face, hunting for any sign of shame or regret or even—for with Oswy anything was possible—that he might be jesting, but his face was expressionless, his eyes as still as a calm sea. Even Penda's animal violence was not so dreadful. She couldn't bear to go on looking at his face in case she broke into screaming madness under those eyes. To steady herself, she fixed her gaze on the goblet, on the spilled wine like a splash of blood near his hand, on the fly.

'You could do *that*?'

'Why not? I killed Elfwyn, and she was my kinswoman—though indeed, she had been half smashed already in the fall of Gefrin, when she betrayed it. I take it on myself. Kings may give the death-doom; it's a right we share with God.'

It was all true. The King of Northumbria could sentence a bastard pretender to death, just as he sentenced a traitress. The divine right was a bitter burden if the traitress or the bastard happened to be bound to the king by ties of blood or wedlock. She even felt a kind of weary pity for Oswy as she went on staring at the blowfly, which had crawled out of the wine and was lying on its back, very still. Very dead.

A king would have the right to sentence a queen to death, if she'd tried to foist a bastard on him with a lie.

213

She smiled.

'How much simpler for you if you just killed me as well as Elfwyn, before I had the child. There'd be no reproach to you—any man could have a dead wife after all I've been through. But then, you'd lose your claim to Cumbria.'

'And it would grieve me to the heart to lose—Cumbria.'

'But you're not getting the choice.' She laughed aloud in her triumph. 'Liadan isn't the only woman who can come and go as she chooses. I choose to go.'

She seized the goblet and drained it; the taste was strange, there had been more in it than wine. Oswy's face began to blur and go into the distance as she called into the space between them, 'I'm free of you, Oswy!'

'For a little while.' He spoke quite gently. 'Lie down and get your breath back to fight me again.' He drew the coverlets over her. 'It's a sleepy drink; Liadan mixed it for you to take after you'd told me.'

Oswy shut the bedroom door quietly behind him. He saw Mildred hovering and made himself smile at her. She came a step nearer, paused, then said, 'The Irish magi—minstrel asked me to give you this.'

Mildred had hesitated over giving the stick; if it had been for Riemmelth she might have put it straight in the fire. Certainly, the marks on it weren't runes, just odd scratches along the edges, but it was bound to be magic; Liadan was an uncanny creature. But there was no doubt she was Oswy's well-wisher, and she seemed to be kind.

Oswy was staring at the ogham letters, reading them over and over again:

'I shall not return. There is a son for you in Ulster; I named him Aldfrid. If you ever need him, send.'

Riemmelth had neither cause nor chance to fight Oswy again for some time. The doctors and cunning-woman he brought to her all agreed that she needed peace and skilled care after her ordeal in the wilds, and a convent was the best place for both. Oswy only saw her in company; he was always the tender, polite husband, thinking of his wife rather than his own pleasures.

He arranged for Riemmelth to go to Coludesburh as soon as she was rested, before winter made journeys uncomfortable and dangerous. She was carried in a litter along the Roman road that wondering churls called the Devil's Causeway; rested a night in the monastic guest-house at Tuidimuth; was ferried across the river next morning and completed the remaining twelve miles up the coast without tiredness or trouble.

Ebbe's monastery, a double foundation of monks and nuns, was in an ancient fort on a great promontory high above the sea, like Bebbanburh; but she had a comfortable grange and guest house a mile or so inland in a sheltered valley by a burn. Here Riemmelth was settled with her servants into the richly furnished rooms Oswy had had prepared for her; and here she broke it gently to Mildred that she did not want her to stay.

'The King told me Cadman had asked for you.'

'And I've given him his answer.' Mildred's grey eyes were bright with tears. 'I told him I'd be making my bed narrow and sleeping alone till I saw you well and in your rightful place as Queen at the head of the table in the King's hall. And if I waited for years, I'd still keep my word.'

Riemmelth kissed her.

'It's a promise then, but I won't keep you waiting that long. The first time I take the Queen's seat again, I'll be there to preside at your wedding—you must promise me that, too.'

'I'll stay and tend you then; we'll go back together.'

'There are enough servants here and sisters in the convent to give me all the tending I need. There's one service only you can do for me.'

Mildred waited.

'Queen Cyneburg is in the convent at Heruteu; Lady Hild is far in the south; Ebbe and I are here. And Elfwyn—is gone, too. The palace needs a lady. Who'll keep the maids up to their work, see the war-band have their shirts clean and mended, fill the King's wine-cup in the hall?'

She smiled.

'You're betrothed to the Horse-Thane; I want you to do this task for me.' She put her keys into Mildred's hand. 'Keep my house bright for me, till I come back.'

When Mildred had gone with Oswy's warriors, the peace of Coludesham settled on Riemmelth. She made up her mind to follow Oswy's teaching and enjoy the present, shutting her mind to what was coming. So she strolled by the burn or in the herb garden; went up to the monastery and talked books with Ebbe; rode a fat, placid pony on the turf above the sea cliffs and boiling foam. When the days drew in and the storm-wind blew, she made herself snug with her maids in the grange, embroidered, played her harp, or listened to the scop reciting *The Fall of Heorot* and *The* (very complicated) *Doom of the Scyldings*. It was pleasant to remember that other folk had their worries.

Beyond the monastery there was peace too, of a kind, throughout Britain once harvest time and the onset of winter brought the campaigning season to an end. Penda stayed in the south, checked by the unexpected hostility of the Cumbrian Welsh. He was re-ordering affairs in Mercia after the death of his brother, browbeating some of his subject-kings who had mistaken that death for a Mercian set-back. The Deiran rebels had been taken aback by Elfwyn's death. Now they had no spy close enough to Oswy to give them warning of Bernician moves; they needed a new leader of Edwin's blood to rally them. Oswy had a few months' grace to assess his own resources, to send and receive secret messages.

Riemmelth's pregnancy gave her little trouble from start to finish. She went into labour on a mild May afternoon. The first pains came on when she was sitting basking in the herb garden; she got back into her rooms without fuss.

Everything was ready, the cunning-women had been in waiting for some time, and they were pleasant and skilful. There was a suitable wet-nurse at hand, a healthy ploughman's wife at the grange-farm who had just borne a child and had a good flow of milk. When the pains got severe, Riemmelth was given a spiced posset, warm and soothing. She recognised the taste, and let herself drift into sleep.

She woke to see Ebbe's face bending over her.

'Is it—?'

Ebbe kissed her. 'A girl—such a lovely little thing, healthy and likely to thrive. She's going to look just like you, I'm sure—she'll have your eyes and your colouring. Oswy sends you his thanks and goodwill for the gift you've given him.'

Riemmelth shivered.

'Is he here?'

'He had to go away at dawn. But he rode here soon after your pains began. He'd had messengers and horses ready to bring him word at once.'

Riemmelth's eyes were closed but Ebbe could see the tears squeezing out under her lashes.

'It's a pity he had to go so soon, but you know there's trouble in the south. It isn't every husband, let alone a king, who'd leave everything to be near his wife when her time came.' Her voice sounded faintly reproachful. 'He left me this to give you—he'd had it made specially. It's Oswald's hair.'

The yellow lock had been plaited under crystal and set in a gemmed reliquary on a golden chain so that she could wear it on her breast. She wondered why Oswy had chosen it; perhaps he thought it made a suitable public gift from a devout husband to a respected wife, perhaps it carried some other message for her. If so, she was too weary to puzzle it out.

Ebbe was surprised, and a little disappointed, that her sister-in-law showed no pleasure at the lovely present. She

217

asked no questions about her daughter either, not even her name. Ebbe had suggested Alchfled, and Oswy had agreed; Riemmelth let it pass.

Ebbe wondered if she were angry or ashamed that she hadn't borne a boy, though Oswy hadn't complained. He'd taken the news good-humouredly, he was really an excellent husband. She hoped Riemmelth knew how lucky she was, poor Oswy didn't deserve a sulky or moody-spirited wife; the Welsh could be odd-tempered sometimes. But perhaps Riemmelth was unhappy that her daughter had been vowed to religion, and was regretting it; that would be why she didn't dare let herself see or speak about the little girl. As Ebbe was already beginning to look on Alchfled as her own daughter, this made her feel tender, and also a little guilty, towards the real mother.

Riemmelth's chief feeling was thankfulness, for the child's sake, of course, but mainly for Oswy and herself; that he was spared killing it, and she was spared having to live with him after he had done so.

Her strength soon came back. The cunning-women bound her body flat and pressed the milk from her breasts, so that she got her lithe shape again. She took up her riding and other amusements; it was a fine hot summer and time passed pleasantly.

Then bad news began to come from the south. Deira had rebelled, Penda had invaded in force, and Oswy was retreating.

By July he had reached Coludesburh; he rode in with a small force, just his own hearth-companions. There was no sign of the war-host; no one had been called out from the northern farms.

Riemmelth went up to the monastery to see him and they dined with Ebbe in the Abbess's private room. The women were grave but Oswy's mouth and eyes were full of laughter; he looked tanned and healthy, and as cheerful as a boy let out of school.

'Couldn't you have stopped the Mercians on the Humber,

218

brother, or in the marshes of Elmet?'

'What would be the point? An advance down there would be more dangerous than a retreat; Penda would just draw me back into the Midland forest, or link up with the Welsh and trap me. And win or lose, I'd have Deira at my back, all ready to put a dagger in, and blocking my way home.'

He shook his head.

'No, I prefer to face Penda on the banks of the Forth. I want him to meet my nephew.'

Riemmelth looked horrified. 'Little Athelwold? You wouldn't give him—'

'God, no! What do you think I'd gain by that? I mean Talorgan, my eldest brother's son.'

Ebbe's head turned sharply. 'You've sent to him?'

'Yes, he's willing and eager.'

Oswy smiled at Riemmelth's puzzled face. 'You've not heard about my brother Eanfrid? Well, I'm not surprised, he's not spoken about much—he went back to the Old Gods. That was in '33, the Accursed Year, when he claimed Bernicia after Edwin was killed, and Penda of Mercia came in with Cadwallon of Gwynedd and nearly destroyed us. We don't count his reign, the year's been given to Oswald. Folk blamed Eanfrid for the disaster because he turned heathen. I think it happened because he asked Cadwallon for a peace-meeting. That was a bad mistake, as Cadwallon said yes, and we never saw Eanfrid alive again, or the twelve hearth-companions he took with him. I'm not even sure we ever found all the bits to bury —the Church wouldn't have him in sacred ground, anyway—but I daresay the angels will get him sorted in time for Doomsday.'

Ebbe winced. 'Don't mock at death or Doomsday, brother; they're coming to us all.'

'Well, before death came to Eanfrid, he'd had time to mate with a Pictish princess and get a son. Young Talorgan's grown into a fine warrior, he'll be their next king, I think; Picts claim through the mother. He hasn't forgotten his father, though. Cadwallon's dead, but he'd like to meet

Penda. I'm going to give him that pleasure.'

'And give Penda the pleasure of ravaging the whole of Northumbria on his way to the meeting!' Riemmelth's eyes were blazing. 'Why haven't you called out the war-host?'

'There won't be any ravaging. Penda fights as simply as a bull, he goes straight for the nearest thing that moves. And that's me—I'm taking care not to get too far ahead of him.'

Riemmelth froze like a young rabbit when the hawk's shadow sweeps overhead.

'It'll be easy enough for the folk in his path to move out of it into the woods or the hills with their stock. The Mercians may burn a steading or two, but they won't move aside to raid cattle and risk losing me—they've heard I've got the royal treasure with me.'

He laughed. 'I have, too. It's a sin to leave temptation in anyone's way. But the story I let fall in Deira for Penda to pick up was that Bernicia won't fight for me, so I'm off to hire warriors in Strathclyde or Dalriada. Good Englishmen won't let all that lovely gold go into the hands of Welsh or Scots. The Mercians will stick to my trail like hounds on the scent. Penda couldn't whistle them off if he tried.'

Ebbe looked grave.

'Aren't you betting too heavily, Oswy, that Penda will always think of his best interests first, like you? Haven't you thought that the one way a simple-minded savage could trick you would be by doing something so mad or stupid that you couldn't foresee it?'

'Everything we do is a bet against our fate, sister. I've got to keep Penda's mind on the one idea, so that he won't have time for anything else.'

His smile was like the winter sea. 'That's why I sent him some of his brother. I found it in a field by Penrhyd. I told him to cut the wood himself to stake it up on.'

'He'll never rest till he kills you.'

'And that won't leave him time to kill anyone else till he catches up with me. He'll catch me on the banks of the Forth, with Talorgan's Picts at my back—and my war-host at his back. The men will be called out when Penda's too far north to know, or for word to reach him. Cadman's seeing to it.'

Oswy finished his drink, stretched and got up.

'Thank you for the meal, sister. I'll be on my way. We're keeping well to the west and going over the Lammermuirs. Penda will be after me in a day or two; he won't come here, but I should move the folk up from the grange while he goes past.'

He looked at Riemmelth. 'I'll leave word with your girls to gather your things and bring them up; you stay here.'

'No!'

Riemmelth's hands were clenched so tight that her nails drove into her palms.

'Do you think I'm going to sit here and wait till Penda comes and sacks my dwelling around me again?'

'Penda isn't coming here,' said Oswy patiently. 'And if he did, he couldn't sack anything. This place is as strong as Bebbanburh; he doesn't know how to fight cliffs and walls.'

He smiled into her eyes, trying to make her smile back. 'If it wasn't for the noise breaking your sleep, I wish he'd try it. I could turn back and pin him at the foot of these rocks—I'd have him then, like a nut between the hammer and the anvil, and finish him at once!'

'Don't lie to me! You'll never finish Penda—you'll never even meet him while there's land at your back to run away on! And don't tell me what will happen when Penda comes to an undefended township—you forget, I was in Gefrin!'

Oswy drew a deep breath.

'I'll take you back to Bebbanburh; there's still time if we make haste.'

'I tell you *no!*' She was shouting, her eyes blank with terror. 'I won't be left in a trap! I won't let it happen to me again! If you won't help me, I'll make my way over the hills, I did it before, I'll get back to my own people!'

Ebbe tried to put an arm around her but she backed away, glaring at the Abbess like an enemy.

'If you chain me up, I'll starve myself,' she whispered, 'or strangle myself in the chains and get free that way! I won't let them near me, I'm not going through that again, never again, I won't let it—'

Her eyes were blank and blind with panic, her voice was rising, in a moment she would be screaming.

Oswy put his hand over her mouth.

'Very well, I'll take you with me. You'll have to ride, a litter would be too slow. I'll have one of the horses brought up for you. Try to sleep tonight and take a hearty breakfast if you can. We ride at dawn.'

Ebbe followed him out of the room; her face was drawn and anxious.

'I think you're making a mistake, brother.'

'I know I'm making a mistake.'

'Then why—'

'She's suffered too much since I brought her from her own people. I owe it to her to pay back some of the debt.'

'By giving her more to suffer?'

'If that's what she asks me. Sometimes it's all we've got left to give people—their own choice of how they suffer.'

20

The blind terror blew away on the free moorland winds as she rode across the Lammermuirs. Riemmelth could even feel surprised at herself, unable to believe in her panic, while knowing all too well that it could seize her again at any time, as it had outside the ale-house at Ceasterford. She wondered if she would ever get her proud courage back; if not, she would never be really free.

From a spur of the Lammermuirs they saw the great estuary of the Forth opening out into the sea, with the hills of

Pictland beyond. Oswy explained to her that Talorgan would be coming over the river at Giudi, some forty miles to the west, then marching for Camelon on the Emperor Antoninus's Wall. Meanwhile, they would head for the shore, making for the eastern end of the Wall. There was a good track, all the way to the west, past the ruins of many Roman forts. Somewhere on the way to Camelon he would make camp in a defensible fort and let Penda besiege him, to be trapped in his turn when Talorgan's host came up and surrounded him.

Riemmelth felt cold at the thought of watching Penda's men trying to storm the walls where she was lurking, but she hid her feelings.

They came down towards the Forth and made camp at Esk Mouth. Oswy let them rest for a day as they had been riding hard and, besides, he wanted to let Penda get so close that he would forget everything but the joy of the chase; he mustn't have time to sense a trap closing on him.

The next day they had a pleasant ride along the sands at low water, with the crags of Din Eidyn towering on their left. The hill-top city had been besieged and sacked by Oswald six years ago, but there were a few farm steadings on the lower slopes, and the summit still had a crown of ruined walls.

Oswy knew the ground from that campaign; he told Riemmelth that there was a village a few miles away at the mouth of the Almond. They would rest there and breathe their horses; the Wall was only another ten miles beyond, where messengers from Talorgan would be waiting for them. He sent Guthlac and Brand ahead to Caer Almond to tell the womenfolk to get a place ready for Riemmelth.

They were fording the Leith when they saw a rider urging a tiring mount towards them. Oswy quickened his horse's pace, Riemmelth riding close beside him; the men gripped and readied their spears. They all sensed, even before the telling, that bad news was coming.

The rider was Guthlac. His mouth was open, he had been

shouting even before he was in earshot.

'Turn back! There's a war-host at the Almond!'

Riemmelth's heart lurched.

'Penda's got ahead of us!'

Guthlac shook his head, gasping. 'No. *Welsh*. We thought they were Talorgan's men. Brand went ahead to greet them—he knows some words of Pictish. He was just able to call a warning before they took him—I don't know if they killed him or kept him to question. We can't get past, there are too many of them.'

Oswy swung his horse and caught Riemmelth's bridle-rein.

'Ride!'

He led them inland, where the rocky heights of Din Eidyn loomed in their path. A narrow defile opened among the cliffs and screes that went up steeply towards the ruined citadel. They drew rein at the foot and dismounted, looking back for signs of pursuit. Their faces were as grim as their prospects. They had played bait for Penda all too well, the scouts reported he was close behind, coming up Deira Street; he would be at Esk Mouth before nightfall. They couldn't go back and they couldn't go on, with the Welsh between them and their Pictish allies. The hunters had been caught in their own trap.

Oswy looked at the great hilltop, more than a mile of crow's flight across in both directions, with a moat of marshes and lochs to the east and south, sheer cliffs to the west. He smiled.

'It's a good place for hide-and-seek.'

'Or for a last stand,' said Godric, looking up at the citadel.

'It hasn't come to that, yet—but ride round to some of the farms and get them to take supplies inside the walls. I don't mean to be penned up there except as a last resort, but it won't come amiss to have stocks laid in.'

'We haven't the men to hold it,' said Wulfstan gloomily.

'They don't know that.'

'The Welsh have got Brand.'

'He won't talk!' snapped Guthlac fiercely.

'If he does, I hope he has the wit to lie.' Oswy looked thoughtful, but not desperate. 'They don't know about Talorgan, but I'm sure Talorgan knows about them, or will do fairly soon. No strangers can come up from the south without the Picts knowing—folk say they can hear the grass grow. Talorgan will be on their track before long.'

'Before long could be too long for us,' said Dunnere. 'If Penda and the Welsh together make an all-out attack, we'll be dead before Talorgan gets here. Time's the one thing you can't hold to a stop with your spearpoint.'

'You might be able to buy some, if you've got gold enough.'

Oswy's eyes gleamed, he might have been playing a board game and just thought of a new move. He pointed to one of the pack-horses.

'Unload one of those bags. Dunnere, take half the men and get the rest of the gold into the citadel. When Godric comes up with the supplies, tell him to stay with you and watch out for us—we may be coming in a hurry. If all else fails, put the gold down the well or bury it in a bit of bog, and hold out as long as you can.'

He watched Dunnere collect his troop and ride off up the defile. Riemmelth was startled to hear him chuckling. She stared at him. He really was amused.

'Ebbe said that the one way a simple-minded savage like Penda could trick me was by doing something so mad or stupid that my cunning mind couldn't foresee it.'

He laughed again. 'The one thing I didn't foresee was that he'd be cunning enough to think of *my* plan—here we are, holing up in an old fort, caught between his war-band and an allied host: just what I meant to do to him!'

'I'm glad it entertains you,' was all Riemmelth said, low-voiced between tight lips. She couldn't point out to him that Oswald, too, had been trapped in an old fort between Penda's war-band and an allied host. It had been a huntsman's plan, although the wrong game had been driven into the net that first time. Elidir had brought Oswald to bay and seen his body torn by his pack of Mercian hounds. He had a hunter's patience and would track a quarry from Powys to Pictland, or to the end of the world if the trail led so far. She saw him taking Oswy like a wolf on the point of his spear, and took the dreadful truth like the shock of that spear driving into her own heart.

'*I belong to you now*,' she had told him, '*don't ever desert me.*' Elidir had been faithful, too faithful. Neither trickery, nor parting, nor her marriage oath had unbound him from his vow. She was the one who had spoken the words; in binding him to her, she had bound herself. *Which of us— how many of us here—will have to die to win release?*

Oswy turned to the rest. 'Follow me. Lead your horses, it's steep.' He took them to the eastern side of the valley, where the ground rose steeply over a little loch. A threadlike track wound up among the rocks. He signed to his men to wait and climbed up, followed by Riemmelth. On a shelf of turf between two crags, there was a little round hut like a beehive, and an oratory of rough unmortared stones under a thatched roof.

'Peace to this place!'

'And to you, my son.'

The hermit had been studying his psalter by the light of his open door. He laid aside his book and came towards them, a tall, thin, old man with skin like leather from the sun and wind, wispy grey hair and beard, his eyes hollow from long vigils but as blue and calm as the loch below.

'We're fugitives, Father. I'm waiting to talk peace with my enemies, if they'll let me. If they don't, I beg you in the name of Christ to give sanctuary to this lady. She's a Christian—the Queen of Cumbria.'

'God bless you, daughter. Don't be frightened. This is God's house, you're at home. Where are your enemies?'

'Coming fast.' Oswy pointed across the low land to the north-east where the Leith flowed to the shore. 'Here they are!'

The hermit turned inside his hut for a moment and came out carrying a large wooden cross. He smiled at Riemmelth.

'Stay here, my daughter, and ask St Antony to guard you.'

He went back down the track with Oswy; Riemmelth hesitated a moment or two, then followed quietly at a distance. She was drawn by something stronger than curiosity about her fate. These warriors, riding fast and proud to Din Eidyn, were her own people. After two years of exile, she felt herself swept towards them on a great wave of longing.

Oswy drew his sword and cut a leafy branch from a stunted alder growing by a runnel of peaty water. He handed his sword to Wulfstan, hauled up the treasure sack that Dunnere had left, and went on with the hermit down to the mouth of the defile. The riders saw them waiting with the cross and the green branch of peace. They halted; there was a moment of talk, then four of them dismounted and came slowly forward. The hermit raised his cross.

'Peace in the name of Christ.'

Two of the newcomers scowled, the other two crossed themselves. One of these said in Welsh, 'We'll give you peace gladly, Father, and ask your blessing with it, but what does the Englishman want?'

'Peace also.'

The Welshman laughed. 'The English are such a holy, peace-loving race! All the dead monks of Bangor-is-y-Coed must be praying for them at this moment.'

Another man spat.

'Oswy loves peace, no doubt about it.' He was speaking Welsh too, clumsily, with a strong Mercian accent. 'There's nowhere too far for him to run looking for it.'

'I'm looking for it now, I tell you frankly.' Oswy was calm and unresentful. 'My people have turned against me—driven me out. I've only a handful of men left, as you can see. I'm going into exile, back to Iona.'

'And you've come to beg for safe passage?'

'I've come to buy it.'

227

He opened the mouth of the leather sack so they could see inside, and held up first a goblet, then a brooch, then a golden platter. The envoys tried to look unimpressed but didn't quite succeed.

'There are five more sacks like this in the citadel yonder. I'm willing to exchange them for five days' grace to wait in my stronghold at Giudi, while I send to Strathclyde for leave to cross their land. If I fall into your hands after that, you can do what you like.'

'We can do what we like now, without asking your permission.' The Mercian's face was twisted with scorn. 'We can have your treasure as soon as we choose to take it, and give your guts to Woden's ravens. D'you think Penda's a merchant, selling peace on a market stall?'

'You can't have my treasure, because my men have orders to sink it in a peatbog if you refuse my terms. And we can feed a fair number of you to Woden's ravens before we go.'

'This is heathen talk,' said the hermit sternly, fixing his eyes on the Welsh. 'I charge you, in the name of God and on pain of His curse, to let this man go in peace into exile with his wife and his followers.'

'His wife?' The Welshman sounded horrified. 'The Queen of Cumbria is here?'

They looked up the slope, beyond the knot of Oswy's men, and saw Riemmelth standing at the turn of the track. The two Welshmen stepped aside and talked urgently, then had what sounded like a violent argument with the Mercians. The hermit joined them; Oswy waited, impassive, with his green branch and his sack of treasure. Finally, the hermit turned back to him.

'They're going to put your terms to their lords. I'll go with them. I'll make myself a surety for good faith.'

'I shall want sureties too, one from each side. They're not all Christians.'

After another few words, one of the Welshmen and the second Mercian, who had not spoken to Oswy, stepped forward, and the others went away over the plain. The two hostages hobbled their horses, left their weapons at the foot of the slope and climbed up to join the Northumbrians. Oswy's men offered their flasks. The Welshman hardly spoke; he glanced curiously from time to time at Riemmelth, who sat apart, shrouded in her cloak, with Oswy beside her. The Mercian, an open-faced, good-humoured fellow, was ready to talk.

'Penda won't make terms,' he said cheerfully, after a good swig at Guthlac's flask. 'He just wants your blood.' His voice carried clearly.

'Taking it hard about his brother? He killed Oswald, too, remember.'

'Oh, I don't think he cares so much about Eobba, that was fair fight—though he didn't like it, mind, when Oswy sent his balls back with that message. But it was the business with the woman that stuck in his gullet.'

'What woman?'

'He took a woman on his last raid into Northumbria—or you might say, she took him.'

Riemmelth froze.

'She took his fancy so much he decided to marry her, which was generous, since he could have her for nothing. She took his offer, too; she even took his bride-gift, his best brooch, come down from old Offa of Angeln. So what does she do with it but put the pin through her heart!'

Riemmelth jerked as violently as if she had been stabbed too; she would have jumped up, but Oswy gripped her. The coarse, cheery voice went on:

'Penda was stark mad with rage when he found her—fit to be tied. He said every Northumbrian from Oswy up was a cheating liar, not even honest enough to sell broken-winded nags at a horse-fair.'

Oswy and his men laughed heartily at this testimonial. Riemmelth's face was bowed under the shadow of her hood; she managed not to sob aloud but the tears were streaming down her face.

At last the hermit came back alone.

'They've granted most of your terms. Penda was unwilling but the Welsh insisted, and they outnumber the Mercians. They won't give you more than three days, though, and this counts as one. You must bring the treasure down here and yield it in front of my cross; Penda won't touch it, he said the Welsh were welcome to it, but he's given them his word not to attack you. You can pass tonight in the citadel and leave at dawn. The peace-pledge ends at sunset the day after tomorrow—if you're not in Strathclyde, or if Strathclyde sends you back, they're free to kill you.'

'So be it. I'm grateful to you, Father.'

'I shall pray for your peace and safety, my son.'

He blessed them, set up his cross in the soft peaty ground and sank on his knees in prayer. The two hostages got their weapons and went off over the plain towards the Welsh camp by the Leith. The Northumbrians mounted and rode at a walk up the steep defile to the citadel. Riemmelth and Oswy went last. He said nothing; she could feel the silence closing in like the walls of a cell. To break it she said, 'Are they going to keep the terms?'

'Probably not; but then, we aren't, either. We'll be with Talorgan long before the second sunset; there'll likely be a message from him tonight. Penda hasn't got enough men to draw a noose round Din Eidyn or stop every herdsman and fisher along the coast.'

He paused a moment and then said quietly, 'I may need to know. Who was she?'

'My cousin. Her mother was Owain ap Urien's love-child. We were very close—she gave me my necklace.'

Riemmelth's throat hurt so much she could hardly speak. 'She was a priestess at Arnemeton. I'd pretended I served The Lady so that Penda would leave me alone.'

'Clever.' Oswy's voice was appreciative.

'She came to help me and took my place—we were very like each other.' Her voice began to shake. 'I gave her that brooch. I didn't dream she'd kill herself—I thought she'd be Penda's queen—'

230

'And so she could have been, if she chose. It's not your doing, Riemmelth.'

She raised her eyes to his face, but she was blind with tears.

'I gave her death for her bride-gift, and this feud was born out of her corpse. Penda won't give up; if you get away now, the attacks will start again and again till the whole North's destroyed.'

She swallowed and steadied her voice. 'Let me go, Oswy. My own people will protect me. I'll face Penda and tell him—'

'No!' Oswy caught her arm like a vice. 'Have you been with Penda and don't know that nothing will protect you from him? He'd kill you if he died the moment after!'

'Even so—'

'Riemmelth, I've never used the word to you yet, but I *forbid* you. Not as your husband—you never wanted me. Not as your king, you're a reigning queen yourself. But as leader of this war-band with all your lives in my hands. I have to make the plans and know that no one else is planning otherwise behind my back.'

He smiled and touched her wet cheek. 'Trust me, my dear. I've been in tight corners, I'll get us out of this. Don't let the men see you crying, it'll damp their spirits.'

By now, they had reached the wall of the ruined citadel on the rock-crest. The gate had gone long ago, but the gap could be blocked by furze and dead thorn bushes; the folk still made use of the place as a refuge from cattle-raiders. Riemmelth watched the loaded pack-horses being taken down the valley by some of Oswy's men, sullen-faced at the thought of handing Northumbrian gold to Mercians and Welsh without a fight. Oswy himself was leading them, looking as calmly amused as usual.

She waited for their return under the blazing August sun, staring down at the loch gleaming like a mirror dropped on the grass, at the great sweep of the estuary beyond, thinking of Arianrhod. Had death been her estuary, through which her life had poured out and widened into a boundless sea?

At last the ransom party came back, the pack-horses trotting easily now. Oswy had Godric and Wulfstan on either side, Godric holding forth in a loud angry voice; they didn't notice her. The rest of the group looked murderous; she turned to Dunnere who was bringing up the rear.

'What's happened? Did Penda change his mind—try to stop them taking the treasure?'

'Oh, they took it all right. They were on to it like a flock of magpies, rot their greedy claws! They took every last scrap of gold—even the ring off Oswy's hand.'

Her heart seemed to twist in her breast; she had to gasp for breath.

'Oswy said it was his wedding ring; but one of the Welsh lords had a mind to it, and Penda swore if it wasn't given up the deal was off. The Welshman had the insolence to say that everything the English had in Britain was stolen goods— that we weren't buying our passage to Giudi, we were just paying back a bit of our debt. Penda didn't like that. Makes you choke, doesn't it, my lady? Never mind, we'll pay them back all right, more than they ask for.'

He gave her an encouraging grin, then went off to see to the horses. Riemmelth was nearly choking indeed, but not with anger, thinking of her ring on Elidir's hand at last, and the long road it had travelled to get there since she gave it to poor Guriat. Even the wide hilltop seemed airless; she went outside the walls and wandered about the grassy slopes like a restless ghost.

The sun was westering, and the sky flooding with gold and rose, when she met a herd-girl bringing milch-goats up to the citadel. The girl smiled and beckoned; she took a little wooden cup from the folds of her plaid, held it under a goat's teats, then offered the fresh, warm milk. Riemmelth took it thankfully, she was thirsty and exhausted after hours under the hot sun. There was something hard and loose in the cup, like a pebble. It was the Cumbrian ruby ring.

Riemmelth glanced round, the hillside was empty. She

232

turned the cup as if she were shaking out the last drops and slipped the ring into her hand. The girl came close to take the cup.

'Under the rocks by the loch-side, lady, after moonrise.'

She went on towards the citadel, driving her goats; Riemmelth followed slowly. She moved through the rest of the daylight in a mindless trance. Oswy was conferring with his men; either he had no time for her, or he thought she was grieving for her cousin and left her in peace. A sleeping-place had been prepared for her in a corner of a building that still had a roof. She retired early and lay as if she slept.

At nightfall, she slipped outside and glided like a shadow among the ruins. Oswy had men on watch, but they were guarding against intruders or a surprise attack, not against someone leaving. It was easy enough to place them and dodge their notice; she was lithe and cat-footed, the crumbling walls did not bar her. She kept under the craggy skyline, setting her feet gently on the turf in case she kicked a stone. The moon was brightening, the bushes and rocks began to have black shadows. One of the shadows moved away from its bush, but it was behind her and she did not look back.

It was late August, already there was a touch of autumn in the air but all the while, as Riemmelth made her way down to the loch, she felt that there was hawthorn blossom in the silver moonlight all round her, and spring woodlands. She might have been following the stream down from St Nynia's Well through the oaks of Inglewood, where Elidir was waiting to take her in his arms.

When she went under the shadow of the crag by the loch-side, and the blackness stirred and caught her, she could only think, over and over again, *I'm home! Home!* feeling his arms hard around her, his body warm against her loins, his mouth hungry on her face and neck. The two years' exile vanished, she had never been away. She pressed her hands down his back, straining him close.

Elidir stepped away from her embrace; she thought he was

233

going, cried out a wordless protest and caught at him. He laughed, and she saw his teeth gleam against the blackness of his beard.

'We've got all our lives for that. It's time to be going now.'

'Going?'

'My men are all ready to ride. It's full moon—we'll be half-way to Caer Luel before sunrise.' He took hold of her arm, expecting her to hurry away with him. She stayed still.

'There's nothing to be afraid of. We outnumber Penda, he can't stop us. He can stay here and cut Oswy's throat.'

'Oswy's my husband.'

'Not much longer. You'll be a widow before I get you home. I'm sorry I can't kill him for you myself, but there'd be trouble with the Church over blood-guilt. So we'll let the English kill each other in their own squalid feud, and you'll be free to marry me without any scandal. Cumbria and Powys together—I can master all Britain!'

She shook her head. 'I can't do that.'

'Can't?—Or won't?'

Elidir was disappointed and angry that she could hesitate for one second. Looking at his dark face, she saw that this man was not the light-hearted young hunter of Eskdale— any more than she was the girl who had believed that life was like a bard's story. This Elidir was a hard, tough war-leader. Did he even love her, the woman she was now as life had made her, or simply love the power she embodied, and the long-awaited victory over a man who had stolen his property?

'You gave me your word. You gave me your body as a pledge. You said you belonged to me—and so you do!'

'I'm married,' she said, hopelessly. 'I've been a wife for more than two years. There's a barrier between us.'

'I've broken a way through it—what do you think I've been doing all these two years? I made myself into the son my uncle wanted. Risked my neck in every challenge, so that the young men would follow my lead. Fought in every war on all the borders of Powys, so that my name would carry weight. Flattered that ravening savage Penda into an alliance, so that he'd sack Oswald's palace in the north and keep him from helping his brother.'

He stared at her suspiciously. 'I got my cousin the monk to write a letter warning you to be ready—you only had to mount your horse and come to me. But you stayed in England—and kept your man safe by you. You let your brother-in-law walk into the trap instead, and so I made you Queen of Northumbria for my trouble! I hope Oswy has paid you his thanks.'

'It wasn't like that. I never got your letter.' Her voice was as faint as a dying breath; she saw, like a map spread in front of her, the road that had led her back to Elidir, with the stopping-places on the way written in blood: Oswald's betrayal, the horror of Gefrin, Arianrhod's death, a new-born child she dared not see. Her eyes blurred.

'Is that all you've got to give me—tears, after all I've done for you, all I've given up? I could have married my uncle's daughter—that's what he wants—a lovely girl and devoted to me. It hurt her when I put off my answer and came away on this campaign—for what? A memory, and a lot of empty promises?'

He mimicked her voice with savage bitterness. '"*There's nothing in the world that I'd deny you, Elidir, but a princess of Cumbria doesn't mate in the greenwood like a peasant girl!*" No, but she can lie back and open her legs like any whore when the price is high enough, the broad lands of Northumbria, say, and all the gold that Ida's crew of pirates ever stole!'

'Can you remember so much and say that to me?' she whispered. 'Did I ask you for gold or lands? The only time in my life I was ever free to choose, I chose you.'

Elidir's smile was brilliant. 'And now you've got your choice. Forgive what I said just now, I didn't mean it. Stop talking—just come.'

He held her to him again and kissed her gently. Memory and longing were so strong that she felt time could indeed turn back for her, was turning back now as she turned in

Elidir's arms and moved to go back with him to his camp by the Leith, where the horses were waiting.

Penda was walking slowly towards them.

'Does the moonlight keep you from sleeping, Elidir?' he said grimly. 'It's bothering your men too, it seems; they're restless tonight.'

He looked at the woman in Elidir's arms. 'Are you planning your next campaign—or has it already started?'

Riemmelth had turned her head at Penda's voice; she tried to shrink behind Elidir and the moon shone full on her necklace. Penda stepped back; for the first time in his life he showed a face of blind terror.

'Why are you walking here? I sent you back to the holy grove—you had your rites. Why have you followed me?'

'What do you mean, Penda?' Elidir was furious but embarrassed. 'This is my kinswoman, the Queen of Cumbria—you'd better respect her!'

'Don't believe her! She's a moon-witch, a night-shadow! That's just a shape to cheat your eyes. She's walking dead, I saw the pin through her heart, I tell you!'

Riemmelth had to silence him.

'Are you talking about my poor maidservant, whom you took from Gefrin?' she said coldly. 'I heard today from your man how she died. She was dear to me, even though she was only a bastard of my House. I'd have given her my consent to marry you, if she'd wanted to.'

She was terrified, but managed to sound as if Penda was a serf who had asked to marry one of the kitchen slaves. She could imagine Arianrhod's mocking laughter at him and all the presumptions of men.

Penda was staring at her face.

'That's generous of you; I never saw a woman who took my fancy more than she did. You're very like her, even to the necklace. You're the same flesh and blood, you'll do for me instead.'

'How dare you?' shouted Elidir, red with anger.

'What's troubling you? It's no insult to a woman, I should

think; to make her the Queen of Mercia. You're her kinsman, you say; I know you're my ally. I'm asking you for her hand.'

Elidir was too taken aback to have an answer ready. In the silence, Penda laid his hand on the hilt of his great sword.

'D'you think I'm fit to fight your battles but not good enough to bed your kin?'

He took a step towards them. Elidir whistled softly, and spearmen came out from among the trees and bushes. Riemmelth had not been aware of their approach; either they had moved like ghosts, or Elidir had stationed them before she came.

Penda stood firm, looking at them calmly. 'Don't stand too far off. I've nothing to say that you're not welcome to hear.' He raised his voice. 'I've just asked Elidir, your chief and my sword-brother, to bind our friendship in the marriage knot and give me his kinswoman here for wife. But moonlight's a poor candle to light our talk. Take her back to your camp now, I'll speak with you in the morning.' He turned to pass Elidir and added quietly, out of the spearmen's earshot, 'And see you're there, waiting for me; I'll tell my men to be watching tonight.'

He was striding away; Elidir gripped Riemmelth's arm. She felt trapped; whether Elidir did try to ride away by night as he had planned, relying on his greater numbers to fight off the Mercians, or whether he confronted Penda in the morning, she was as helpless now, between them, as a war-captive.

'You're speaking to the wrong man, Penda.'

Oswy stepped out of the darkness under the crags. 'The Queen of Northumbria already has a husband.'

Penda looked at him scornfully.

'Didn't you hear me say I'd taken a fancy to her? I'm not one to drive a hard bargain when I've a mind to the goods. I won't charge you wergild for my brother, and you can name your own price for the woman. Then you'll be able to buy yourself another, I know you're short of gold now.'

Oswy shook his head, smiling indulgently as if talking to a very stupid child.

'Your brother's life went a little way towards paying me for mine. As to my lady, Christians don't deal like that. We respect our wives, we don't trade them.'

'Then fight for her. She'll have the better man, there's no disrespect in that.'

Riemmelth turned desperately to Elidir. 'You call yourself my kinsman. Are you going to stand by and see my husband butchered?'

'I've got no part in Englishmen's private quarrels,' said Elidir, coldly. 'It seems they're at feud about their brothers. I and my men will keep the ring, if you like, to see fair fight.'

She saw the satisfaction in his eyes; the fight could only go one way, but Penda would not be the winner. Penda would kill Oswy, sure enough, then the men of Powys would avenge her husband and save her honour by killing Penda. The Mercians would be told that Oswy had murdered Penda by some furtive treachery and that the men of Powys had avenged their ally. Penda couldn't see it, of course; she was fairly sure that Oswy did.

She drew her hunting dagger and set the point between her breasts. Arianrhod's road was always open; she was not going to live all her days like a cow being fought for by the bulls and taken by the strongest.

'Don't be frightened, cousin!' Elidir sounded alarmed. 'I won't let anyone hurt you.'

'I'm not frightened.' Riemmelth was angry enough to believe it at that moment. 'And no one need trouble to hurt me, I can do that for myself. I always have!'

Bitterness rose in her throat like vomit and she nearly choked on it.

'At least the King of Northumbria asked my leave in front of a priest. We made an honest bargain and kept it.'

'You keep talking,' said Penda scornfully. He drew his sword. 'For Woden!'

'For honest bargains!' Oswy raised his sword to her, then

had to dodge out of reach of Penda's first blow.

She didn't want to watch, but couldn't look away. It wasn't so hopeless as her own fight with Penda had been. Though he seemed slight beside the Mercian, Oswy was a tall and powerfully-built man. He had speed and range, he was a fine swordsman, too; but then, so was Penda. Oswy could deal more punishing blows than she could, but he had the same problem: to kill Penda, or even disable him, you had to get in under his guard, and that was not easy. And if you stopped one of his parrying strokes, you could have your sword broken, or your sword-arm hacked off or smashed.

In the last resort, the only real defence against Penda was to run for it, but Elidir's ring of spearmen would stop that. Oswy against Penda was like a wolf against a king bull: in an enclosed space he would be worn down in the end by the furious charges.

Oswy feinted towards Penda's left side, then drove in under his right arm, going for the heart, but Penda swept a back-handed down-stroke that would have taken Oswy's leg off if he hadn't jumped away. Penda brought his blade up while Oswy was still off balance; he had to parry with the sax in his left hand; it was nearly knocked flying. Oswy kept his grip, but for a minute or two his left arm hung jarred and numb.

Now Penda stormed against Oswy with a furious shower of blows to his head, his neck, his guts, his arms and legs, that had him parrying desperately, jumping and ducking like a hooked salmon, always driven back and round, back and round the unyielding shield-wall of the Powys warriors.

Riemmelth's sight was blurred; she wasn't watching Oswy now. Gefrin was burning round her, her ears were filled, her mind was stunned by the savage chanting:

'*Seize the shield-maiden, slit her with man-spear.*'

She was the one being driven round the circle; it was her eyes that were blinded with sweat, her ears that were deafened with roaring blood, her lungs that were labouring, her sword-arm that was numb, her legs that were dragging and stumbling as the horror came nearer, nearer, nearer . . .

Oswy was down; the sword fallen from his nerveless grasp, he lay sprawled on the ground, his limbs thrown wide as hers had been. Perhaps he was stunned, he was making no effort to struggle; perhaps despair and horror held him, as they had held her at Gefrin, as they were holding her now, down in the dirt with no escape.

Penda paused to breathe and wipe his face; then he came over to Oswy, taking his time to place the blow. He straddled his great legs over Oswy's body to get a good balance, and swung his sword.

It was over in a flash. Oswy turned like an otter, snatched his sword and drove up straight between Penda's legs. It must have been the only blow Penda feared; the dreadful swiftness bewildered him. He leapt back in clumsy panic with a grotesque jerk of the legs, like a clown dancing, to shield his privates; tripped himself and fell crashing, stunned by his own weight, with blood streaming down his thighs.

Oswy had jumped to his feet, ready to plunge his sword again into Penda, but the nearest Powys men covered his body with their spears. The icy chain of terror and sexual shame that had held Riemmelth for so long, dissolved, she was free of it for ever. She was still shaking and gasping as she fought against a rising tide of giggles. The roaring in her ears was an echo of the roar of laughter and bawdy joking that would sweep across Northumbria, as the tale was told how Oswy had solved the problem of getting in under Penda's guard.

She had sheathed her dagger and was wiping the back of her hand across her wet eyelashes; but when she saw the spearpoints directed at Oswy, she darted forward and grabbed Penda's sword-hilt. It took all the strength of her two arms to lift the weapon, but she managed to raise it at the spearmen, screaming, 'Get back, you cowards, or I'll skewer you!'

They turned to stare at her and she cried out in amazement, 'Idwal! Rhodri! What are you doing here?'

Looking round at Elidir's spearmen, she saw more than one Cumbrian face, warriors of the Caer Luel palace guard.

They looked uncertainly from her to Oswy, who was still standing by Penda's body, leaning on his sword and panting. He was watching the scene as if it were a knockabout mime in Bebbanburh hall at Yule.

'We heard you were being held against your will, lady.' Idwal glanced at Elidir. 'The story went through Caer Luel that you'd never be seen in Cumbria again.'

'If Penda had taken me, I certainly never would have been. Stand aside, now, the King has some work to finish.'

'The fight is over,' said Elidir sharply, before Oswy could move. 'I let you defend your honour, as you were challenged, but Penda is our ally and you're under terms of peace. I forbid you to kill him. I won't permit it.'

Oswy smiled. 'It's good to know you were standing by to see we didn't hurt each other. You should have told me before, I wouldn't have been so scared.'

Elidir looked at him with loathing; he couldn't decide whether Oswy was more contemptible if he was serious or joking.

'You'd better get out at first light. You've broken the peace; you can't claim two days' safety now.'

The Cumbrians drew together in a body around Riemmelth.

'I advise you not to linger either,' said Oswy. 'You've got a damaged ally to account for—I should get him up to the hermitage, if I were you, before he bleeds to death. You could tell the Mercians I defeated him in single combat, sword to sword. You just happened to pass by with a picked band of spearmen and watched me do it. They might believe you.'

He smiled and added, 'Before our truce ends, though, I've a favour to ask.'

'Favour?'

'Yes. I've got a hard journey before me, and I'm not sure when or if I'll be back. I haven't time to escort your cousin to

Caer Luel. Your road to Powys lies that way; would you have the goodness to go along with her people,' he nodded to the Cumbrians, 'and see her home?'

Riemmelth saw the exultant satisfaction blaze in Elidir's eyes, saw the road home stretching in front of her as if a door had been flung wide. If Oswy was trying to salvage his Cumbrian alliance by proving that she was not being held against her will, he would not lift a hand to stop her leaving. And she would never come back. She heard her own voice, somewhere outside herself, very calm and pleasant:

'You're forgetting, my lord—it's a women's matter, it'll have slipped your mind among graver business—but I promised our dear Lady Mildred that I'd attend her wedding. It would be cruel to keep Cadman ap Cadwal waiting much longer.'

She looked desperately into Elidir's eyes, searching behind their bafflement and anger for the boy who had loved her under the hawthorns in Eskdale.

Don't forget our love or curse it—I did love you, truly; I'll love you for ever—

Elidir's eyes were as hard and blank as jet; she couldn't reach him.

She took the Cumbrian ruby from her finger, raising her voice so that both her own people and the men of Powys could hear her.

'My brother, King Pascen, loved you like a brother. I meant you to have this when he died. I want you to take it now, in memory of that time, and in thanks for your care of me tonight.'

She held out the ring to him on her open palm, pleadingly; her heart leaped as he took it.

'A trifle—not worth remembering.'

He tossed the ring from him, it struck a stone and bounced off into the loch; she heard it hit the water. The Cumbrians stirred angrily. Oswy took her arm.

'As your cousin says, we'd best be going.'

'We'll come with you, lady,' said Idwal. She felt Oswy's

hand tighten and she made herself smile.

'There's no need, my husband's nephew is coming with his troops to escort us to Pictland. Your place is in Caer Luel. Tell my people I'm coming—perhaps before the Nativity, certainly by the spring. I wish you all a good journey to Cumbria, and to Powys. The sun on your path before you.'

The door that had opened for a moment clanged shut again. She bowed her head courteously to them, and walked away from her youth and love without a backward glance.

21

They climbed the defile slowly, in unbroken silence. The world was all cold moonlight and black rocks. Oswy paused once, at a pool, to wash the blood off his hand and sword. They walked in past the guards with nothing but a brief word of greeting. At the door of her shelter, Oswy stopped.

'Get what rest you can. We'll be on the move early.'

He left her without a glance or a smile. She sank on to the pile of bracken and cloaks, asking herself what she was doing there, why she had put herself, of her own free will, into exile for ever with a stranger. A mocking, unscrupulous stranger, who'd probably eavesdropped on every word that had been spoken down by the loch.

'You gave me your word. You gave me your body as a pledge.'

How would Oswy value her word if he had heard that—or her body, either? He had said ill luck was nobody's fault; he'd pitied her rape, as he would have pitied her if she'd been thrown while hunting, and lamed.

But if he had been within earshot—how close had he been, how soon had he come after her?—he knew now that Elidir was her lover. He'd surely think, as Elidir did, that she had only stayed with him because, in spite of all set-backs, Northumbria was still the greatest kingdom in all Britain.

'—*she can lie back and open her legs like any whore when the price is high enough*—'

She could feel the blood stinging her cheeks as if she had been slapped, remembering Elidir's voice and look; imagining Oswy watching and listening. Was that why he had given her a chance to go? To get well rid of a whore, so that she could brand herself publicly as Elidir's harlot and leave himself free to repudiate her without risking Cumbrian anger or the Church's curse?

She had thwarted this neat and simple riddance—but Oswy had already made it clear to her, calmly and with no visible signs of guilt or grief, that he could and would rid himself of living threats whenever he saw the need.

The moon was setting and through the broken door of her shelter she could see that the hilltop was growing dark; she might never see another sun rise. The idea brought no fear with it; if Oswy took her life, at least he had given her this one gift tonight: that never again would she be captive to blind terror.

How stupid, in any case, to picture anyone as clever as Oswy killing her to gratify a personal spite, at a time when his own life and kingdom were on the edge of destruction. Even the rumour that she was being held against her will had been enough to bring the Cumbrians up in arms. Oswy would take care to display her at the Pictish court, and then in Caer Luel as soon as possible, as his beloved and respected queen. They were both good enough liars to play out the farce in public, like a strolling tumbler and his woman mumming a scene of married life to pass the time after a feast.

I had the choice, and this is what I chose! I can't complain, I'm not a peasant girl or a slave, to be given or sold at her master's whim. 'Free folk make their own fate'; my choice has been in everything I've ever done, even my marriage. I could always have chosen to kill myself, like Arianrhod.

Well, if Oswy and I have to play a public farce for the rest of our lives, for the sake of our people, we need not do it between ourselves. When Oswy comes back I'll tell him whatever he doesn't already know or hasn't guessed about me. After that, I'll live the life I've made for myself.

What was that life going to be like, alone with Oswy's cold contempt? Even Elidir's temper seemed less desolating, at least he had valued her enough to want her with him—why hadn't she gone?

'It's full moon—we'll be half-way to Caer Luel before sunrise.'

She tried to send her spirit riding with Elidir under the moon, to see Caer Luel rosy in the dawn as she drew rein at his side before they crossed Idon bridge—only to feel agony, like flesh torn out of her side, when it came home to her that this could never be . . .

It was all as distant and beautiful as a bard's tale: 'Once upon a time there was a princess of Cumbria who loved a young huntsman.' She might have died long ago for all she felt.

She was now as free from love as she was from terror. It had been her own choice, God alone knew what was coming next.

She was chill, and she began to wonder where Oswy was, what was happening down the valley. The moon set and still Oswy did not come; she was alone in the darkness. At last she slept.

She woke with Oswy's hand under her ear, his fingers cold.

'Wake up. We're going.'

'Is it dawn?' She peered into the darkness.

'No, but past midnight. I've had word from Talorgan, it's time to be off.'

'Can we get past them in the dark? They were stirring late, and there'll be trouble over Penda. We could be scattered and destroyed in a night surprise.'

'We're not going past them, there's no need.' He chuckled. 'Mercia and Powys are Midlands, but no Northumbrian ever forgets the sea. I've had my ships keeping up with us along the coast—they're waiting behind that island in the Forth. Talorgan's folk are going to ferry us out.'

'The horses?'

'I'm leaving them. Don't worry, they'll be in good hands before morning. They'll pay our ferrymen—they're all we've got left to pay with! Hurry now.'

They slipped out of the citadel and went down south-eastwards behind the hill-crest. A couple of plaided, sure-footed shadows guided them on a winding track through the marshy ground at the foot of the hill and then turned north, following the course of a burn that ran out into the sands about two miles away. There were some large coracles beached at the water's edge as if ready for the night's fishing; Riemmelth was hauled into one and carried bobbing out into the shimmering water to the island in the middle of the Forth where Oswy's galleys were waiting for them to come on board.

Riemmelth was dazed with broken sleep and exhausted by all that had happened. She was soon asleep again on a pile of cloaks in the stern, with a last question flickering in her bemused mind about what she was doing there.

The question was still with her when she woke up to a morning of bright sun, brisk wind and swooping, crying gulls. She sat in the stern, watching them come skimming over the crests of the breaking waves, listening to the steady creak and plash of the oars, noting without surprise that they were heading south-east, out to sea.

She should have been desolate, but she found that her spirits were soaring up with the gulls. The beat of the oars began to take shape as words in her mind, a song that old Dunnere liked and often asked the scop to sing. It was about a sailor who'd had some foul nights out on the northern sea, stiff with cold, battered by storms and hail, hating every moment. Yet on dry land, as soon as spring opened the first leaves, his heart went flying out to sea, calling to him to take ship again, hungry to be away.

'Now the blood beats at my breast,
my heart's desires drive me
over the swelling billows, the salt breakers.
Endless longing lures my soul to set out,
to seek a foreign folk in a far land.

And so my soul bursts from its breast-coffer,
my spirit swoops over the sea-tides,
wheels across the whale's haunt; homing again
hungry and hankering, the lone flyer calls me,
whets my willing heart to the whale's way
over the waste of waters.'

I'm free, she thought, *the world's full of roads, the sea reaches every shore. My road is whatever I choose to do. I could go to Rome, to the Holy Land, I could see Constantinople—I can see little Alchfled! If she's happy in the convent, like Ebbe and Hild, well and good. If not, I'll have her out of it and she'll marry as she likes, see if Oswy can stop me!*

She hugged her knees, smiling to herself as the wind tugged at her hair. She was hungry for new things, like Dunnere's *Seafarer*.

She was also quite simply hungry, and thirsty too, by the time they beached the ships for the night in a sheltered cove where a burn ran out from the cliffs. The salt air gave an extra savour to food and drink. Afterwards, she walked on the sands, glad to stretch and move. Oswy followed her and they fell into step.

'Had you always meant to double back to Bebbanburh?'

'If I didn't trap Penda as I wanted. No sense being holed up in Pictland. But never tell the truth to your enemies, Riemmelth—or not more than you can help.'

'Will there be war in Northumbria now?'

'Not this year. The Powys men will go straight home—

your Cumbrians will see them on their way in peace. You handled that very well.'

They were calm and friendly: a king and queen talking statecraft; warriors who had stood side by side in battle and taken each other's measure.

'And the Mercians?'

He laughed. 'I don't know quite how far my sword point got on that last blow, I didn't have time to place it as neatly as I'd wish. But if it went where I wanted, Penda'll walk all the rest of his life as an ox instead of a bull. His son's only a child and his brother's dead. If Penda dies now, there'll be a merry civil war in Mercia. His war-band will want him alive as long as possible. They'll go back over the Cheviots and down the Long Hills, keeping out of folk's way.'

'Couldn't we take them as they come back?' she asked hopefully.

'My own position's not firm enough yet for all-out war against Mercia and Deira. That will come when I'm ready— I've got some tidying up to do first.'

'Will you rebuild Gefrin?'

They had reached the end of the bay and turned to stroll back to the ships. Oswy paused for a moment, looking out to the barren, homeless waters.

'I must,' he said quietly. 'It will look like defeat if I don't. But it's an unlucky place now, there was too much evil at its end. Bishop Aidan can build a chapel there and pray peace to the dead. I've got an estate at Melmin that will serve to oversee Glein Dale. It's near enough for them, if they want to come and visit.'

'They?'

'The ghosts.'

Riemmelth felt sorry for him, he'd lost more than she had in this last dreadful year. Rhun had died in his bed, Caer Luel and Glannaventa stood untouched. But Oswy had lost his palace and his family treasures; Oswald, Elfwyn, his own unborn child, had all been destroyed by treachery and violence; his wife and the daughter she had borne could not

248

have given him much joy. It crossed her mind that he had never given her a word of blame or complaint for her part in his troubles.

They had reached the ships. The men were going to spend the night on the sands by the fire; she had her bed made up in the stern of Oswy's vessel. She took his hand to help her up over the side, and kept hold of it. He came and sat beside her on the cloaks.

'The dead are safe for ever,' she said, gently, trying to find some comfort for him. 'Nothing can hurt them or change them. When our pain stops, we can go back in our memory and meet them again, just as we knew them. It's when they live and turn against you—that's when they're walking ghosts.' Her voice shook.

He looked at her. 'That Welshman was your lover.'

'You loved Liadan,' she said quickly, defending herself.

'I *love* Liadan,' he said, not defending himself. 'I love music and poetry, good wine, well-painted books, jewels. I've got many loves—and one wife.'

Whom you don't love. Or did he mean that people could share their knowledge and joy? That it might be possible to share, not Elidir and Liadan, of course, but whatever of Elidir and Liadan that they kept within themselves? It seemed impossible, and yet—

'When I met you,' she said haltingly, groping for an idea she couldn't see very clearly herself, 'you were Liadan's lover. Whatever, whoever, you were before that, I'll never meet him. The man I married was Liadan's lover.'

She tried to read his face, to see if he was following her thoughts, but his eyes were on the sea; they had the same light, blue-green surface, the same unknowable depths.

The woman you married was Elidir's lover—and still is— we're everything we've ever done and suffered. How many women besides Liadan have helped to make you the man I chose?

'Why didn't you go with Elidir?' he asked quietly.

'Why did you tell me to go?'

'The wisest person I know—an Irish ollave—told me

once that the surest way to make a woman strike root in your bed was to tell her the door's open behind her for her going.'

Riemmelth's eyes flashed wide with outrage; she had her hand up to smash across his face before his meaning hit her. Then she began to laugh. She sank into a sea of laughter, wallowed in it and came up gasping as another billow of it washed over her and sent her rolling. It rolled her into Oswy's arms.

Far into the night, when the moon had risen, she shivered and drew away a little. Oswy blinked awake and stared up at her: her eyes were wide and alarmed, her breasts and shoulders gleaming among the black streams of her hair.

'What is it, sweetheart?'

'It won't always be like this.'

He shifted his back and shoulders. 'I hope it'll be in a softer bed. These planks'll earn us time off purgatory.'

'There you go again—you jeer at everything! We'll vex each other, be at cross-purposes, always grating against each other. We'll fight again.'

'And again and again. Well, it keeps me in battle-trim. The man who's married to you could take on all the war-hosts of Britain. But I've had enough weapon-drill for now. Lie down and—'

'—get your breath back to fight again.'

They made Bebbanburh on an early afternoon, giving a wide berth to the sandbanks of the Holy Island and coming in past the Farnes with the sea-birds yelling at them from the stacks and whirling round them in clouds, the seals bobbing up to look at them.

Cadman was waiting on the beach with an escort. Mildred was at the door of the hall with the guest-cup, very dignified to greet the King, then collapsing into Riemmelth's arms, laughing and crying. The two of them hurried off to the women's quarters, where Riemmelth had her worn and grubby riding clothes stripped off with cries of horror from Mildred, who swore to burn them as soon as possible.

When she was bathed and in her clean shift, Mildred showed her the gown she had been preparing ever since Riemmelth went to Coludesham: bright scarlet wool, the neck, cuffs and hem stiff with bands of amazing gold and purple embroidery. Mildred had remembered how much Riemmelth had enjoyed the pictures in the book Oswy brought when she was ill in Eoforwic. She had stitched vine-scrolls coiling and twining in all directions, with leaves and bunches of grapes bursting out of them, and fantastic birds and animals climbing and perching in every curve.

Riemmelth admired it, as well she might; then, entering into the spirit of celebration, she topped it with one of her purple brocade tunics from Constantinople. She looked fiercely handsome, like the North Country in autumn, heather moors and rowan berries under a clear blue sky.

'Now you do look like a queen!' cried Mildred.

Riemmelth raised her eyebrows, mocking herself a little. 'A queen without a crown.'

Mildred glanced at her own trinket-box; Oswy had packed it with jewels after she saved Riemmelth. She half reached for it, but Riemmelth caught her hand.

'No—you won those in the marshes at Eoforwic. Nobody else shall wear them till you send Cadman's son to court a bride.'

'You don't need a crown with this on your head,' said Mildred, running her fingers through the raven-black tresses; then, with sudden fierce joy, 'I'll make you a crown!'

She plaited the mass of hair with gold ribbons and wound it round Riemmelth's head, building it up and pinning it into a towering mitre. The horn sounded just as she finished, and they went to the hall together, followed by their admiring women.

Oswy had told the servers to set the Queen's seat beside him on the dais like a bridal, not a warriors' feast. He looked at her with interest as she came up and took her place.

'That's a very handsome crown you're wearing. It's a pity you haven't got any jewels to go with it.'

Riemmelth tried to think of something consoling: that jewels didn't matter, that she didn't care for jewels—both lies, as Oswy well knew. Anyway, there was never any use in making comforting noises to Oswy. Instead, she said in a tone of sardonic Northumbrian flatness that even Dunnere would have envied, 'It's lucky I can grow my own crown for my head, it's the only sort I'm likely to have.'

'You Welsh have always got your answer, but don't be so sure about it. Here—hold fast what I give you.'

He closed her fingers over her palm; she opened them and found the Cumbrian ring.

'It was a shame to spoil a good gesture—but more of a shame to waste a good ring.'

Remembering what he'd learnt about her that night, what he'd risked to go back and hunt for her ring, her eyes filled.

'Don't cry—you'll have your jewels. This is just a token in earnest. When I'm Bretwalda, you'll have so many jewels you'll be throwing them to the kitchen girls.'

Her winged brows slanted up. 'Bretwalda is it, now? Aren't Cumbria and Northumbria together enough for you but you must be High King of Britain as well?'

'I shall be driven to it.' His voice was sorrowful, he had the face of a much put-upon man. 'Nothing less could satisfy the pride of a queen from the House of Urien.'

Riemmelth thought of several answers, all of them rude. She needed time, though, to select the most scathing and hone it to a deadly cutting edge. There was no need to hurry, she had all night to insult him. Meanwhile, duty came before pleasure. Signing to Mildred to follow her, the Queen of Northumbria took the drinking horn and stepped down from the dais to greet the King's hearth-companions.

Languages and Place-names

Riemmelth's people spoke Cumbric, a northern form of Old Welsh, or British, the language of Britain. Oswy's people spoke Anglian, a northern form of Old English. Educated people knew some Latin. Oswy's family had been in exile in Iona: Irish was their second language; King Oswald acted as St Aidan's interpreter when he first came to Northumbria.

The English adopted many place-names from Welsh: Carlisle, Penrith, Derwent. Sometimes they substituted an English word of similar sound to the Welsh name: Efrog—Eoforwic. In other cases the English name is quite different from the original: Metcaud—Lindisfarne.

The three names in italics are guesswork, as the original names are lost and the modern ones are later than the period of this story.

Cumbria (known in Welsh as Rheged) extended from the northern side of the Solway Firth down into Lancashire.
Alauna—Watercrook, Kendal
Argoed Llwyvein—Bewcastle Fells
Caer Luel—Carlisle
Derwennydd—Papcastle by the Derwent

Dunoding—S.W. Lancashire
Eamot—R. Eamont
Glannaventa—Ravenglass
Guasmoric—Wigton
Gwensteri—Winster Valley
Idon—R. Eden
Llwyvennydd—Lyvennet Valley
Penrhyd—Penrith
Tu Hir   }
The Long Hills } —The Pennines
Uxellodun—Castlesteads

The Ninianic shrines—1) St Ninian's Well, Brisco
                   2) Old Church, Brampton
                   3) Ninekirks, Brougham

Northumbria was made up of three kingdoms:
Bernicia—roughly modern Northumberland and Durham,
      but extending to the southern side of the Forth
Deira—roughly North and East Ridings of Yorkshire,
      which in Edwin's reign had annexed
Elmet—a British kingdom that contained the modern
      district of Leeds, extending up the valleys of the
      Calder, Aire and Wharfe into the Pennines.
Aber Lleu—mouth of the R. Low
Bebbanburh—Bamburgh
Caer Almond—Cramond
Caer Rhos—Ros Castle, Chillingham
Catraeth—Catterick
Ceasterford—Castleford
Ceasterholm—Vindolanda
Coludesburh—St Abb's Head
Coludesham—Coldingham

Corabryg—Corbridge
Dana—R. Don
Deira Street—Dere St. Roman road from York to Cramond
               partly followed by the A66
Deawesbyrig—Dewsbury
Dierne—R. Dearne, tributary of the Don
Edinburh ⎫
Din Eidyn ⎭ —Arthur's Seat
Esk Mouth—Inveresk
Gefrin—Yeavering
Glein—R. Glen
Giudi—Stirling Castle Rock
Heavenfield—St Oswald's Church on the Wall, nr. Hexham
Heruteu—Hartlepool
Hrypum—Ripon
Melmin—Milfield
Metcaud—Lindisfarne, the Holy Island
Waking Rock—St Cuthbert's Island
Weorf—R. Wharfe
Yr—R. Aire

Elsewhere
Alclud—Dumbarton
Arnemeton—Buxton
Bancornaburh—Bangor-is-y-Coed
Caer Legion—Chester
Cogwy—Old Oswestry
Manau—the Isle of Man
Manceinion—Manchester
Pengwern—chief royal court of Powys, either Wroxeter or
             Wrekin hill fort
Tomeworthig—Tamworth, chief royal court of Mercia